KILLER HONEYMOON

Savannah was barely listening. She was forcing herself to look at the dead woman's face. A lovely face, even in death. A face that did, indeed, look very familiar to her.

"Amelia," she said, more to herself than to Dirk.

"What?"

"I knew I'd seen her before. So have you. That's Amelia Northrop."

Dirk studied the victim for a moment. "The Channel Seven newscaster that we watch every night?"

Savannah nodded solemnly.

He bent down and took a better look. "You're right. It's her. Now that I think about it, I heard that she has a vacation home here on the island, her and her big-time land developer husband, William Northrop."

"William. Yes, William."

"Huh?"

"She said his name . . . before . . ."

"Like, 'Tell William I love him'?"

"No. I asked her who shot her and she said, 'William' . . ."

Books by G.A. McKevett

Published by Kensington Publishing Corporation

G.A. McKevett

Killer HONEYMOON

A SAVANNAH REID MYSTERY

KENSINGTON BOOKS
www.kensingtonbooks.com

KENSINGTON BOOKS are published by

Kensington Publishing Corp.
119 West 40th Street
New York, NY 10018

All Kensington titles, imprints and distributed lines are available at special quantity discounts for bulk purchases for sales promotion, premiums, fund-raising, educational or institutional use. Special book excerpts or customized printings can also be created to fit specific needs. For details, write or phone the office of the Kensington Special Sales Manager: Kensington Publishing Corp., 119 West 40th Street, New York, NY, 10018. Attn. Special Sales Department. Phone: 1-800-221-2647.

Kensington and the K logo Reg. U.S. Pat. & TM Off.

ISBN-13: 978-0-7582-7652-0
ISBN-10: 0-7582-7652-4
First Kensington Hardcover Edition: April 2013
First Kensington Mass Market Edition: March 2014

eISBN-13: 978-1-61773-042-9
eISBN-10: 1-61773-042-4
Kensington Electronic Edition: March 2014

10 9 8 7 6 5 4 3 2 1

Printed in the United States of America

This book is lovingly dedicated to Evan,
Who will live his adulthood as he did his childhood,
With kindness, integrity, courage, and strength . . .
The truest measure of a man.

I want to thank my dear friend, Leslie Connell, for years and years of loving support, not to mention her invaluable proofreading services.

I also wish to thank all the fans who write to me, sharing their thoughts and offering endless encouragement. Your stories touch my heart, and I enjoy your letters more than you know. I can be reached at:

sonja@sonjamassie.com
and
facebook.com/gwendolynnarden.mckevett

Chapter 1

Those darned cats were hogging the bed. Again.

As Savannah lay on her side—half-dreaming, half-waking—she felt Diamante draped—furry, warm, and heavy—across her thigh. Cleopatra was sprawled across her waist. Without even opening her eyes, Savannah knew which was which.

Since they were kittens, both had tried to sleep on her head, or at least on her pillow. Savannah had demanded they stay down by her feet. Over the years, they had negotiated this compromise. It worked, for human and feline alike.

Except for the snoring.

Cleopatra snored. Loudly.

She might be named after an Egyptian queen; her glossy coat could shine like fine black velvet, and her eyes glow like the most majestic mini-panther in the jungle. But Cleopatra snored like a cartoon bear. This morning was the worst that Savannah had ever heard. Plus she smelled like Old Spice.

Savannah woke fully with a start and tried to flip over onto her back, but she was thoroughly pinned. With her newfound consciousness, she realized these were not simple kitty cats—not even the miniature leopard style—holding her down.

She ran her fingers over the hard, hairy arm wrapped around her waist. Then she investigated the harder and hairier object across her thigh. It was her husband's leg.

Yes. *Husband.*

She had one of those now.

The memories of yesterday's vows and the two rings on her left hand made it quite official. As did the presence of a man in her bed and the sound of his snoring that reminded her of a Georgia tornado, whirling a few inches from her ear.

Savannah Reid was a married woman; and normally, that thought might have alarmed her. But his familiar smell and the blissful heat of his body pressed against hers reminded her—it was Dirk. Not just her husband, but her best friend and partner for more years than she cared to count.

So it was okay. In fact, it was much more than okay.

"Hey, good morning, wifey," he said, nuzzling her ear, his breath tickling her neck. His arm tightened around her waist, pulling her even closer against him.

"Good morning to you, hubby," she replied with a giggle. "First time I ever said that."

He kissed a sensitive spot over her temple. It gave her delicious shivers. "Well, get used to it. This is a life sentence."

"Wouldn't have it any other way."

As she snuggled in, a feeling swept over her that she could only describe as wondrous, warm, and cozy. Better than a dark chocolate gourmet truffle savored lingeringly on the tongue. More delicious than a sip of the smoothest cognac that slid like liquid fire down the throat to the belly and then set every cell in the body to tingling.

Ah, it was heavenly.

Then he went back to sleep and started to snore. Much louder than before.

A moment later, her leg went numb. She tried to gently slip out from beneath him and couldn't. That big, hard, muscular thigh she had admired so much the night before weighed a ton.

She looked around the motel room and felt a bit homesick. She missed her lace curtains and her pink sheets. She missed Diamante and Cleo's soft, feminine purr-snores.

And Savannah realized that what her blessed granny had told her for so many years was true: Sometimes love was sacred, the most holy and powerful force in the universe. Sometimes it was a warm, fuzzy feeling. Occasionally it was a wildfire of passion that, like cognac, inflamed every cell of your body.

And sometimes it was just a decision. Plain and simple.

At that moment, lying in her new husband's arms, she knew that this big bear of a man would willingly die for her; and even more important, only yesterday, he had vowed to live for her.

With his arm and leg draped protectively over her, cutting off her circulation, she felt her soul fill to the brim with "warm and fuzzy."

And she decided, once again, to love him forever, just as she'd promised to do yesterday in front of God and everybody she knew.

Now . . . if she could only get back to sleep.

In an effort to get away from it all—"all" being Savannah's enormous family, who had decided to camp

out in her house for a Southern California vacation following the wedding—Savannah and Dirk had hopped a
ferry and escaped to the tiny, picturesque island of
Santa Tesla. Twenty-four miles from their own native
San Carmelita, and fifty-one miles northwest of Los Angeles, Santa Tesla was a world away and a kingdom unto
itself.

With its lush, tropical greenery, brightly colored
houses decorated with white gingerbread trim, and
grass-roofed huts, the place reminded Savannah of pictures she had seen of Polynesia and Key West. While she
had never been to either—poor little girls from Georgia and grown-up, but underpaid, private detectives
didn't do a lot of traveling—Santa Tesla looked exactly
the way Savannah had always imagined those romantic
locales.

As she and Dirk left their shabby little motel and
strolled, hand in hand, along the waterfront, she
breathed deeply, taking in the delicate scent of honey-
suckle wafting on the salt sea air, blending with aromas
from the various food establishments they were passing.

She looked around her, enjoying the treats that nature had to offer, from the brilliance of the bougainvillea and hibiscus, which bloomed in profusion, to the
giant palms swaying gently in the breeze, the glistening
waves as they rolled onto the sand, and the white seagulls circling the beach.

Farther away, the harbor was lined with every sort of
boat, yacht, and ship imaginable. And in the distance, a
giant cruise ship lay at anchor, waiting while her passengers explored the island and sampled its exotic
foods and drinks, hiked nature trails, went diving and
snorkeling, parasailed, fished, and deepened their tans
on the beaches.

She turned to her groom, gazed lovingly into his

eyes, and said, "Don't you just love it here? It's pure romance. Perfect for a honeymoon."

"I liked it better before that dude at the motel told me how much taxis cost here. What a bite in the ass!"

Okay, she thought. *So much for loving gazes and pure, unadulterated romance. It's not like you didn't know he was grumpy and cheap when you married him, Savannah girl.*

He pointed to the closest thing resembling a "transportation hub" on the island—a bicycle-rental hut. "Yeah, we're gonna have to rent a couple of those."

Looking around her at the steep, steep hills, rising from the beach area to the distant mountains, some soaring to nearly two thousand feet, she reminded herself of her early-morning platitude about love being a choice, a decision, a determination to commit.

"And sometimes it's a vow not to smack 'im silly with the nearest heavy, metal object," she muttered under her breath.

"What?" he asked.

"If you think I'm gonna spend my honeymoon pedaling all over tarnation on a bicycle, buddy, you best reconsider."

"But it'll save us a fortune!"

She turned to him with a look that was sans adoration and brimming with "Get real."

In her thickest, most deep-down-in-Dixie accent, she said, "Last night was wonderful, amazing, all I ever dreamed of, and more."

He beamed.

"But such unaccustomed activity has left me with an aching need to park my butt on a hot-water bottle, not a bicycle seat—if you catch my drift."

He stopped beaming. "Oh. Right. Gotcha."

As she looked up and down the beach with its seaward-facing shops and concessions, she spotted what she was looking for—a golf cart rental. "Now, *that* is more like it. I always wanted to drive one of those things."

He brightened as they headed toward it. "Yeah, that looks like fun, but I wanna drive."

"Nope, I thought of it."

"But I'm the husband. Husbands do the driving."

She grinned up at him, slapping him on the back. "Darlin', we need to get you the latest edition of the *Husband Handbook*. Obviously, the one you've been reading is badly out of date."

A few moments later, as Dirk was filling out the rental form for the cart and Savannah was sliding her California driver's license back into her wallet, she noticed something inside her purse. A creamy white envelope with beautiful script on the front.

Dirk walked up to her and dangled the cart's key in front of her nose. "Possession's nine-tenths of the law," he said, far too proud of himself.

Ordinarily, she would have snatched the key away from him, or at least tried. It might have even ended in an all-out tussle there in front of the tourist hordes. But she was too distracted by the envelope.

She pulled it out, turned it over in her hand, and studied the front. *Savannah and Dirk* had been written in a hand she knew very well. In all her life, she had only met one person with penmanship that perfect, and who wrote with an antique fountain pen.

"Whatcha got there?" Dirk asked, taking her arm and propelling her toward their waiting, freshly rented cart.

"It's from Ryan. I think it's a card." She paused,

trying to remember. "I have a half-memory of him handing it to me in the Bentley, when he and John were driving me to our wedding. It's a little hazy. I was a bit discombobulated."

"Yeah, well, I was about to pee my fancy tuxedo pants. I was so nervous waiting for you to get there. I was already wondering how I was gonna explain it to the rental joint."

She hardly noticed when he tucked her into the passenger seat and stuck himself behind the wheel, because she was busy unsealing the linen vellum, tissue-lined envelope.

"It's from Ryan and John," she said as she pulled out the card and opened it. " 'Dearest Friends,' " she read aloud. " 'While we trust you two are having a wonderful first night, reminiscing in your motel of choice, we thought you might enjoy a more romantic venue for the remainder of your island honeymoon. Forgive us for taking the liberty of arranging an alternative, which you are more than welcome to accept or refuse.' "

Dirk slipped the key into the cart's ignition switch. "Cool. I wouldn't mind having better digs than that one we just stayed in."

"You told me you wanted to stay there," she said. "Sentimental reasons, and all that."

"Seemed like a good idea at the time. Since we didn't do anything the other time we slept there, it was sorta like making up for lost time. But I think I got a fleabite on my leg last night."

"Get used to it. You'll be sleeping with flea-bitten felines for the rest of your life."

He grinned at her and stomped on the pedal, causing the cart to lurch forward. "As long as it's Cleo and Di. They're my girls, fleas and all."

As they bounced away from the hut and onto the street, she gave him an annoyed, sidewise glance. "Driving as smoothly as always, I see."

"Hey, you're talking to a manly man here, and we manly men are hell on wheels." He nodded toward the envelope in her hands. "What else does it say?"

She continued to read, as best she could, considering the bumpiness of the road and Dirk's erratic swerving to avoid pedestrian tourists, dressed in eye-searing tropical prints. " 'Take this card to the gift shop at the base of the lighthouse and tell Betty Sue we sent you. Love and best wishes overflowing, John and Ryan.' "

Savannah closed her eyes for a moment and savored the thought of her precious friends, whose love and devotion had sustained her over the years. Tall, dark, and outrageously sexy Ryan Stone and his genteel British gentleman partner, John Gibson, had brought more elegance and charm into her life than she could have ever imagined. It looked as though they were providing still more.

"Whatever our surprise is," she told Dirk as he swerved to avoid a couple of old hippies in tie-dye, "it's bound to be wonderful."

"Knowing Ryan and John, it'll be classy. Hope it ain't too highfalutin. Us manly men have a reputation to uphold."

She pointed toward the end of the island where the Santa Tesla Lighthouse towered above all other landmarks, both manmade and natural, glistening white and stately against the perfect blue sky. "Point this jalopy that-there direction. Let's go and find out what Miss Betty Sue's got for us in her gift shop."

*   *   *

About two hundred yards from the lighthouse, in a quaint little shop, Savannah and Dirk found Betty Sue standing behind the counter, amid a jungle of seashell-festooned wind chimes. She peeked out at them from between dangling starfish, bits of sparkling sea glass, and delicate sea horses, which danced on the breeze that floated through the cozy store.

Like Savannah, Betty Sue bore a name that suggested she might be a fair daughter of the Confederacy. But she was no dainty Southern belle. With her silver hair cropped to less than an inch, her skin darkly leathered by the sun, her baggy men's work shirt, and her faded denim overalls, she looked more like a deep-sea fisherman than a down-in-Dixie debutante.

But her smile was bright and her pale blue eyes sparkled when she greeted them. "I was expecting you two to pop in about this time," she said. "Ryan and John told me that the new bride would be as pretty as a picture. Shiny, dark, curly hair and eyes bluer than mine—that's the way they described you, Savannah."

She gave Dirk a quick glance. "And they mentioned you'd be comin' along, too."

"Yeah, we grooms tend to hang out and make a nuisance of ourselves on our honeymoons," he grumbled in return.

Betty Sue walked around the counter, winding her way through displays of kites, straw hats, and plaques with nautical themed quotes like, *Life's a Beach*. In her hand, she held a large skeleton key and a smaller one, both attached to a chain with a skull-and-crossbones medallion dangling from it. The keys and the ornament looked ancient—tarnished and rusty.

When Betty Sue placed them in her hand, Savannah felt a slight chill, of the delicious type, shiver down her back. If only her friend and assistant, Tammy Hart, were here, she would be thrilled. These artifacts were straight out of an old Nancy Drew book. In her imagination, Savannah could envision the title—*The Mystery of the Skeleton Keys*—and the cover copy, encouraging the reader to *Discover what terrors lurk behind the doors, unlocked with these sinister keys.*

"So, what're those?" Dirk snapped. "The keys to a dusty ol' crypt or some vampire coffin?"

Betty Sue chuckled. "Oh, no. Something much nicer than that. Follow me. . . ."

Betty Sue led them out of the shop and along a dirt walkway, which cut across a small field. As Savannah followed her, keys in hand, through a profusion of natural vegetation—wild sage, golden marguerites, orange poppies, and the occasional pear cactus—she could see that their path could only lead to the lighthouse itself.

She glanced back at Dirk, who was a few feet behind her, and gave him a questioning look. He shrugged, but he looked as intrigued as she.

When they arrived at the majestic tower, Betty Sue steered them toward the two-story white-stucco cottage with a red tile roof, nestled against its base.

Both the lighthouse and the cottage appeared quite old. Their doors were arched and built of heavy, dark, distressed wood. The freshly polished brass hardware shone brightly, but looked as though it had weathered years of sea storms. Instead of being perfectly clear and smooth, the glass in the windows of the house had tiny seed bubbles, striations, and imperfections that hinted at its age.

At the upper-story windows and downstairs, as well,

redwood window boxes added a graceful charm to the cottage, spilling over with salmon-colored geraniums, white petunias, and maidenhair ferns.

"This is the lightkeeper's cottage," Betty Sue told them. "It was built at the same time as the lighthouse itself, back in 1853."

"Wow, pre–Civil War," Savannah said as Betty Sue took the keys from her hand.

"Yes. President Franklin Pierce ordered it built after a notorious shipwreck on the reefs over there." She pointed toward the water to a row of jagged rock teeth, some of which jutted above the surface, while others, looking just as sharp and ominous, lurked below.

"Wouldn't wanna run aground on those things," Dirk said. "They'd grind you up and spit you out—turn you into shark bait."

"That's pretty much what happened to the crew and passengers of the *Lillyan Suzanne*." Betty Sue stepped to the door of the cottage and fit the smallest key into the lock. "She was a steamer, transporting a bunch of guys from San Francisco to Panama. They'd just struck it rich in the gold rush up there and were carrying their fortunes with them. The ship hit the reefs, and it was every man for himself. In the melee, they were more interested in stealing each other's gold dust than rescuing the survivors."

"Tough group," Dirk replied. "Reminds me of our police department barbecues when the supply of ribs runs low."

Betty Sue turned the key and opened the cottage's door. It creaked loudly on its hinges, and Savannah thought, *What else would you expect from a door opened with a skeleton key?*

"If you choose to accept your friends' generous gift," the shopkeeper said, "this is where you'll spend the remainder of your honeymoon. I have to say, I envy you. It's as romantic a setting as you'll find anywhere."

Chapter 2

Betty Sue threw the door of the lightkeeper's cottage wide open and waved them inside with a flourish.

Savannah stepped over the threshold and back in time. The furnishings were Victorian and nautical in flavor. A sofa covered in burgundy velvet, with a diamond-tufted back, carved wood trim, and claw-feet, dominated the far wall. In front of the sofa, a massive marine chest—its top covered by a sheet of cobalt blue mirror—served as a coffee table.

The walls were hung with gilt-framed paintings of clipper ships in full sail, battling their way through tempest-tossed seas. In other renderings, warships fired upon each other amid billows of dark smoke and bright flame.

In the center of the ceiling hung a chandelier made of a giant ship's wheel, studded with hurricane-glass chimneys, while brass lanterns warmed the corners of the room with soft golden light.

Above the stone fireplace, on a heavy wooden mantel, sat a model ship, imprisoned in a giant glass bottle.

Antique leather books and a brass sextant graced the opposite ends of the mantel.

Savannah stood there, absorbing it all—the romance of a bygone era.

As a little girl, marooned on a patch of flat Georgia farmland, she had often dreamed of the sea, fantasizing about how it would be to ride the waves in one of those magnificent ships, to feel the wild wind in her hair and the spray of the salty sea on her face.

Standing in that room with its art and furnishings that hadn't changed in over 150 years, she imagined herself wearing a gown of lavender silk taffeta and Dirk, in his sailor's garb, as she kissed him good-bye. He was leaving to go away to sea. Heaven only knew if she would ever, in this lifetime, lay eyes on his precious face again and—

"Is there a shower in this place?" he barked at Betty Sue. "'Cause I can't stand taking baths. A lot of these old places don't have showers. If it ain't got a shower, I ain't stayin'."

Savannah revised her fantasy slightly to include her lifting her dainty black boot, with its row of teeny-tiny buttons and intricate lacings, and giving him a loving little kick on the tush as he turned to leave her.

Betty Sue cleared her throat and shuffled her feet. "Um . . . well, actually, it doesn't have a shower. But it has a huge, beautiful claw-foot tub that's big enough for two. Most romantic and—"

"Romantic, she-mantic. I ain't spending money on a place to stay that don't even have a shower."

Betty Sue's friendly demeanor evaporated. Her smile slipped from her face.

Savannah had noticed that happening a lot in Dirk's presence. Smiles slipping, pleasantries vanishing, jollies going *ka-poof*. It was a predictable effect he seemed to have on those around him.

She stepped forward, laced her arm through his, and gave it a squeeze that was a wee bit harder than her usual affectionate hug. "May I remind you," she said in a low voice, "that you aren't spending a dime on this. It's a gift from Ryan and John."

He scowled down at her, but he didn't reply.

"You can spend your honeymoon standing in the shower back there at the Fleabag No-Tell Motel, if you want," she continued, "but your bride is going to stay right here, taking full advantage of this amazing present. Suit yourself, darlin'."

"Ain't gonna be much of a honeymoon without my wife."

Savannah smiled up at him sweetly, making full use of her dimples and batting her eyelashes for added emphasis. "That was my thought exactly." She leaned over and gave him a peck on the cheek. "You sit in one end of that big ol' tub, I'll sit in the other, and I'll dump a bowl of water over your head. How'll that be?"

He mumbled something under his breath, which wasn't quite audible; for that, she was grateful.

Betty Sue appeared to sense that the battle of the sexes was over—at least for the moment—and her smile reappeared. "The master bedroom and bath are upstairs," she said. "I think you'll find them quite comfortable."

She walked back to the door and motioned them to follow. "Now I want to show you the best part of your present. You don't just get to sleep in the lightkeeper's cottage. You get free run of the lighthouse itself!"

* * *

As Betty Sue led them to the light tower, Savannah could hardly contain her excitement. She had been a fan of lighthouses since she was a child and had first seen a picture of the Cape Hatteras Light on the wall of her hometown library: the grace and beauty of the gleaming towers themselves, the rich history filled with the drama of shipwrecks, pirates, and moon cursers, not to mention the folklore of courageous lightkeepers who rescued drowning, sea-tossed victims. Ah, the thrill of it all.

For her, simply to be able to enter one was a dream in itself. To think she would have one all to herself— well, plus Dirk—was more glory than she could take in.

"Like other lights all over the country," Betty Sue was saying, "this one is now fully automated. So you don't have to do anything but pretend to be lightkeepers."

"No whale oil lamps to clean?" Dirk asked as he trudged along behind the women.

"No," Betty Sue replied dryly. "But if one of those cruise ships runs aground, you'll be expected to swim out there among the reefs and pull victims to shore." She gave him a quick glance over her shoulder and a smug little smirk.

He grunted. "No problem. I was a lifeguard back in the eighties."

Savannah dropped back to take his hand. "Wrestled sharks, too," she said, grinning up at him.

"I'd throw a ring buoy around 'em, and tow 'em to shore with the throw rope between my teeth."

Savannah reached down and pinched his butt. "Manly man o' mine."

"Don't you forget it."

Betty Sue glanced back at them and rolled her eyes. "*Pleeez*. I'm almost finished with this tour, and then I'm outta here and you two can be as saccharine sweet as you want."

Savannah nudged Dirk and whispered in his ear, "I'm more interested in locking loins at the top of that light. Won't that be a hoot?"

He looked pretty much hoot-free as he leaned his head back, looked up at the top of the light, and scowled. "You mean you intend to climb up there?"

"Of course I do! Are you kidding? We get to go up in a lighthouse! Do you know how many people would kill for a chance like . . . ? Oh . . ."

She'd forgotten.

Dirk wasn't afraid of bank robbers, purse snatchers, or disorderly drunks. He'd sneer in the face of a rabid, foaming-at-the-toothsome-mouth junkyard dog. But he had two fears that were so irrational and consuming that they could be fully classified as "phobias."

For some reason, unless they were in pieces, laid out on Savannah's backyard grill, and slathered in barbecue sauce, Dirk hated chickens.

He also loathed heights. And he considered anything above the second rung of a stepladder to be "high."

Savannah had a lightbulb moment concerning her new groom and their new honeymoon locale. Maybe a lighthouse wasn't the best choice for Dirk.

"You gonna be okay, sugar?" she asked him, squeezing his hand.

He gulped. "I don't know."

As Betty Sue unlocked the giant door of the tower with the largest key on the ring, she gave Dirk a sarcastic little smirk and said, "What's the matter, Manly Man? Scared o' heights, are we?"

Savannah held her breath. If Betty Sue had been a

guy, Dirk might have done something spectacularly wrong and deeply embarrassing . . . like challenge her to arm wrestle there on the spot.

But, fortunately, when it came to those of the female gender—even those wearing past-its-prime fisherman attire—Dirk was as gallant as any gentleman born and bred south of the Mason-Dixon Line.

"Stand aside and let me in there," he said as he pushed past both Savannah and Betty Sue and rushed toward the door of the lighthouse.

As he passed Savannah, she could hear him muttering something under his breath about ". . . show her . . . battle-axe . . . overalls . . ."

Okay, she thought. *Minus two points on that "Gallantry Checklist."*

As she followed him, passing Betty Sue, the woman placed the keys in her hand. "It's all yours now," she said. "Have fun and"—the shopkeeper glanced at Dirk's retreating back and gave Savannah a somewhat sympathetic smile—"well, good luck."

Something that felt a lot like righteous indignation swelled inside Savannah. A moment later, she heard herself saying, "He has his quirks. He's cantankerous enough to make a preacher cuss. Some days he could start an argument with a fence post. But I can tell you, under all that contrariness, he's a good man, with a heart of gold—if he likes you, and you don't get between him and his supper dish."

Betty Sue chuckled. "Funny. That's almost word for word what your friend Ryan said about him. Except for the cursing preacher and the supper dish part." As she turned to walk away, she gave Savannah a grin and a wink and added, "So, if he's good in the sack, you might wanna keep him."

Savannah flashed back on the intimacies of the night

before—when a man known far and wide for his impatience, gruffness, and roughness had been nothing but patient, loving, and infinitely tender.

"Oh yeah," she whispered to the retreating Betty Sue, who was making her way through the fields of wildflowers and prickly pear cacti back to her gift shop. "He's a keeper."

"Hey, are you comin'?" she heard him bellow from inside the light. "I ain't interested in doing this all by myself, you know!"

She sighed. And followed him inside.

Savannah entered the semidarkness of the lighthouse tower and felt a thrill as she gazed at the winding staircase that spiraled gracefully upward. At the top, the stairs disappeared into a small, round hole, the access to the lantern room itself.

Dirk was nearly there. For a guy who seldom exerted himself without good reason, he wasn't wasting any time getting the job done. Savannah chuckled to herself. Whether it was eating some limp green vegetable off his plate, tackling a drunk, unbathed homeless guy, or performing the ten-year oil change in his ancient Buick, if Dirk had an unpleasant task to do, he was big on getting it over-and-done-with as soon as possible.

She knew that the instant he got to the top of the light, proving he could do it, he would descend even faster than he had ascended. She was determined, though, not to let it happen.

Fulfilling a lifelong dream shouldn't be rushed. And it should be performed with your newly avowed spouse by your side. At least that was her intention, if she could get up the staircase fast enough and block his downward escape.

When he disappeared into the hole at the top, she expected him to pop right back down. But he didn't. And although it took her a long time and a lot of huffing-and-puffing climbing to get to the top, he was still in the lantern room when she finally popped her head above the floor and looked inside.

He was staring at the center of the round room, where something that looked like a cross between a glistening, modernistic sculpture and a glass beehive stood.

"Check this out!" he said. "Cool, huh? I think this thing makes the light."

"It's called a Fresnel lens," she told him, eager to share her lighthouse groupie expertise, "invented by a French guy named Fresnel."

She stepped up onto the lantern room's floor and joined him beside the strange but beautiful configuration of glass prisms. Dominating the center of the room, the structure stood about three feet high and was mounted in a polished brass frame. "There's a hurricane lamp inside there," she said. "Or at least there used to be before they replaced them with electric bulbs. All those pieces of glass, situated just so, concentrate the light into a beam that'll reach miles and miles across the water. Awesome, huh?"

She leaned down, peering into the center of the lens, trying to see the bulb.

She was so intent that she didn't realize Dirk had left her, until she heard the door that led outside close with a resounding thud.

Through the windows, she saw that he had walked out onto the gallery, the exterior catwalk that surrounded the lantern room.

Must've gotten over his fear of heights, she told herself as she followed him outside to enjoy the view.

But by the time she stepped through the door, he had already made his way around to the other side of the light. All thoughts of her new groom vanished as she took in the magnificent sight below her.

From this amazing vantage point, the island in all its splendor lay at her feet. She could see from one end to the other—the forested areas, covered in thick, tropical foliage; the more arid regions, with their sparse vegetation sprouting from sand and rocks. And circling the edge of the isle, the stony cliffs soaring above the shimmering beaches and cerulean waters.

She took a mental snapshot to add to the photo book she had been collecting all her life—an album of memories, tucked deep inside her heart, which contained some of the most precious moments she had experienced. The majority of those carefully assembled memories revolved around family and friends. But some, like this one, simply celebrated a moment shared between her and her surroundings, the beauty of nature, and a sense of oneness with it.

The moment was fleeting at best.

Life had a way of interrupting the flow of even the most blissful spiritual connections.

Far below the lighthouse, where a particularly steep cliff met the beach, she saw a flash of blue in a copse of tall shrubs with bright yellow flowers, then another, as something darted among the dense greenery.

Instinctively, she knew something was wrong and watched closely as a figure emerged, just long enough for her to see that it was a woman. A blond woman wearing a pale blue business suit. A woman who didn't look like she was going for a morning jog.

She looked like she was running for her life.

"Dirk!" Savannah called. "Get over here. Look at this."

She shielded her eyes with her hand as she squinted into the morning sunlight, trying to determine what, or who, might be chasing the blonde. But she saw nothing, not even a rustling in the bushes.

For a moment, the woman stopped and poked her head out of the greenery, looking behind her. Then she left her hiding place and raced on down the beach, away from the lighthouse.

Savannah watched until she disappeared behind a large outcropping of rock and cliff, farther down the shore.

"Dirk!" she called again, and turned to see him walking up behind her.

"What are you yellin' about?" he said. "Sheez. Wanna holler it again? There might be some goat on a mountain in Tibet that didn't hear you."

"Well, you shouldn't have dawdled. You missed it."

"Missed what?"

Savannah turned and continued to scan the coastline for any sign of the woman's pursuer. "Seeing a gal hightail it down the beach. She was running like her tail feathers were on fire."

Savannah turned and headed for the door. "Let's get down there. See if we can find out what's goin' on."

"No," he said, blocking her path.

"No? What do you mean, 'no'?"

"I mean, this is our honeymoon, and we're not getting involved in anybody else's business. Especially if it's business that involves running or feathers on fire."

"But—"

"No 'buts.' We made a deal that we wouldn't go looking for trouble of any kind, shape, or form while we were here. We had more than our share of drama just trying to get married. I intend to enjoy this honeymoon."

He stepped closer, looking down at her with so much love—not to mention a lusty twinkle in his eye—that she could hardly resist.

Then she thought of how hard that blonde had been running on the beach, dressed in her fine business suit. For a moment, Savannah's curiosity warred with her desire to stay on her new husband's good side.

After twenty-four hours, she was all too aware of how nice his good side could be.

But of all Savannah's virtues and vices, the character trait that had always been first and foremost in her psyche was curiosity. Pure and simple.

And this time, it won out over lust. It triumphed over her soul-deep need for a peaceful vacation from their recent travails. Even her deeply engrained Southern teachings about pleasing the people around you at all personal costs crumbled in the face of pure, unadulterated nosiness.

"I have to find out," she told him, fixing him with her infamous, cobalt blue-eyed, steely, hundred-yard gaze. "I understand why you'd want nothing to do with it. I know you want our time here to be about loving and bonding and celebrating our nuptials, and I appreciate that. And I promise you we'll get to that."

She took a breath and looked down at the catwalk beneath their feet. "In fact, I promise you that later tonight, we'll sneak up here in the dark and I'll make such wild, passionate love to you that you won't be able to see straight for a month."

He grinned. "Wouldn't mind trying that."

"It's a promise. But, boy, I'm telling you something else just as sincerely. If you don't get outta my way, I'm gonna hurt you."

He moved aside so that she could pass.

As she reached for the door, he got it first and

opened it for her. As she moved past him, he put his hand on her back and gave her a little pat. "I'm gonna hold you to that promise. Ordinarily, with the way I feel about heights, I wouldn't be lookin' for an excuse to come back up here. But that was a pretty intriguing offer you made."

"I never made love in a lighthouse," she said as she stepped back inside the lantern room. "Have to make the most of life's opportunities when they present themselves. Never know if they'll come back around again."

He followed her, giving a sheepish glance back toward the side of the light where he had been standing alone earlier. "Okay," he said. "But when we come back up here—to get romantic and all . . ."

"Yes?"

"You don't wanna go around to that other side, where I was when you called me."

"Because? . . ."

" 'Cause that's where I threw up."

"You threw up on the walkway? Dirk, that is so gross! Why did you do that? Why didn't you lean over and do your business over the rail?"

He stared at her with haunted eyes for what seemed like forever. Finally he said, "Lean *over*? Look *down*? Look *al-l-l* the way *down*? Are you kidding me?"

"Oh. Right." She sighed, rolled her eyes, and shook her head. "What was I thinking?"

Chapter 3

Savannah made it down the lighthouse staircase in less than half the time it had taken her to climb it. Funny how much easier it was when you had gravity and rabid curiosity on your side.

Dirk was directly behind her as she rushed out the front door and closed it behind them.

"I guess I should lock it," she said, fumbling with the keys in her hand. "Betty Sue wouldn't have given us keys if we weren't supposed to use them."

It took her a couple of tries to get the ancient lock to turn, but finally it slid home with a solid *thunk*. And when she tried the door, it was securely fastened.

"There," she said. "No lighthouse burglars or nor'easter's gonna push that sucker open."

Dirk motioned toward the nearest cliff. "How do you propose we get down to the beach from here? I've climbed all the heights my delicate psyche can handle for a while."

"I saw some stairs over there," she said, "leading down from that dirt road to the water."

He trudged along at her heels as she headed in that

direction. "Just what I need. Another big, long, high, *tall* staircase."

She stopped and turned so abruptly that he ran into her. "If you don't want to go down there with me, you don't have to. I'll go by myself and you can stand there at the top of the steps and look down and . . . Oh, sorry. You wouldn't want to do that either, huh?"

He didn't miss her sarcasm. Judging from his scowl, he didn't like it either.

"You know," he said, "just because you don't have any phobia junk yourself doesn't mean you should make fun of people who do. It ain't easy. In fact, it can make a person feel pretty damned stupid to be scared spitless of something that doesn't bother most other people."

For a moment, she flashed back on all the times she'd made chicken jokes at his expense, and she felt more than a little ashamed of herself.

She reached out and placed her hands on his chest. She could feel his heart pounding beneath her palms.

Wow! This really is hard for him, she thought. *Rough, tough ol' Dirk. Who would've imagined?*

"I'm sorry, sugar," she said, her voice soft with Georgia sweetness. "I really am. You don't need to go down those stairs or anyplace else you're not comfortable going. And I promise I won't ask you again."

He gave a snort and headed for the top of the stairs. "Oh, I'm going down to the beach with my wife," he called over his shoulder. "I just want her to appreciate the sacrifice I'm making for her. I want major husband points."

She laughed as she scrambled after him. "You got 'em, babycakes. And being how it's our honeymoon, you should have plenty of opportunities to cash 'em in."

As they hurried down the steep stairs, Dirk in the lead, she glanced to their left, to the stand of yellow-blossomed trees where she had first spotted the woman. Then she looked farther down to the rock outcropping where the blonde had disappeared. All seemed still and natural. No hint of anything amiss.

Except for the churned sand where the woman had left uneven, ragged footprints as she'd fled along the water's edge.

Savannah directed Dirk toward the stand of trees. "The gal was dodging in and out of those big bushes," she told him. "Like she was trying to hide from somebody who was after her."

They walked into the thicket and picked their way among the scrub brush, looking for anything that Mother Nature herself might not have left there.

Savannah located the first find . . . and the second. "Here are her shoes," she said, pointing to a designer peep-toed pump, which had been discarded beside a mallow bush. A few feet away lay its mate. Savannah wanted to reach down, pick it up, and examine the glossy, charcoal gray patent leather. But years of experience and expertise involving the handling of potential evidence kept her from doing so. Something told her these shoes and anything else they might find could wind up being evidence.

"She may have pulled them off so she could get around in the sand easier," Savannah said. "I wouldn't want to be running for my life in high heels on a beach."

"Which brings you to the question, 'Why would she wear high heels to the beach in the first place?' " he replied, poking among the bushes.

"Maybe when she dressed this morning, she didn't know she'd wind up strolling on the sand," Savannah suggested.

He leaned down, looking at something on the sand

beneath a plant with delicate green leaves and flowers like small magenta stars. "Hey," he said. "I got something else here."

"What's that?" Savannah walked over to him and squatted to see.

"Looks like a purse to me."

Instantly Savannah recognized the luxury handbag as a Louis Vuitton. "I don't think a lot of ladies grab their Louis on the way out the door to the beach."

"Grab their Louis?"

Dirk didn't spend a lot of time reading magazines that featured lifestyles and handbags of the rich and famous. His favorite boxing magazine, *The Ring*, didn't include a lot of ads for Louis Vuitton handbags or luggage.

"That purse cost more than my car is worth," she said with only the slightest twinge of green-eyed, gut-twisting envy.

"Something tells me," Dirk replied, "that right now you wouldn't want to trade places with the woman who dropped that purse and ran right out of her shoes, trying to get away from somebody."

"So true. So true."

Leaving the designer accessories untouched on the ground, Savannah started to follow the clear line of footprints in the sand. When she had the rare opportunity to stalk her prey in sand, mud, or snow, she felt like a Native American tracker—who was cheating. She didn't even need the assistance of Granny Reid's bloodhound, Beauregard. As a private detective, it was about as easy as her job ever got.

"Wish everybody left tracks like these," Dirk said as he caught up and walked beside her. "It'd make police work a lot simpler."

"I was just thinking the same thing. How much you

wanna bet that purse back there'll tell us all we want to know about who she is?"

"I almost looked in it to see. But you seem so convinced there's skullduggery afloat, I figured I'd better not disturb it till we see what we're dealing with."

" 'Skullduggery afloat'?" She snickered. "You've been hanging out with Tammy 'Wannabe Nancy Drew' Hart too long. In a minute, you'll start talking about 'sleuthing' and 'finding clues in old clocks under staircases.' "

"Harrumph. I'll have you know that was a Sherlock Holmes reference. Nancy Drew, my ass."

"If Tammy were here, she'd slap you upside the head, using 'Nancy Drew' and 'ass' in the same sentence like that. I'm pretty sure she'd consider that blasphemous."

"The kid's a pansy-bimbo, and she doesn't hit that hard. Where you, on the other hand—".

Savannah was too absorbed to appreciate the compliment as they had reached the outcropping where she had last seen the woman. Holding up one hand, she motioned Dirk to stop.

She lowered her voice and said, "Shh. If she's right around the corner, I don't want to scare her."

"What you mean is, you're nosy and you don't wanna interrupt anything that might be going on until you find out what it is."

She gave him an annoyed look. She hated how he always knew exactly what she was up to. Even more upsetting was that after figuring it out, he would then tell her—usually in terms that made her intentions sound less noble than they were. Or, at least, less noble than she liked to portray them.

There was nothing more irritating than a friend who knew you better than you knew yourself.

Except maybe a husband.

What had she gotten herself into, putting that ring on her finger? Everything she had ever loved and hated about the man beside her was now magnified a hundred-fold.

Yikes, she thought, before shoving the whole subject to the back of her mind. It didn't bear thinking about. Not now anyway. Because she thought she could hear a female voice, and the sound was coming from the vicinity of the rocks ahead. Perhaps just on the other side.

The woman sounded upset and scared.

She glanced at Dirk and realized from the concerned look on his face that he could hear it, too. He nodded and stepped closer to her.

Together, they looked around the rocks and saw that the shoreline curved sharply, forming a small, rock-strewn cove. There, the beach was narrow, as thick brush and trees crowded close to the water.

In the midst of some of the thickest foliage, she saw patches of blue again, moving among the green.

"There she is," she whispered to Dirk.

"Where? I don't see anything."

"Over there, on the other side of those rocks, in the trees. She's wearing a blue suit."

A second later, the blonde burst out of the foliage and headed straight toward them, running as fast as she could.

They heard her scream, "No! No!"

The sound went through Savannah—human fear, raw and primal. No one screamed like that unless they were horribly hurt or afraid they were about to die.

Savannah took one step toward the woman, intending to skirt the rocks and run to her aid.

But a loud, popping sound echoed around them.

Dirk's hand shot out and yanked her back behind the cover of the stones.

"Gun!" they yelled in unison.

There was another shot. And yet another.

Savannah had to look.

She took one quick peek and saw the blonde stumbling toward the water. Her hands reached out in front of her, as though trying to grasp some form of safety that wasn't to be had.

One more shot, and she fell, face forward, into the foaming surf.

A horrible feeling of helplessness washed over Savannah as she watched the waves roll over the victim. She couldn't see the shooter. Whoever had fired the shots was hidden among the trees.

Even if she could see the shooter, she didn't have her weapon on her. And she didn't need to ask Dirk if he had his.

Usually, both of them brought their guns with them, even on vacations. Old habits die hard for a cop and an ex-cop/private detective.

But they had decided that heavy weapons strapped against their ribs would not enhance the romance of the occasion. Surely, a newlywed couple wouldn't need guns on their honeymoon, so both had left their weapons at home.

She turned to Dirk, saw the look of horror on his face, and knew he was feeling exactly what she was.

Well, maybe not exactly.

As she turned and looked back at the woman lying, dying in the water, a sense of dread flowed through her that only someone who had endured a similar, terrible circumstance could feel.

Only a few months before, Savannah, too, had been

felled by gunshots and had lain on the ground, bleeding, knowing that her life was literally flowing out of her.

In that moment, standing on the beach, she could feel the other woman's pain—that searing, fiery misery—in her own body. Savannah could feel her icy terror and the agony of thinking that no one was coming, no one could save her.

But someone had saved Savannah. Dirk had been there for her when she'd needed him most. Someone had to be there for the woman on the beach, too.

Savannah couldn't stand there, in the safety the rocks afforded, and just let her die alone. Shooter in the woods, or not, she shook off Dirk's restraining hand and darted out from behind the rocks.

It was crazy, she knew, to put herself in harm's way, out there in the open with no cover. No weapon. No armed backup. It went against all her training and even her common sense.

She could hear Dirk yelling at her. She knew he was terrified and furious with her.

She'd deal with him later.

If she made it to the woman without getting shot herself.

As she ran, she braced herself for the feeling she knew all too well, the impact of bullets piercing her body, scorching and fierce as they ripped into soft, unresisting flesh.

But there were no more shots.

No one ran out of the bushes toward her—though she was dimly aware in her peripheral vision of Dirk racing across the sand toward the trees.

For a moment, a sharp bolt of fear crashed through her. What if Dirk was killed? What if his reaction to her impulsive move got him shot?

Fortunately, she didn't have long to play that night-mare fully in her mind, because she had reached the woman and was standing, knee deep in the surf, grab-bing for her.

The victim was still alive, but thrashing weakly; her face downward in the brine. Savannah slid one forearm under each of the woman's armpits and dragged her back onto the sand.

She flipped her onto her back, and that was when she saw the wounds. Two dark areas blossoming into hideous red circles of blood—one on the woman's chest, the other in her abdomen.

Exit wounds.

Sometimes they were smaller than entry wounds. Sometimes the same size. But more often, they were larger.

These were huge.

Savannah's heart sank when she saw them. Not just the size, but the location.

She looked into the woman's eyes and could see that she, too, knew what was about to happen. No matter what Savannah—or anyone else did for her—she was going to die.

Savannah glanced back toward the trees. She could see Dirk moving among them, quickly, but carefully. Or-dinarily, she would have been rooting for him to catch the bad guy. But an armed bad guy? And Dirk without his weapon? No, this was one time she hoped the two wouldn't meet.

She knelt beside the woman, leaned over, and checked her breathing. She could hear air rushing in and out, but it wasn't a comforting sound. It had an awful, gargling quality that Savannah had heard before. It was a sound that preceded death.

The woman's eyes were open, wide open, registering

her pain, fear, and shock. She seemed aware of Savannah's presence.

"It's okay," Savannah lied as she pressed her palms over the dark wounds, an action that did absolutely nothing to stanch the flow. "You're okay."

"No," the woman whispered. "Not okay."

Savannah looked deep into the victim's eyes and knew—this wasn't the time for lies.

"I'm going to stay with you," Savannah said. "I'll be right here with you. Okay?"

The woman seemed to understand and nodded slightly.

"The worst has already happened," Savannah told her. "I know you're scared, and I know it hurts. But it's going to get better." She glanced down at the blood pouring through her fingers at an impossibly high rate, staining the sand and water around them.

"Soon," Savannah told her. "It's going to get better soon. All right?"

The woman on the sand nodded again. Some of the fear seemed to leave her face as she stared up into Savannah's eyes.

For the briefest moment, it occurred to Savannah that she might know this woman. Something about her was familiar, but she couldn't place her.

There would be time for that later. The trained police officer in Savannah came to the fore, pushing everything else to the background.

"Who shot you?" Savannah asked her. "Who did this?"

The victim moved her lips, though the sound she made was little more than a whisper. The dreadful gurgling sound was diminishing. Instinctively, Savannah knew she had only moments to live.

"Who were you running from?" Savannah asked again. "Who did this to you?"

Savannah leaned closer, her ear nearly against the woman's mouth. She heard one word, feebly uttered, but clear all the same.

"William."

"William? William shot you?" Savannah asked, feeling a rush of discovery, even in such sad circumstances.

But then the woman shook her head. "No. Not William. William . . ."

And that was all.

Savannah moved her hands away from the wounds and reached to grasp the woman's hand. It was limp. As lifeless as the eyes that now stared blindly up at her.

A moment later, the gargling stopped. So did the blood flow.

Savannah felt the strength go out of her own legs. She sat down abruptly beside the body.

In an unconscious movement—her mind frozen from the trauma of having just watched someone lose her life—she spread her fingers and held her hands down below the surface of the waves. She watched as the water flowed over them, washing away the blood. She watched for what seemed like a very long time, as with each wave they got cleaner.

She watched because she didn't want to see the beautiful young woman stretched out on the sand beside her.

"Van."

The miracle of life gone forever from her eyes.

"Savannah."

The woman she hadn't been able to save.

"Savannah. Honey, are you okay?"

She turned her head and looked up. Dirk was stand-

ing over her, staring down at her, a dark expression on
his face.

"Yeah," she said.

He glanced toward the body. "She's gone," he said. It
was more of a statement than a question.

"Yeah."

He reached down and offered Savannah his hands.
She took them, and he pulled her gently to her feet.

"I didn't see the shooter," he told her. "I found the
spent casings over there, under that big oak tree."

"Okay."

"There's a road only about fifty feet in. He's probably
long gone."

Savannah was barely listening. She was forcing herself to look at the dead woman's face. A lovely face,
even in death. A face that did, indeed, look very familiar to her.

"Amelia," she said, more to herself than to him.

"What?"

"I knew I'd seen her before. So have you. That's
Amelia Northrop."

Dirk studied the victim for a moment. "The Channel
Seven newscaster that we watch every night?"

Savannah nodded solemnly.

He bent down and took a better look. "Holy cow,
you're right. It's her. Now that I think about it, I heard
that she has a vacation home here on the island, her
and her big-time land developer husband, William
Northrop."

"William. Yes, William."

"Huh?"

"She said his name . . . before. . . ."

"Like, 'Tell William I love him'?"

"No. I asked her who shot her, and she said,

'William.' Then I said, 'William shot you?' and she said, 'No.' She passed before she could say any more."

"Great. Just what you want at a homicide. An incomplete dying declaration."

Suddenly Savannah began to shiver violently. Though she blamed it on the fact that her clothes were wet, she knew better, because the chill reached deep inside her.

Dirk wrapped his arm around her waist and pulled her close. She buried her face against his warm chest and closed her eyes. But she could still see it—all that blood pooling between her fingers. The light going out in the young woman's eyes.

"I couldn't save her, Dirk," she said softly.

He hugged her more tightly. "You did what you could."

"I was hoping I could save her."

"You did all you could. You kept her from dying alone."

"It wasn't enough."

He reached down, put his hand under her chin, and forced her to look up at him. His eyes were moist, like hers, when he said, "Savannah, listen to me. You risked your life for her. It *was* enough."

His eyes searched hers, looking for a sincere response.

"Do you hear me?" he asked.

Finally she nodded. "I hear you." And the words were from her heart.

Yes, she told herself as she pressed her face, once again, to his chest. *I did all I could do. And "all" has to be enough.*

Chapter 4

One phone call to 911 and twenty minutes later, the shoreline was crawling with Santa Tesla's finest. But there weren't that many of them. And Savannah and Dirk weren't at all impressed.

They had expected the police force arriving at the crime scene would be minuscule compared to the LAPD or even San Carmelita's teams. The island had a reputation for being virtually crime-free, so why would they need a massive department?

But even the smallest and least busy law enforcement agency needed a rudimentary knowledge of how to process an area where a felony had occurred. And their total lack of efficiency was driving Savannah and Dirk crazy. Standing on the sidelines, watching the so-called investigators walk around in circles, was almost more than they could stand.

What impressed them least was the fact that no one had even debriefed them about what had happened. Not interviewing eyewitnesses was a highly unusual procedure, considering the gravity of the crime and the fact that they had seen it happen firsthand.

Two uniformed policemen, a man wearing a white smock, which suggested he might be a coroner or CSI, and a woman in a black suit strolled around, the four of them chatting among themselves, while occasionally stopping to study the body and the surrounding beach area.

"Shouldn't we go grab one of them and tell them about the cartridges we found, and the shoes, and the purse?" Savannah asked Dirk, who was leaning on the rocks they had previously hidden behind when they had witnessed the shooting.

His arms were crossed over his chest and the scowl etched on his face told it all. Dirk didn't like standing by and watching people bungle a job when he could—with his characteristic total lack of humility—tell them how to do it much better.

He was especially offended when the shoddy job being done was police work.

And he certainly didn't like being ignored.

"Naw," he replied. "Let 'em contaminate the scene a little more. There might be some area of it that they haven't tromped on yet."

"Maybe they're waiting for the dogcatcher and the librarian to arrive and lay down a few more footprints here and there."

"Smash some more evidence down into the sand."

"Handle the body and see if they can drop a little more hair and fibers on it before they bag it."

They sighed and shook their heads in unison, as only a pair who had worked together far too many years and processed far too many crime scenes together would do.

"Somebody might've already took off with that purse back there," he grumbled.

"If any woman who wears that size shoe sees those

pumps, she's gonna nab them and giggle all the way home, figuring she's hit the jackpot."

Dirk watched the woman in the suit walk over to the body, once again, and stand there, staring off into the ocean, as though hoping the sea would offer clues as to what had happened on land. "Not our problem," he said.

"Apparently, not even our concern," she replied.

"If they ain't worried, why should we be?"

As they stood there in silence and watched one of the patrolmen pick up a small bit of seaweed, look it over, and then throw it down, Savannah felt her indignation rise to uncontrollable levels.

"If I don't do something, I'm gonna pop," she told him. "That woman layin' there has a right to a proper investigation. If these nincompoops aren't gonna give her one, we are. Come on."

"But—"

Before he could register any sort of complaint, Savannah was gone, striding across the sand toward the body and the gal in the black suit. She was a woman with a purpose. Following a few paces behind her, Dirk knew better than to try to stop her when her mind was set, her mission as clear as this one was.

By the time he caught up with her, she was already in the midst of her verbal tirade, giving the woman in black what-for.

As usual, when Savannah's ire was raised to dizzying heights, her Southern accent was as thick as Mississippi sorghum.

". . . nothing like this in all my ever-livin' days," she was saying, her hands on her hips, her face only inches from the woman's. "My partner . . . uh . . . husband and I told that young patrolman over there that we were

eyewitnesses to the whole thing. And we've been standing over there by that rock, our teeth in our mouths,
waiting for somebody to give a tinker's damn and come
question us about what we saw. But *nooo*. Y'all are too
busy pussyfooting around here, accomplishing absolutely nothing to—"

"Excuse me?" the woman interjected. "Do you want
to tell me who the hell you are?"

"Savannah Reid . . . er, Coulter . . . um, Reid. I'm a
private detective from the mainland and a former cop.
This is my husband, Detective Sergeant Dirk Coulter, of
the San Carmelita Police Department. We saw this
woman get shot and watched her die. So it might be-
hoove you knuckleheads to have a word with us about
what happened here, before you do much more muckin' around."

Savannah glanced down at Amelia Northrop's lifeless corpse, her sightless eyes, and a wave of sadness and
pity swept through her. "Except maybe to cover up that
poor woman's body," she said. "If you have something
clean that won't contaminate it any more than y'all
have already done."

The woman in black stood there quietly for a long
moment, studying first Savannah, then Dirk, with eyes
so dark they didn't seem to have pupils. Her black hair
was short and lay in tight waves close to her scalp.

She was a large woman, as tall as Savannah and just
as full-figured. Her rigid posture suggested a military
background; the scowl on her face and the way her
black eyes bored into both of them might have intimi-
dated lesser souls.

"Yeah!" Dirk snapped. "You wanna hear what we got
or not? We have better things to do than cool our heels
at your crime scene. We're on our honeymoon, you
know."

"No, I didn't know," she replied coolly. "In fact, no one even told me that we had eyewitnesses."

At that moment, a patrolman rushed up to them and tried to wedge himself between the woman and Savannah. Savannah gave him a look that caused him to think better of it. He moved aside just a little.

"Sorry, Chief," he said to the woman. "I don't know how they got out here." He turned to Savannah and Dirk. "You two can't be here. We've got a dead . . . I mean . . . we're conducting an investigation, and you don't belong on the beach."

"Actually, Franklin, it appears they do," the newly identified chief of police told him. "In fact, someone should have notified me of their presence long ago. It seems they're eyewitnesses to the killing."

"Oh," Franklin said sheepishly. "I didn't know. . . ."

"What's worse, *I* didn't know." The chief gave the young man a withering look, which made Savannah feel a little sorry for him.

After having been fired from the police force by a crooked chief, she wasn't fond of "the brass." And this woman in her austere black suit, with her piercing black eyes and her black mood, seemed to be a particular pain in the "brass."

Savannah didn't envy Franklin having to work for her.

"You and I will discuss this later," the chief told the patrolman.

He ducked his head and scurried away, reminding Savannah of Beauregard the bloodhound, after an especially harsh scold-ing from Granny Reid—usually regarding the evils of chicken chasing.

The woman held out her hand to Savannah. "I'm Chief Charlotte La Cross, of the Santa Tesla Police Department. I regret all the inconvenience your waiting must have caused you," she added with more than a touch of sarcasm in her voice.

Although she didn't look all that remorseful, Savannah shook her proffered hand anyway. After all, there was little advantage to offending the chief of police—any more than she already had.

Though Savannah figured any former rudeness on her part should be overlooked.

What? This gal never heard of wearing a uniform, or, at the very least, a badge? she thought. How was she supposed to know the woman was the frickin' chief of police before she ripped into her, verbal guns ablazin'?

Any decent person would have held up a warning hand and said something like, "Excuse me. Before you dig your grave any deeper, you should know you're addressing the head honcho here." Especially once an uninformed body started using words like "knuckleheads" and "muckin' around" to make their point.

Savannah swallowed a little lump in her throat, which tasted just a tad like crow, and said, "Nice to make your acquaintance, Chief La Cross. Or, at least, it would be, under pleasanter circumstances. You'll have to pardon me if my words had a bit of an edge to them earlier. You see, we've had a pretty rough last couple of hours."

"Yeah," Dirk said, accepting the lukewarm handshake that was offered to him as well. "When we set out this morning to have a nice, relaxing day here on your pretty little island, we weren't expecting to wind up in a situation like this."

"No. I don't suppose you were." Chief La Cross studied them for a long time before adding in a guarded tone, "Hardly any serious crimes occur on Santa Tesla.

Certainly, no violent crimes. Why, this island is the closest thing you'll find to paradise anywhere on God's
green earth."

Savannah couldn't help wondering what travel
brochure she had taken that line from. It reminded her
that tourism was everything to Santa Tesla and its permanent inhabitants. Without mainland dollars flowing
through its stores, hotels, and eateries, the island's
economy would collapse within weeks.

It also occurred to Savannah that if word got out that
an innocent woman had been gunned down in cold
blood on one of their beautiful, pristine beaches, that
might not be good for Santa Tesla's bottom line.

Although, considering the identity of the victim, it
certainly wasn't a secret that could be kept. Short of a
media blackout, this would be the lead story on the six
o'clock news.

Amelia Northrop was as well known for her ferocious
approach to expository journalism as she was for her ex-
ceptional beauty. More than one of her scathing, in-depth
reports had brought people in high places, their compa-
nies and organizations, their extravagant lifestyles, crashing to the ground.

Savannah couldn't help thinking that if she were
Chief La Cross, the first place she'd look would be that
list of former demigods and demigoddesses, now ru-
ined and publicly disgraced.

The chief turned from Savannah and Dirk, long
enough to wave over the second patrolman on the
beach.

"How long until you'll be bagging this body for trans-
port?" Chief La Cross asked him.

"Uh, well, Martin has to take some pictures of it before we—"

"Then tell him to get them taken, and then either re-move it or cover it with a tarp. The press will be arriving any minute. If any unauthorized photos are taken, I'm holding you two responsible."

"Yes, Chief."

The patrolman hurried away and returned almost in-stantly with the man in the smock, who took out a cam-era and began taking shot after shot of the body.

Chief La Cross led Savannah and Dirk across the beach, back to where they had been standing beside the rocks. "So," she said, "what do you have to tell me about this? What exactly did you see?"

"We saw that woman run out of the woods toward the water," Dirk told her. "We heard the shots and saw her fall."

"If you want more detail than that," Savannah added, "we'd be glad to fill in all the blanks. But before we do that, you've got some evidence lying just around the corner and down the shore a piece."

"What evidence?" La Cross asked.

"Some discarded high heels and a purse."

A look passed over the chief's face that Savannah rec-ognized. It was one she'd seen many times. It was an ex-pression that flashed across someone's features, right before they told a lie.

"That's good," the chief said evenly. "Maybe it's hers and will have her ID in it. Then we can find out who she is."

Savannah stared at her for a long time, searching her eyes. Finally she said, "Are you telling me that you don't know who that is, lying back there on the beach?"

"No. Why would I? Do you?"

It was another lie. Savannah could tell, and one quick glance at Dirk told her that he knew it, too.

"Of course I do," Savannah replied. "I'm surprised

that you don't. It's the news reporter Amelia Northrop. One of your more prominent and famous residents, I should think."

For what seemed like a very long time, Savannah and Chief La Cross stood, staring into each other's eyes with the intensity of a couple of gunfighters. Finally it was the chief who broke the silence.

"You may be right. You may be wrong," she said. "But until we know for sure, I'm going to insist that you keep your opinion to yourself. You're to say nothing to anyone at all about what you think you saw here today. Do I make myself perfectly clear?"

Savannah didn't like her tone. She didn't like the chief's black suit or the way her eyes bored into hers. She didn't like her ramrod posture that gave the impression Chief La Cross was constantly looking to fight with anyone over anything . . . and expected to win every fight she began.

Dirk took a step toward the chief, his own stiff body language telegraphing his fury. "Now see here," he began.

Savannah held up one hand, signaling him to let her have this one. It was a gesture she'd used many times over the years, and he knew better than to ignore it.

He backed off.

"Now, Chief Charlotte La Cross," she began, her accent thick and bittersweet, "you don't want to go threatenin' me like that. Last I checked, there was still freedom of speech in this country."

"If you mean by 'this country' the United States of America, let me remind you that Santa Tesla Island may be a territory of the U.S., but we are self-governing in every way. We have our own system of law enforcement, and I'm the head of that system, so you will do exactly as I say, or you'll find yourself spending your honeymoon in separate cells in our jail."

She smiled, but there was no warmth in it. In fact, it reminded Savannah of a great white shark. And there was a conviction in her dark eyes that convinced Savannah she meant every word she was saying.

Dirk stepped closer to the chief; his eyes were no friendlier than hers. And he wasn't bothering with any sort of smile, warm and genial, or carnivorous. "The shoes and the purse are down the beach, that direction," he said through a clenched jaw, "under some bushes. Back where your patrolmen are tromping through the trees, there are some spent cartridges. From what little we observed, the shots seemed to come from that direction. Beyond that, my wife and I have nothing more to say to you."

He reached over, took Savannah's hand, and tucked it tightly into the crook of his arm. "If you need anything else, we'll be trying to enjoy what's left of our honeymoon in the lighthouse keeper's cottage. Good luck with your case. Something tells me you're going to need it."

"I hope you solve this murder," Savannah added as they walked away, "for the victim's sake, if not for yours. She died horribly. She deserves some justice."

Savannah could feel La Cross watching them, until they had rounded the rocks and were beyond her sight.

For some reason that she couldn't quite understand, but didn't want to think too much about, her eyes filled with tears. She tried to blink them away, but Dirk saw them.

"If you want me to," he said, "I'll go back and stomp a mud hole in her, as you Confederates like to say."

"Naw. Wouldn't be very gentlemanly, you whompin' a woman."

"You sure she's a woman? Something tells me that under that suit, she's got bigger gonads than mine."

She gouged him in the ribs with her elbow. "But not as big as mine!"

"Baby, nobody's got a set like yours!"

"Don't you forget it." She leaned closer and rested her head on his shoulder. He kissed the top of her head.

"Thanks for the offer," she said, "but I don't want you to thump her on my behalf. If you did, I'd have to jump into the affray and, like she said, we'd be spending our honeymoon behind bars instead of making wild whoopee in a beautiful lighthouse."

"We could find out which car is hers and put Limburger cheese on her manifold."

"Now you're talkin'."

Chapter 5

Much later, Savannah and Dirk settled down for the evening in the living room of the lightkeeper's cottage, having brought their luggage over from the motel. After searching through her suitcase, Savannah had donned the sleazy leopard-print negligee her sisters had given her as a bridal gift, thinking it might impress Dirk. When she'd appeared in all her glory, Dirk had given her a hearty wolf whistle and motioned her over onto the double chaise lounge where he was sprawled.

He'd dressed up special for her, too. He was wearing his briefs.

As they snuggled on the chaise in front of the fireplace, a soft afghan across their laps, Savannah contemplated—not for the first time that hour—how to murder her new husband and get away with it.

Of course, she would never actually do such a thing. But she found that, as she listened to him bitch and moan about absolutely everything under the sun, fantasizing about husbandcide could relieve a lot of pent-up stress.

"This bathtub crap just doesn't cut it. A man has to take a shower. Baths are for girls."

That complaint had prompted her to wonder how long it would take for a man to drown if he was dangled upside down by his feet . . . out a two-story window . . . in a Category 17 hurricane.

"This refrigerator doesn't get cold enough. My beer won't get cold enough. You know I can't stand it when my beer isn't cold enough!"

How long, she had wondered, could a guy survive, folded into quarters and stuffed into that undersized, theoretically lukewarm refrigerator? Could you fold a fellow in eighths and shove him into that tiny freezer? Would he suffocate right away, or would the hypothermia get him first?

"That looks like a feather bed! I can't sleep on a feather bed! They're way too soft! I need a good, hard surface for my bad back! Call that Betty Sue gal and tell her to get me a plank of plywood to put on top of that thing. Otherwise, I'll toss and turn all night, and you know how cranky I get when I don't get a good night's sleep."

If you rolled a grumpy curmudgeon up in a feather bed mattress, she speculated, and dragged him to the edge of a cliff and pushed him over, would he bounce when he hit the bottom? How many times? Would he roll on into the water? If he did, would a shark be able to bite through the mattress or just get a big mouthful of feathers?

"That might be entertaining," she mumbled to herself as they cuddled and stared into the fire, "a shark spitting out a mouthful of feathers."

"What?" Dirk turned and looked at her as though she'd lost her mind. "What did you say?"

"Oh, nothing. Do you think sharks sneeze?"

He shook his head and sighed. "Savannah, you're a very strange woman."

"Yes, I am. Don't ever forget that."

"Not likely." He reached down, took her hand, and folded it between his. "Since you're asking silly questions, I've got one for you."

"Shoot."

He nodded toward the mantel. "How do they get a ship inside a bottle, like that one there? I checked and there's no hole in the bottle or seam where they glued it or anything like that."

"It's a secret."

"Well, yeah. I figured that. Do you know the secret?"

"Yes. Grandpa Reid was a merchant marine, years before he even met Granny. He built one of those one time. She still has it."

"So, how did he do it?"

"I'm not gonna tell you. It's a sacred secret."

"Like magicians have?"

"Something like that."

She glanced over at the grandfather clock in the corner. "The news will be on in a couple of minutes," she said, her tone far heavier than a moment before. "Might as well turn it on."

"You really want to?" he asked, reaching for the remote control, which was lying on the end table next to him. "We said we were going to try to put it out of our minds as much as we could, and—"

"Well, I tried. And I couldn't. Could you?"

"No. I've been thinking about it all afternoon. How can you not? Something like that . . ."

He pointed the remote and punched a button. A moment later, a small television, which was mounted on the wall above a bookcase to their right, came alive.

"Might as well turn it to her station, I guess," he said,

flipping through the channels. "They'll have the best coverage."

Savannah steeled herself for the images that were sure to be splashed across the screen any moment now. She tried to brace herself for the emotions that would, undoubtedly, come flooding back the instant she saw them—not that she had been particularly successful in burying them.

She could even feel a sort of phantom pain in her own wounds, which, although mostly healed, would forever be a part of her. Some things—the memories, the scars, the horror that had been driven, DNA-deep, into every cell of her body—would never go away completely.

"And now . . . the *Eyewitness News* at six o'clock," a male voice was saying as majestic scenes of Southern California beauty flashed across the screen, along with the program's familiar logo and overly dramatic theme song, set to the rhythm of a clicking telegraph.

She felt Dirk's hand tighten around hers, and she blessed him for imparting that bit of comfort, and even for sensing that she needed it.

Even when she wanted to murder him, she couldn't help loving him to pieces.

She squeezed back. "Here we go," she said.

"Yeah. Let's see what they've got."

"It is with great sadness," said the handsome news anchor, with his perfect Ken doll hair and perfect, though slightly orange, tan, and his perfectly dazzling white smile, "that we report the passing of someone very close to us—a dear member of our *Eyewitness News* family."

He paused, and the look of deep sadness that crossed his face touched Savannah's heart, causing her to put aside her shallow judgments about his appearance. *Death has a way of putting such things into perspective*, she thought.

"Our own Amelia Northrop lost her life today on Santa Tesla Island, where she and her husband, William Northrop, have made their home for the past five years."

A picture of the beautiful blonde popped up on the screen, smiling her famous smile, her eyes alight with the intelligent curiosity that was her trademark.

Savannah couldn't help comparing the vision on the television with the one in her memory—the dead woman, with lifeless eyes and seaweed in her hair.

In all Savannah's years of dealing with life and death, she had never gotten over her amazement and bewilderment at the difference between the two states. It was a paradox of the darkest sort.

"Her body was discovered, floating facedown in the surf in one of Santa Tesla's picturesque coves," the announcer continued. "And while the investigation is in its preliminary stages, officials say her death appeared to have been the result of accidental drowning."

"'Accidental drowning'?" Savannah and Dirk shouted in unison as they bolted upright from their comfortable, reclining positions.

"What the hell?" Dirk said. "She drowned, my ass! What about the bullet wounds that were . . . ?"

"Two, at least," Savannah said, jumping off the chaise. "The way she was bleeding, at least one of them got her right in the heart! I can't remember when I saw that much blood!" She paced back and forth in front of the television. "Drowning? *Drowning?* How can they say that?"

She paused to listen as the anchor continued his speech. "We go to Santa Tesla Island, where our on-the-scene reporter, Lori Austin, has more details. Lori, this is a sad, sad day for us all here at *Eyewitness News*. Tell us what you've discovered there."

The scene switched to a locale Savannah knew all too well—the beach where Amelia Northrop had died. A pretty brunette in a bright red dress stood with her back to the ocean. Her grief showed on her picture-perfect face as she gave her report.

"Earlier this morning, shortly after Amelia was found here on the beach, I had the opportunity to talk to Santa Tesla's chief of police, Charlotte La Cross."

Again the scene changed, and Lori was interviewing a woman with a face Savannah was beginning to loathe. Lori asked the chief, "What can you tell us about what happened here this morning?"

With the expected degree of grave concern, La Cross responded, "From what we understand at this time, this morning some tourists, who were enjoying our beautiful beaches, happened upon Ms. Northrop. She was lying, facedown, in the water right about there."

She turned and pointed to an area of the beach that had been cordoned off with yellow tape. "They pulled her from the water and tried to administer lifesaving cardiopulmonary resuscitation to her. Unfortunately, she was already gone."

"What!?" Savannah whipped around to Dirk to see if he was hearing what she was. "Administer CPR? Who administered CPR? What is all this crap?"

"Who said she was gone?" Dirk shouted back. "Nobody told her the gal was gone! The victim was alive when you pulled her outta the water. She talked to you, for Pete's sake!"

"Yeah, but the chief there doesn't know that," Savannah reminded him, "because she didn't bother to question us about diddly-squat!"

"I got the strong impression she didn't want us to confuse her with any facts."

"Exactly."

"At this time," the chief continued, "it appears she was taking a morning swim and may have been caught in a riptide. We did issue a riptide warning earlier in the morning. Here on Santa Tesla Island, our guests' safety is always our foremost consideration. Unfortunately, not everyone heeds our advice in these matters. It's sad that a young woman had to lose her life in this terrible accident."

" 'Accident'!" Dirk yelled at the TV. "This is unbelievable! Savannah, what are we gonna do about this?"

"We're going to do exactly what she warned us not to do," Savannah replied, a wicked light in her eyes. "We're going to talk about this to everybody we can, starting with that news channel right there. Something tells me they'd want to know what really happened to their fellow journalist."

"And," he said, "we're going to go back home and get our weapons. I'm not going to be running around this island with an armed killer on the loose and crooked law enforcement in high places without proper protection."

"And we'll sic the Moonlight Magnolia gang on that police chief. They'll find out why she's lying like a no-legged dog. Something tells me this ain't her first roll in the manure pile. She's just gotta have some secrets to uncover."

"We'll put Tammy on her trail."

Savannah shuddered. "Normally, I wouldn't wish Tammy on my worst enemy. That gal's ruthless when it comes to digging up a body's dirt. But something about that La Cross makes my flesh crawl."

"So we'll catch a ferry back home first thing tomorrow morning," Dirk said as he reached for the remote and switched off the TV.

Savannah just stood there, staring down at him, until he finally said, "Unless you want to go now."

"Put your britches on, boy. We got tracks to make."

Savannah turned to Dirk, who was driving, and noticed that the greenish tint to his face was fading a little. Just a little.

She reached over and patted his arm. "Sorry, sugar," she said. "We'll get you a big ol' package of seasick medicine for the trip back."

"Gee, thanks. Ain't that sorta like closin' the barn door after the horses—or my dinner, as the case might be—has already left?"

"You weren't the only one. It can happen to anybody. I noticed a lady leaning over the back of the boat with you, keeping you company while you upchucked."

"She was pregnant."

"Oh. Sorry. Maybe the waters will be calmer on the way back."

"If not, I'll have my gun with me. I can always just shoot myself and get it over with."

"Um . . . o-okay."

After that uplifting exchange, they drove on in silence, from San Carmelita's waterfront, up the hill, and through its charming downtown area. The tiny tourist town was best known for its antique stores, souvenir shops, and restaurants, all Spanish Mediterranean–style white stucco and red-tiled roofs, accented with stone or brightly colored tiles and wrought iron.

The first time Savannah had seen this town, more years ago than she wanted to count, she had thought she was in Shangri-la.

Although there were many beautiful areas of Georgia, Savannah hadn't been raised in one of them. Poor people, living in shotgun shacks, scratching a meager living from red clay, barely able to put food on the table—that had been her childhood reality.

So, San Carmelita and its gleaming mission-inspired architecture, sparkling in the Southern California sun, its palm tree–lined streets, all cooled by constant, gentle breezes from the Pacific, had spoken to her. It had said, "You're home, Savannah girl." Having found her heart's home, she knew she would never leave.

Dirk drove his battered old Buick past the commercial district and into the residential area, where Savannah and the majority of her fellow San Carmelitans lived. She couldn't afford the mansions on the hillsides, with their panoramic ocean views. But in her part of town, the small, modest homes had a charm all their own. Like hers, most were also stucco with red-tiled roofs, and though the lots were small in this area, the yards were all well kept. Flowers of every bright color spilled in profusion from window boxes, draped over fences, and climbed over arbors and trellises.

When they arrived at her simple two-story cottage, she noticed that her own bougainvillea was glowing dark red in the light of the setting sun. She remembered the day she had planted those two small cuttings, one on each side of her doorway. Now they were massive splashes of color, running up the sides of the door and meeting over it in a graceful arch, turning her plain little house into a thing of beauty.

"It's kinda nice to be home," she said. "I've only been gone a little over twenty-four hours, but I miss it."

She turned in the seat and looked at him lovingly. "This'll be your home from now on, too. Cool, huh?"

"Yeah. I've gotta get all my crap dragged over here, before it's gonna feel much like home to me," he grumbled. "I'll have to rent a truck. Not looking forward to that."

"*All my crap*"*?* she thought. Those three simple words filled her with unspeakable horror. "*All*"*? Really?*

She did a quick mental inventory of the contents of his house trailer. His bus seat "sofa." His two rusty TV trays, which served as dining tables. His stacks of plastic crates filled with VHS tapes.

Then there was his Harley-Davidson collection. He didn't actually own a Harley, but he had all the trappings: the ashtrays, the shot glasses, the figurines, the mugs, the old tin signs, the tee-shirts—framed, of course—collector plates galore, and last, but not least, an awe-inspiring collection of Harley-Davidson Christmas ornaments.

She thought of how lovely those ornaments would look next Christmas hanging on her tree among her carefully color-coordinated, lavender and rose Victorian vintage baubles.

Oh, dear Lord, she thought, *what have I gotten myself into?*

Dirk pulled into her driveway and parked next to her bright red '65 Mustang. It was her baby, her pride and joy, the reason why she could almost understand why he loved his Harley stuff to distraction. An obsession was an obsession. As long as she talked lovingly and sang to her 'Stang every Saturday morning when she washed, vacuumed, dusted, and waxed it—stopping just short of flossing its teeth—she really couldn't say much about his framed Harley tee-shirts.

"Who-all's here?" he said as he cut the key and gave a wary glance toward the house.

"You mean, which of my zillion Georgia relatives are still using my house as a free motel while they prolong their California vacations?"

"Yeah, something like that."

Savannah couldn't blame him for being leery. So was she. On her wedding day, when she had left her home, it had been filled to the brim with Reids.

As the oldest of nine kids, she had more relatives than she could shake a stick at. Frequently, she found that was exactly what she wanted to do. She could handle them one at a time when she had to, but having her small, two-bedroom, one-and-a-half–bath house overrun with her two brothers, six sisters, one brother-in-law, two nieces, and two nephews had just about been her undoing.

Her grandmother had been there, too, but Granny was the one person in the world, other than Dirk—and the jury was still out on him—whom Savannah wouldn't mind living with for the rest of her life. Gran had taken all nine of her neglected grandchildren into her home and heart, years ago. For that, and for all the loving guidance and comfort she still continued to supply in bountiful abundance, Savannah would be forever grateful and in her debt.

"Well, Granny's here," she told him.

"Gran can stay as long as she wants, as far as I'm concerned," he said, reminding her of why she loved him.

"And Waycross."

"Waycross's a cool dude. I don't mind him. Just tell me Vidalia and her old man and those two sets of twins are gone."

"Left this morning."

"Thank goodness for that. Not that I don't like children, but those kids of hers are enough to turn you against the younger set."

"Cordele, Alma, Jessup, Atlanta, and Macon left last night. Marietta's still here," she said, hoping she could slip that in without him noticing it.

"Marietta? Oh, man. Just kill me now."

"Ah, come on. I know how much you love her."

" 'Love her'? I can't stand her. What's that thing you always say about her and cockroaches?"

"She's crazy as a sprayed roach?"

"That's it. And she is. You keep that woman away from me."

"I'll do my best, sweetums. Let's go inside. It's time to face the music."

Chapter 6

Savannah and Dirk got out of his car and walked, hand in hand, up the sidewalk to the house. As Savannah was unlocking the front door, she could hear Marietta's voice inside, high and shrill, rattling on about some topic that Savannah knew had to be positively enthralling. Probably something about the new brand of hair spray she'd discovered on sale or maybe the edible, tiger-striped undies at the naughty-girlie shop she'd located somewhere on the bad side of town. If Granny wasn't around, she'd probably be jabbering about how she was going to use the hair spray to get the biggest hair possible, and how she would wear the new panties to a rendezvous with some guy she'd met yesterday during an Internet chat. Her most recent soul mate, no doubt.

Marietta was a woman with her priorities in order.

"They call this Passion Aplenty," they heard her say as Savannah swung the door open and they stepped inside. "It's the latest color. I'm going to paint my toenails, too, and wear my open-toed platforms when I meet him tonight. What do you think?"

Savannah walked into the living room to see her sweet, long-suffering assistant, Tammy, huddled in the corner desk as Marietta leaned over her, shoving a bottle of nail polish under her nose.

"Uh, what do I think?" Tammy replied in her most transparently "patient" voice. "I think if you like that color, you should absolutely wear it. Individual expression is important."

"Yeah, I know what that means. Means you don't like it." Marietta walked away, her nose slightly elevated and obviously out of joint.

"But that isn't important," Tammy replied. "What matters is if you—"

"Don't go smoochin' my rear end after insultin' me like that." Marietta plopped her ample backside onto the sofa and threw one leg up onto the back of it, showing an indecent amount of thighs, crotch, and zebra-printed panties.

Savannah glanced at Dirk and saw him quickly avert his eyes.

He did a lot of averting in Marietta's presence.

When Marietta caught sight of them standing in the foyer, she reached up and patted her enormous bouffant updo, "just so," and donned a sappy, sexy grin, which Savannah noticed she only wore in the presence of men she considered attractive. Savannah also noticed that in spite of her hair adjusting, she didn't bother to lower her leg or rearrange her skirt in a more modest position.

In fact, she wriggled around and settled into a pose that showed even more of her nether regions.

"Oh, look what the cat dragged in," Marietta drawled in a Southern accent that made Savannah sound plumb Yankee-fied. "Our honeymooners are back already. I predicted this marriage would have the life span of a gnat, but I thought you'd at least keep him happy a day or two, big sis."

Savannah gave her a dirty look and grabbed Dirk's hand. She led him past the sofa, and its sprawling, simpering occupant, toward Tammy's desk in the corner.

"Why don't you hightail it to the kitchen, Mari?" she suggested as they passed. "See if you can find some lemons to suck on."

Tammy jumped up out of her chair and rushed to them. She grabbed Savannah in an almost desperate hug.

"What's the matter?" Tammy asked, searching Savannah's face, then Dirk's. "Something's got to be wrong or you two wouldn't—"

"Don't worry, kiddo," Dirk said. "We're all right. We just had to come back to"—he glanced over at Marietta—"to get some stuff and to talk to you about . . . some stuff."

Tammy stood there for an awkward moment, looking at them, then Marietta. Finally she nodded. "Oh. Right. Some stuff. Got it. I think."

"Hey, Dirk," Marietta said, fingering the lacy trim along the neckline of her extremely low-cut tee-shirt. "That leopard-print negligee I bought Savannah—did she wear it for you yet?"

Savannah bristled. "Watch yourself, Marietta Reid. I'm fixin' to jar your preserves over there."

Marietta didn't look particularly terrified. She waggled one eyebrow. "But I reckon she wouldn't do that nightgown justice." Then, in a voice that reminded Savannah of a Dial-To-Talk-Dirty phone actress, Marietta added, "Now if *I'd* been wearin' that nightie, what with the build on *me*, you'd have stood up and took notice, big-time. Least ways, parts of you would've!"

Slowly, with the blankest of expressions on her face,

Savannah left Dirk and Tammy and walked over to her comfy chair. She picked up Diamante, who was lying there, stretched across a throw pillow.

"Excuse me, Di," she said softly as she placed the kitty on the floor and gave her two soft strokes on her glossy black fur. "Mommy's gotta borrow your pillow for a minute."

Savannah picked up the pillow and walked over to Marietta. She stood over her for a moment, staring down at her.

Marietta's smirk started to subside. "What?" she said. "You're not miffed about something I said, are ya? I was just makin' conversation."

"And I . . . ," Savannah said calmly, ". . . am just gonna do something I've been aching to do for most of the years I've known you."

Suddenly Savannah's entire demeanor changed. In an instant, she tore into her sister, beating her with the pillow—first on the head, then systematically up and down her body, with all the fury and violence of a demon-possessed serial killer. Had her weapon of choice been anything other than a throw pillow, the attack would have, undoubtedly, been fatal.

"Ow! Now, Savannah, that hurts! Ouch! Stop it! Savan-nah! You're messin' up my hair and . . . *Owww!* Now, girl, that hurts! You better . . . oh!"

Tammy gasped and clapped both of her hands over her mouth, staring bug-eyed at the brutality occurring only a few feet from her.

Dirk whispered, "Holy shit"; then he grinned.

As she pounded away with all her might, Savannah was lost in the fog of battle. But in her peripheral vision, she registered a familiar figure walking down the stairs, crossing the foyer, and casually strolling into the living room.

It was her blessed grandmother—Granny Reid—in the flesh.

For a second, Savannah froze in midswing.

Marietta saw Granny and shouted, "Gran! Savannah's whoopin' me somethin' fierce! Make 'er stop!'"

Barely glancing their way, Granny glided through the living room in her brightly colored caftan and purple-and-red–sequined house slippers.

"If Savannah's thumpin' on you, Marietta," she said in her soft, calm voice, "then you had it comin'. Take it like a big girl and turn from the error of your ways."

"Error of *my* ways?" Marietta whimpered, her arms up to protect her badly damaged bouffant. "Why do you always figure it's *my* ways and not *Savannah's*?"

"Let's just say I know the both of you," Gran replied as she left the living room and entered the kitchen. "If your sister's finally resorted to cleanin' your clock, I reckon you ain't gettin' nary a lick amiss."

Tammy leaned over and whispered to Dirk, "What does that mean?"

"Don't know," he replied. "I can translate most of Savannah's Southernisms, but Granny's . . ."

Savannah was still standing there, holding the up-raised pillow over Marietta's head.

Marietta looked up at her sister and the pillow. She put on her most patient, yet condescending, look. "Now, Savannah," she said, "if you've had quite enough of this childish behavior, I would like to—"

Wham! Another blow, and then another, and another.

But Savannah had lost some of her steam.

Finally she stopped, walked back to her comfy chair, and laid the pillow back on the seat cushion. Then she reached down and picked up Diamante, who was still right where she'd left her.

"There you go, sweet pea," she said as she gently, lovingly laid the cat on the pillow. "You go back to sleep now. Mommy done knocked the stuffin' outta Aunt 'Jezebel' Marietta, and she won't be bothering Mommy or Uncle Dirk any more."

Meanwhile, Aunt "Jezebel" Marietta was hauling herself off the sofa with great difficulty, while trying to straighten her now-sadly-askew hairdo.

"I have never," she was muttering to herself, "in all my born days, been subjected to such a display of adolescent—"

Marietta stomped across the room, wobbling slightly on her five-inch, chrome-and-acrylic platform stilettos.

As Savannah watched her, she thought that any woman wearing shoes like that should be flat on her back, not walking . . . and certainly not stomping. But she decided not to mention it.

It wasn't good battle strategy to start World War IV with a tired arm.

Marietta paused at the foot of the staircase to deliver one more verbal volley before retreating. "You know, Miss Grouchy Pants, I didn't traipse all the way from Georgia to California to attend your nuptials, only to have the tar beat outta me. You are the worst bride I have ever had the misfortune of—"

She ducked as a book sailed past her head, nearly taking off her right ear.

As Savannah watched Marietta scurry on up the stairs, she murmured, "Well, won't you just look at that. Given enough motivation, she can make pretty good time on those hooker heels."

She turned back to Tammy and Dirk, who were smiling like a couple of yahoos with a twelve-pack of beer watching a wrestling match on TV.

"Way to go, Savannah," Tammy whispered. "I've been wanting to do that for a week."

"Yeah, baby," Dirk added. "I think that's the first time I ever had a woman fight another one over me. It was kinda awesome."

"Come along, you two," Savannah said. "Let's raid the refrigerator and see if we can find us something with a lot of empty calories in it. We've got a new case to investigate, and after all that exertion, I need myself an energy boost!"

Instead of sitting in her usual, favorite chair, with its rose-printed chintz and none-the-worse-for-wear pillow, Savannah plopped herself in the middle of the sofa to eat her pecan pie and ice cream. It wasn't a conscious decision. More of an instinctive one. It wasn't until she was settled and halfway through her pie that she realized what she had done and wondered about it.

For many years, Savannah had sat in her chair, and Dirk had sprawled across the sofa. They had talked, laughed, and cursed whatever people or circumstances might be annoying them at the time. They had watched television, petted cats, and munched a wide variety of edibles. When they were extremely tired, they had sat there doing absolutely nothing . . . together. She on her chair, and Dirk on the sofa.

But tonight, when they, Tammy, and Granny had returned from the kitchen to the living room and chosen their spots, Dirk had situated himself in his usual place on the end of the sofa. And Savannah had parked her backside in the middle next to him.

Granny was in Savannah's comfy chair, concentrating on her pecan pie.

As usual, Tammy was sitting yoga-style on the floor, sipping mineral water with frozen grapes and strawberries floating in it.

Briefly Savannah wondered if she would do this, year after year. Had marriage changed her life so much that she would forever give up her favorite chair? How much else would she find herself surrendering, before all was said and done?

She suspected it was just a temporary state of affairs, born of newlywed ardor. She knew herself and Dirk pretty well. They were creatures of habit and comfort. Eventually they'd probably revert to their old routines.

But for tonight, she enjoyed having her shoulder and arm against his. The warm, solid feel of him. The pleasant emotion that it imparted—a sense of being loved, protected, and looked after by someone who truly cherished her.

Best of all, she no longer felt so alone in the big, wide world.

On the other side of her sat her six-foot-three skinny brother, with his carrottop hair and a thin mustache and tiny goatee to match. He had been out running errands for Granny and had arrived after the pie had been distributed. But since he was her favorite brother—her favorite male on the planet, next to Dirk—Savannah had made it up to him by constructing a formidable banana split.

All that remained in his dish was half of a split banana. None of the Reids were bashful when it came to cleaning their plates.

"That's some story you just told us," Granny said as she set her empty plate on the table beside the chair. "Why do you reckon that woman chief of police acted the way she did?"

"And her not thoroughly questioning you," Tammy

added. "Even I know that isn't proper procedure, and I'm not a member of law enforcement."

Waycross nodded in agreement. "Then telling the news folks and everybody listenin' to the television set that lady up and drowned herself in some sorta riptide. What's all that hooey about?"

Dirk scraped the last bit of ice cream off his plate with his finger and held it out to Cleopatra, who was sauntering by the sofa. She gratefully licked it off, then climbed into his lap. "Well," he said, "the least incriminating reason I can think of is that she's trying to protect the island from any bad press. It's the beginning of the summer tourist season there. They depend on every cent they can get from the knuckleheads on the mainland who come over there to play and honeymoon, and stuff like that."

Savannah looked up from her pie. "You mean, knuckleheads like us?"

He nodded solemnly. "Exactly. Her lyin' her face off like that might be nothing more than them not wanting people to know they got themselves a killer there among 'em."

"It's a little bitty island," Gran supplied. "Knowing that you might be rubbin' elbows with a killer, that don't contribute to a carefree, fun-lovin' sorta vacation mood. If it was me, instead of goin' there, I'd just go to Disneyland."

Savannah laughed. "Granny, you always want to go to Disneyland."

"I got me a thing for the Mouse. It's a powerful thing, I'll admit. But my point is, there's a lot of nice things to do here in Southern California for fun besides go to an island where a killer with a gun's done run amuck. That had to occur to that police chief lady."

"Granny's right." Tammy nodded. "There's a lot of competition for the tourist dollar. Especially in this less-than-robust economy."

Savannah gave Waycross a sideways glance and saw that he was watching Tammy, rapt adoration shining on his handsome, freckled, young face. He seemed captivated by her every word, every gesture.

Why shouldn't he be? Savannah thought. Tammy was simply the sweetest, smartest, most beautiful woman Savannah had ever known. How could a single young guy like Waycross not notice?

Tammy set her glass of water on the coffee table and stretched her long, tanned legs out in front of her. Running several miles a day—not to mention regular workouts at the local gym and daily tai chi exercises for as long as Savannah had known her—had left her in perfect physical condition. Tammy's glossy golden hair fell like a shimmering curtain around her shoulders and nearly to her waist. When she walked down a street, men, and even some women, turned to stare at her.

But one of the loveliest things about Tammy was that she didn't know how beautiful she was. To her, life was good; most people were good. She took her own radiant sunlight with her, wherever she went.

Savannah wasn't at all surprised that Waycross was head over heels in love.

Savannah wondered if Tammy knew. Once in a while, she caught Tammy sneaking a look in his direction. If he intercepted it, she would duck her head and glance away, her cheeks pinking a bit.

Yes, Savannah could see that the simple infatuation they had was growing into something more. And she couldn't be happier about it.

Even before Savannah and Dirk's wedding, Tammy had expressed an interest in Waycross, and vice versa.

Savannah had hoped that spark would grow into a flame, a fire that would warm them both. Of the people she loved most, she counted them to be the best. They were a rare breed: kind, loving folk with pure hearts. They deserved to find love.

But at the moment, she had less pleasant topics to think about. Far less.

"Chief La Cross might have a darker motive, it's true," she said, pulling her attention back to the business at hand. "She put herself way out there on a limb today by giving that false statement. Once the coroner's office releases their report, she's gonna have enough egg on her face to make a Denver omelet."

"That's true," Dirk said. "Then everybody's gonna wonder why she lied and what she had to hide."

"And," Savannah added, "she doesn't seem to me like a woman who's stupid and didn't figure that out. I don't like her or trust her one bit, but she strikes me as being hard as nails, and twice as sharp."

Granny stood and picked up her plate and the other empty ones on the coffee table. "Then you better mind what she says. Somebody like that threatens you—especially somebody with a badge to back it up—you'd better watch yourself. She comes after you there on that little island, who are you gonna call? The law? She's it."

"That's true." Waycross jumped up and took the dishes from his grandmother. "We know all about that sorta thing in our neck o' the woods. We've got us a lot of little communities where there's only a cop or two per town enforcing the law. If they're crooked, the folks living in their jurisdictions have got themselves a serious problem."

"I ain't afraid of her," Dirk said, lifting his chin a notch. "She doesn't know who she's messing with, she takes me on."

"Yeah, yeah." Savannah elbowed him in the ribs. *"Muy macho hombre."*

Tammy laughed. "How macho can he be when he's afraid of you, Savannah?"

"Hey, everybody's afraid of my big sister," Waycross told her. "If you don't believe me, go upstairs and check out Miss Marietta. She's hurlin' clothes and high heels and cosmetics into them purple patent leather suitcases of hers to beat the band. Whatever Savannah did to her earlier this evenin' put the fear o' God in her."

"Fear of me—that's more like it." Savannah snickered. "Giving her that pillow whompin' did my soul a world of good. Should've done it long ago."

Waycross headed toward the kitchen with his load of dirty dishes. "I'm just sorry I missed it. One time in twenty years Mari's hairdo's outta whack, and I don't get to see it."

Savannah watched Tammy watch him. Yes, the kid was definitely goo-goo–eyed. But then, watching a man tend to dishes was enough to set almost any woman's heart to pitter-pattering.

"So, what are y'all gonna do about this situation you got?" Granny asked.

"You can't let it ruin your honeymoon," Tammy added. "Ryan and John were so happy to score that lighthouse cottage for you. If you don't get to use it, they'll be heartbroken."

Gran gave a little snort. "They'll be more heartbroken if they have to come over there to that island and bail your backsides outta the crowbar hotel. Assuming they'd even letcha out. I've seen shows on TV about those foreign prisons. Some of 'em don't even feed you. If your family don't show up with a bologna sandwich once in a while, you just plumb starve to death."

"Yeah, well, we're going back," Dirk said. "We're not

gonna let that gal with the black suit and the evil eye scare us outta having our romantic honeymoon." He nudged Savannah. "Huh, babe?"

"Uh, yeah." She had started to fade. Suddenly the day and its horror came crashing down on her, and every muscle in her body felt like a wrung-out wet rag.

He poked her again. "Hey, you going to sleep on me there?"

"I know the look," Granny said. "If you don't get her upstairs and in bed in a minute or two, you'll be totin' her upstairs like a sack o' taters, over your shoulder."

Dirk turned to Savannah, looked her over, taking in the droopiness of her eyelids and her size. "Okay, sweet cheeks, let's get you upstairs pronto. Manly man that I am, it's been a tough day for me, too. I'd just as soon not have to do the Rhett Butler Carrying Scarlett Up the Staircase routine tonight."

He stood and pulled her to her feet. Wrapping one arm around her waist, he turned to Tammy and said, "We'll wanna get on this first thing tomorrow morning—figure out what we're gonna do. You mind assembling the rest of the gang?"

"Sure!" Tammy beamed. She was never happier than when being called upon to officially sleuth. "I'll have Ryan and John here at nine sharp."

"Make it ten sharp." Dirk grinned. "We might wanna sleep in."

"Can I sit in on this powwow you're havin'?" Granny asked. "I'll make biscuits, and I brought a couple jars of my peach preserves from home."

"Of course, Gran," Dirk told her. "Are you kidding? You are an honorary lifetime member of the Moonlight Magnolia Detective Agency."

* * *

When Dirk had Savannah tucked into her bed, and he was settled next to her, the kitties at their feet, he leaned over and kissed her on the cheek. "I'm sorry you had such an awful day, babe," he said.

"Wasn't exactly a Sunday picnic for you either."

"It was harder for you. You were the one with her when—"

"Yeah."

"And you're the one who, well, was in a similar situation as her, not that long ago. So it had to be rough on you. Brought back memories, I'll bet. All that stuff."

Cleopatra wriggled her way between them, moving under the covers until she was at Savannah's waist. Savannah reached down and, a moment later, the cat's warm nose nuzzled her palm with a loving sweetness, which brought tears to Savannah's eyes. Cleo always seemed to know when she could use an extra bit of affection and comfort.

Sort of like Dirk.

"Thank you, honey," she said, slightly embarrassed by the crack in her own voice.

"Tomorrow'll be better," he said. "I promise."

She chuckled dryly and snuggled against him. "Wouldn't take much to improve on today. Like . . . if Southern California doesn't have an eight-point-one earthquake, and we don't see another person murdered in front of our eyes on our honeymoon."

"Yeah." He sighed. "That'd do it."

Chapter 7

When Savannah greeted Ryan and John at her front door, she gave them both rib-cracking hugs. "You two are the sweetest, most generous, classiest friends on the planet," she said as she laid a kiss on Ryan's cheek and then one on John's. "That lighthouse and the keeper's cottage are a dream! How did you ever think of that?"

"We remembered you saying you loved lighthouses," Ryan told her as she pulled them into the living room. "John's a big fan, too. He spent a night there once, years ago, and thought you'd enjoy it."

John put his arm around Savannah's shoulders and pulled her to his side. "So tell me, love . . . what's this nasty business that brought you two home in the midst of your honeymoon?"

"Come on into the kitchen and have a seat. Granny made a big ol' country breakfast for us. We'll fill you in on all the ugly details."

* * *

More than a dozen soft scrambled eggs, fried green tomatoes, a skillet full of sausage gravy, two pans of buttermilk biscuits, and an entire jar of Gran's homemade peach preserves—all prepared to Granny's highest standard of Southern perfection—served to take the edge off everyone's hunger.

In fact, more than one belt had been loosened as they all pushed away from the table, picked up their cups of strong coffee, and took them out to the backyard patio.

The basic details of the case had been discussed over the meal, and now it was time to digest and strategize.

Savannah had lagged behind everyone else, tidying up the kitchen before Granny had the chance to do it. For as long as Savannah could remember, Gran had been a hard worker.

Lazy people didn't offer to raise their nine grandchildren.

If Savannah didn't watch out for her, she'd do far more than her share.

As Savannah was folding the hand-embroidered, crochet-trimmed dish towel—another gift from Granny's busy fingers—Marietta flounced into the kitchen, holding an oversized suitcase in each hand.

When she saw Savannah, she stopped so abruptly that she nearly stepped out of her purple ostrich feather–trimmed mules.

"Oh, it's you," she said as she set one suitcase down, patted her hairdo, then ran her hand down the side of her leather miniskirt. "Where in tarnation is that Waycross? He's supposed to be givin' me a ride to the airport."

"He's out back with the others," Savannah said, hanging the towel on the drying rack. "We missed you at breakfast."

"Yeah, right. Like one pig at the trough misses another."

"I nabbed a couple of biscuits for you and saved 'em back."

"You did not."

"I most certainly did. Put butter and preserves on 'em, too. They're wrapped up in tinfoil, there in the oven."

Slowly Marietta set down the other suitcase, walked over to the oven, and peeked inside.

Savannah watched the battle of "indignation" versus "gluttony" war upon her sister's face.

Finally Marietta opened the door, pulled out the foil package, and lovingly unwrapped it.

Gluttony triumphed again, as always in the Reid clan.

"How many did the rest of y'all get?" she asked.

"I don't know, Mari," Savannah said, suddenly feeling quite tired. Marietta frequently had that effect on her. "We might've put away three apiece."

"But I notice you only saved me two," she complained with a mouth filled with biscuit.

Savannah said nothing, but she walked over to the coffee machine, pulled out the pot, and dumped the remaining coffee into the sink. She couldn't help grinning just a little as she thought how good that coffee was and how dry biscuits, even Granny Reid's, could be without a cup of good java to wash them down.

Marietta didn't notice. She was too busy getting comfortable at the table with her biscuits.

Finally she was settled "just so" in her chair. She glanced around the kitchen. "Got any coffee to go with these?"

Savannah slid the pot back into the machine. "Nope. Nary a drop."

Marietta took a big bite, then choked, sputtered, and coughed. "Well, I'm about to gag myself to death here. Do you at least have some sweet milk to offer me?"

"Yep."

Marietta looked at her expectantly.

Savannah ignored the look and said far too cheerfully, "Feel free to help yourself. I keep it in the icebox."

With a great sigh and a lot of huffing and puffing, Marietta trudged to the refrigerator, got out the milk, poured herself a huge glass, and returned to her seat . . . leaving the carton on the counter.

Savannah waited until she was comfortably seated, biscuit poised in front of her face. "You wanna put that milk away?" she said. "It'll go bad, left out like that."

That did it!

Marietta flew up out of her chair, stomped to the counter, grabbed the milk carton, and practically hurled it back into the refrigerator. "There!" she shouted. "Are you happy now!"

Savannah gave her a half-smile and said very calmly, "Thank you."

"Well, you aren't welcome. You aren't welcome, because you don't give a hooey about milk goin' bad. You're just bein' as contrary as you possibly can be to me, and I do not appreciate it!"

Slowly Savannah walked to the table and sat down in the chair across from her. Folding her hands demurely in front of her, she said, "No, Mari, I'm not being as contrary as I can possibly be. You'd be surprised just how contrary I can get when somebody pushes me too far. And, sugar, you're at that line and hangin' your toes over it."

"You tell me that, after you beating the tar outta me yesterday?"

"With a pillow. Marietta, it was a pillow fight."

" 'Tweren't no fight. I didn't have a pillow. It ain't a fair fight if the other person ain't armed."

Savannah sighed. "Marietta, do you want to go upstairs right now to my bedroom? I'll give you a pillow. No, I'll give you two of my biggest ones, and you and I can duke it out, fair and square. Is that what you want?"

Marietta thought it over. "No. I'd just have to do my hair again. It'd make me late for my plane."

"So it's official, then? You're going home today?"

"After what happened last night? Of course I am! Why shouldn't I?"

"Because Dirk and I are going to be leaving in less than an hour to go back to the island, and then you'll have the house to yourself again. Well, you and Granny and Waycross. So you leaving in a big ol' huff, with your back up and your tail in the air, that ain't exactly to your advantage, now is it?"

Savannah ran her fingers through her hair and closed her eyes. Why did she bother? It would be so much easier just to let Marietta be Marietta . . . far, far away. But this was her flesh and blood. Somewhere, sometime, someone had said something about how you had to go the extra mile for family.

She thought of Tammy, Ryan, and John—the family her heart had adopted. She thought of how little they asked and how much they gave. Why couldn't blood relatives be the same?

"I want you to listen to me, Marietta," she said, opening her eyes and fixing her sister with a steady, solemn gaze. "And I want you to listen good. I apologize for losing my temper with you yesterday. I shouldn't have struck you. Not even with a pillow."

"You're darned right you shouldn't have."

"And I'll never do it again. But I'm warning you that there are more ways for me to get even with you than to whup you."

Marietta didn't reply, but she stared coldly at her older sister, eyes narrowed, lips tight.

"Since we were kids in junior high school," Savannah continued, "and since your figure done filled out, you've been chasin' after my boyfriends."

"I didn't have to chase 'em. They were fallin' all over me."

"You should probably be very quiet and refrain from saying crap like that, or I might take back what I just said about whuppins."

Savannah drew another deep breath and began again. "As I was saying, you've been showin' your tail and chasing after every male I ever set my cap for since I can remember. But we were just kids, and they were just boyfriends.

"Now . . . now I'm a married woman. Dirk is my husband. And I'm telling you right now, you'd best keep your skirt tail down and your legs together when you're in his presence. You better watch what comes outta your mouth, too. 'Cause if you go talkin' slutty trash to him, like you always do, gal, I am gonna mop the floor with you."

Less than terrified, Marietta gave her a little smirk. "What's the matter, big sis? You feelin' a mite insecure? You afraid somebody like me's gonna take your man away from you?"

Slowly Savannah stood and walked around the table to stand beside Marietta. She reached down and, with surprising speed and ease, grabbed handfuls of her sweater front and yanked her to her feet.

Eye to blazing eye, she said, "It would never occur to me that the likes of you would interest my husband. He has much more sense and far better taste in women than to go for anything you've got to offer. But it's insulting to me and to him that *you* think he might. So I'm warning you, once and for all, do not flirt with or act like a brazen hussy around my man.

"Because if you do," Savannah continued, "I promise you, I will make that pillow thumpin' I gave you look like nothing at all. Girl, I will knock you clean into next Tuesday. Once I'm finished with you, a messed-up hairdo will be the very least of your concerns. You, Miss Marietta, just might find yourself snatched plumb bald!"

She released Marietta's sweater.

For a moment, one brief instant, Savannah saw what she was looking for in her sister's eyes. It was just a smidgeon of fear mixed with grudging respect.

That was all she'd wanted.

"Meanwhile, you're welcome to remain in my home and enjoy the rest of your California vacation," she said as she headed for the back door. "Now that you and I understand each other, we won't ever need to speak about this again."

She went out the door and closed it behind her. She closed the door on her stunned sister and on decades of hurtful sibling rivalry.

And she felt very, very good about it.

"Let's get this show on the road. Time's a-wastin'," Granny addressed the informal gathering of the Moonlight Magnolia Detective Agency that was sitting on thickly cushioned chaise lounges under Savannah's wisteria arbor.

"Hear, hear," added John, "we must return these lovebirds of ours back to their honeymoon nest."

Ryan lifted his coffee mug in a toast to Savannah and Dirk, who were sharing an oversized chaise. "Yes, let's find the answers you need so you can get back to what's important. I can't imagine that hanging out with this motley crew is your idea of wedded bliss."

Granny barked, "Well? Who's fixin' to do what? Let's divvy up the duties."

Savannah smiled, loving the woman sitting across from her. Gran's magnificent hair—her one vanity— glowed like fine spun silver in the morning sunlight. Her blue eyes, so like Savannah's, twinkled with excitement at the prospect of another "case."

A few times, Granny had helped with their investigations, and the feisty octogenarian had received enormous satisfaction in doing so. Her years of life experience had proven invaluable to them as they dealt with the finest and the worst of what humanity had to offer.

Gran had a way of bringing out the best in the people around her. But she was a realist. When it came to people, she also expected the worst, and she was seldom wrong.

"Savannah and me are gonna go to that TV station in Los Angeles," Dirk was saying, "find out what-all they know. Or don't know, judging from that so-called 'news' they gave last night."

Savannah nodded. "And if they've been misinformed about how their colleague died, we're going to fill in some blanks for them."

"You two are going all the way to Los Angeles?" Tammy asked, a frown on her pretty face. "That's the opposite direction from the island. Don't you want to get back to your honeymoon?"

Waycross piped up, "Yeah. Tammy and me . . . er, Tammy and I . . . could go talk to them. Soon as we're done, we'll ring y'all up and tell you what they said."

Tammy gave Waycross a quick sideways glance, a vigorous nod, and a bright smile. "Sure! We could do that! We'd be happy to."

Yes, Savannah thought, *definitely something nice developing there*.

"That's okay," Dirk told them. "We'll go. It's not that far. We'll be back by noon."

Savannah gave him a quick look and a slight nod toward Tammy and Waycross. She knew Dirk was rooting for this blooming romance as much as she was.

He cleared his throat. "But you two can help a lot here at home. Go online and find out absolutely everything you can about Amelia and her husband."

"Yes." Savannah nodded. "She was a bulldog of a reporter. Had to have made a bunch of enemies along the way."

"And him being a big-time land developer," Tammy said. "With all the focus on conservation and ecology, they don't usually win a lot of popularity contests these days."

"Exactly." Savannah took a sip of her coffee, which was now turning cold. It was time to wrap this meeting up and get on with business. "You know what to look for, Tammy. Waycross, you help her out."

"Oh, I will."

Waycross grinned broadly . . . and so did everyone else in the circle. Young love was as hard to hide as California sunshine on the Fourth of July.

"I'm reluctant to mention this," Ryan said, "because it would be so much nicer for the two of you to just have the island to yourselves, but . . ."

"Yes?" Savannah prompted him.

"John and I have a friend who owns a vacation home on the other end of the island, well away from the lighthouse. If you'd like to have any of us nearby while you're there, but not too near, I'm sure we could use it."

John nodded. "That's true. Our friend and her husband are on holiday in Switzerland now, so it's probably available. I know they'd be happy to have any of us there . . . but, of course, only if the two of you want—"

"Sure," Dirk interjected. "It's not like you're going to be bunking right there with us in that fancy cottage you rented for us. Since the law enforcement on the island seems to consider us the enemy, it'd be kinda nice to have backup if we needed you."

"That's for sure," Granny added. "You'll need somebody there to bring you bologna sandwiches when they throw you in the slammer." She glanced at Ryan and John; then she turned back to Savannah. "I don't mean me. I'll just stay here and feed the cats and clean the litter boxes. But the rest of y'all might as well—"

John reached over and put his hand on Granny's shoulder. "Don't be ridiculous, love. If *we're* going, *you're* going."

Her face beamed. "But who'll feed the cats?"

"Marietta and I had ourselves a little sister-to-sister chat," Savannah said. "After us discussin' some of the facts of life, she's decided to stick around and prolong her vacation for a while longer. She can tend the girls." She turned to Ryan. "How many bunks does your friend have in her vacation house?"

"It has five en suite bedrooms."

"What's 'on sweet' mean?" Gran asked.

"Every bedroom has its own bathroom."

Granny grinned. "Boy, howdy. That *is* sweet."

Ryan laughed. "It has a pool house, a guest cottage, an infinity pool, tennis courts. There's definitely room for the entire Moonlight Magnolia gang."

Tammy clapped her hands, Waycross cheered, and Gran's blue eyes sparkled.

Savannah smiled to herself, thinking this would hardly be a traditional honeymoon, with the whole crew along. But the idea couldn't have pleased her more.

She turned to Dirk, leaned over, and whispered in his ear, "Is this all right with you, sugar?"

He chuckled. "Sure. What guy wouldn't want everybody he knows to tag along with him and his new bride?"

"If you'd rather not, we can tell them—"

He gave her a squeeze and a kiss on the forehead. "Shhh. And if we get our butts thrown in jail, Granny can bake us a carrot cake with cream cheese frosting and a file in the filling."

Chapter 8

"I'm sorry, sir, ma'am, but you simply cannot see any member of the news team without an appointment."

The fresh-faced young woman in her crisp navy blue suit, with her crisp white shirt and crisp white smile, which was becoming more forced by the moment, stepped in front of Dirk as he tried to get around her.

Savannah could sense a huge fight brewing.

Dirk was getting more cranky with each passing exchange with this gal, whose name tag identified her as PANZY—JUNIOR HOSPITALITY COORDINATOR. Since he began most encounters with his fellow humans with his mood-o-meter set at "crotchety," it was bound to get ugly.

"Miss Panzy," Savannah said, wedging herself between them and donning her most patient, Southern belle smile. "I understand that standard procedure dictates that we set an appointment previous to visiting your fine establishment here. But as you can see from Detective Sergeant Coulter's badge, he's a police officer, and this is important police business. I know that—"

"You have to have an appointment."

"I know that you're just trying to do your job, and I admire you for that. I surely do, but—"

"Nobody without an appointment gets past me."

The junior hospitality coordinator glared up at Dirk, whose face had gone from red to purple. He looked like he was about to explode.

"And if you try to push by me again, like you did before," she told him, "I'm going to start screaming bloody murder. When I do, twenty-five of the biggest, meanest security guards you ever saw are going to come running, because we take security here at the studio very, very seriously."

Savannah's cup of indignation overflowed, much like a garbage disposal trying to process a ton of ten-day-old Thanksgiving leftovers.

"I can see how seriously you take every blessed thing, Miss Panzy," Savannah said, loudly enough for a tour group, which was being led through the reception area by a tour guide, to pause and listen, their ears practically sticking out on stems. "How serious do you reckon the studio execs are gonna get when they find out that two people left their honeymoon on Santa Tesla Island and came all the way here to wonderful downtown Los Angeles to tell your station that its star reporter didn't drown accidentally?"

Savannah stopped to take a deep breath as dead silence reigned in the reception hall. "That's right. We came here to tell y'all that Amelia Northrop didn't drown. She was murdered, shot down in cold blood, and we saw it happen. And your bosses are going to find out that we weren't able to tell them that because you, Miss Prissy Pants Panzy, wouldn't let us, 'cause we didn't have a dadgummed appointment! Now you put that in your pipe and smoke it, gal."

Panzy, the tourists, the tour guide, and even Dirk stood there, silent, their eyes bugged, mouths agape, for what seemed like forever.

Savannah had heard of places so quiet you could hear a mouse pee on a cotton ball, and she figured this had to be one of them.

Then, suddenly, there was pandemonium. The tourists began to discuss what they had just heard . . . loudly. Some began taking pictures and videos of Savannah with their cell phones. The tour guide snapped to attention and tried to herd the horde down the hallway and away from this seemingly crazy lady, who was making all sorts of outlandish claims.

Panzy the junior hospitality coordinator fled. On her sensible two-inch black pumps, she ran to a desk on the other side of the room, grabbed a phone, and began giving an earful to someone on the other end.

Dirk turned to Savannah. "Well, I guess that particular cat's outta the bag and there'll be no putting it back."

Savannah shrugged. "Oh, well. It was getting out, sooner or later, anyway." She glanced warily down the hallway. "You reckon they'll really send twenty security guards? Just for us? That'd kinda be overkill, wouldn't it?"

"She said twenty-five."

"Oh."

"Big, mean ones."

"Woo-hoo."

An hour later, Savannah and Dirk were still sitting in the station manager's office. The man appeared to be as confused as he had been when they'd told him, fifty-five minutes before, why they wanted to see him.

"This makes no sense," Edward Deville said as he

toyed with an elegant fountain pen made of sterling silver and lapis. "As tragic as it may be, it isn't all that rare for someone who's in the public eye, the way Amelia is"—he paused, swallowed, then continued—"I mean, *was*, to be murdered. Sadly, these things do happen. But why would the island police tell us she died in an accidental drowning?"

From her seat on the creamy white leather sofa, where she sat next to Dirk, Savannah studied the station manager. It was easy to see every inch of him, because he was sitting behind a desk made of a clear acrylic material and there was nothing on the desk but a sleek laptop computer, the fancy fountain pen, and a crystal sculpture of a nude woman and man caressing. Or, at least, she thought it was a guy and a gal getting it on. Or it might have been a couple of dolphins, or an odd, curvy lump of glass. She wasn't sure.

Edward Deville didn't look much like an executive to her. She always thought of execs as being harried, overworked, dressed expensively, but slightly disheveled because grooming was low on their list of priorities—well below hiring and firing people, sweating over budget cuts, and fighting with their boards of directors.

But in his pink polo shirt, khakis, and sneakers, and with his pristine desk, he didn't look the part to her. She couldn't help wondering how he had risen to such a position. Jobs like station manager of one of the largest television stations in Los Angeles weren't just given away.

Her eyes scanned the walls of the ultramodern office. Two of the walls were glass.

Edward had the corner office overlooking the Los Angeles skyline. Another one of those überperks not just bestowed on every Tom, Dick, or Edward.

The third wall held glass shelves, which displayed numerous awards, including two statuettes that Savannah quickly recognized as Emmys.

The fourth wall held a strong clue as to Edward's ascent in the world. Hanging, side by side, were two portraits. One was of the man sitting at the desk in front of them, and below his picture, a silver plaque identified him as EDWARD DEVILLE II, STATION MANAGER.

The picture next to him was of an older man who looked very similar to Edward. *And he should,* Savannah thought as she read the silver plaque under his. EDWARD DEVILLE, PRESIDENT.

Explains a lot, she mused. Apparently, the station head wasn't above showing a bit of nepotism. Or even a lot, as the case might be.

"We don't know why they're covering up the fact that it's a murder, sir," Dirk was saying for the fourth time since they had begun trying to tell him their story.

"We're going to try very hard to figure that out," Savannah added. "We were hoping that maybe you could help us with our independent investigation of this horrible crime. You must feel pretty bad about it, Amelia being part of your 'team,' as such."

"Our 'team'?" Edward shook his head, and looked genuinely distressed as he ran his fingers through his short, thick mat of brown curls. "You mean, our 'family.' We're all very close around here."

Savannah couldn't help glancing up at the portrait of Edward I.

And Edward II noticed.

"We may not have been blood related to Amelia, the way my father and I are," he said, "but Dad and I care deeply about everyone who works here at the station."

"I'm sure you do," Savannah said. "So, could you please just tell us if you have any idea who might have killed her? Anyone who had a grudge against her or who might have threatened her?"

A thoughtful look on his face, Edward tapped his pen on his see-through desk. "Two people spring to mind, though I'm sure she had others," he said. "Last year, she had a stalker. An ex-con who fancied himself her boyfriend. He would hang around outside the studio doors, trying to catch her as she entered and left."

"Do you know his name?" Dirk asked, pulling a small notebook from his shirt pocket.

"Yes, it's Burt Ferris. She got a restraining order against him. Last I heard, he was leaving her alone, but you never know with those guys."

"You certainly don't," Savannah said, thinking of how often a simple piece of paper failed to protect people from their enemies. With some, the prospect of running afoul of law enforcement was enough to bring them to their senses. Others ignored the demand to desist. And some even considered a court order of protection a challenge, an opportunity for defiance against society, with whom they were frequently at odds.

"How long ago was this?" Savannah asked.

"He harassed her for over a year, following her around, sending her creepy presents—underwear and sex-toy crap you'd buy at an X-rated shop. She finally got the restraining order . . . let's see . . . I think it was about three months ago."

"Last you heard, where was this guy living?" Dirk asked.

"Around Luna Bonita, I think."

Immediately Savannah began to text Tammy: **Background, Burt Ferris, LKA Luna Bonita.**

Almost immediately, she received the answer **On it,** followed by a mustachioed, goateed smiley face.

She grinned. Obviously, brother Waycross was assisting Tammy. No great surprise there.

"You said that two people who might have posed a threat to her came to mind," Savannah said. "Who was the other one?"

Edward hesitated, as though reluctant to talk about the second individual. He looked at Savannah, then at Dirk. The expressions on their faces clearly showed they weren't going to leave without this additional information.

"Well?" Dirk snapped. "Who's the other one?"

"Ian Xenos."

The name rang a slight bell for Savannah, but she couldn't recall where she'd heard it before. Something to do with organized crime or fashion?

"Who the hell's Ian Xenos?" Dirk asked. "And what kinda name is that?"

"Probably fake," Edward told him. "Xenos is head of a group of fashion merchandise counterfeiters who sell designer knockoffs in Los Angeles and New York. Amelia not only exposed his organization, but she proved the money was being funneled to a terrorist group."

"Yes, I can see why that wouldn't make her very popular with him," Savannah said as she texted **Ian Xenos, background** to Tammy and Waycross.

"Where's Xenos right now?" Dirk asked.

"About six weeks ago, they arrested him. He's out on bail, awaiting his trial in a month or so. He's the reason we're so tight with our security at the moment. Thanks to her exposé on his group, we're on high alert around here. At least until the trial's over."

"Yes, I'll bet you are," Savannah said, her stomach roiling at the thought of terrorists.

She knew she would never, for the rest of her life, get

over 9/11 or the Oklahoma City Bombing. They were the only two events—other than her own personal-life tragedies—that simply thinking of them would instantly cause tears to spring to her eyes.

Though Granny Reid had taught her to forgive her enemies and not to hate anyone, she truly despised terrorists, both homegrown and foreign alike. And she didn't feel one bit guilty about it, Granny's upbringing aside.

"I understand," she said, "that Ms. Northrop was married. Can you tell us anything about her husband, her marriage?"

"Not much," Edward replied. "Amelia had an established career in journalism before they met, and it took a lot of her time and energy. He's a very successful businessman, and that kept him busy. But they seemed to have a good marriage. Can't say I saw them together all that often, but at office parties and stuff like that, they seemed like a loving couple."

"Other than those two guys you told us about, is there anyone else you can think of who might do harm to Ms. Northrop?" Dirk asked. "Personal or professional?"

Edward seemed to think it over before saying, "Not really. Amelia was ruthless as a reporter, but around here she was very loved and respected." He paused, and Savannah saw him bite his lower lip before continuing. "We're going to miss her. A lot."

"I'm sorry for your loss," Savannah said, meaning it. In her career she had seen far too many people suffer terrible losses, precious loved ones gone forever because of someone else's violence. "I wish there was something we could do for you."

Edward looked her squarely in the eyes, and for a moment, the otherwise lackluster, even mousy-looking guy behind the desk radiated an unexpected, ferocious energy.

"If what you're telling me is true," he said, "and Amelia was really murdered, get whoever did it and see to it that they pay. I want justice for my reporter."

Dirk and Savannah stood. Dirk reached across the desk and offered him his hand.

"Mr. Deville, we're going to do our very best. We promise."

As Dirk drove them along Interstate 10 toward Luna Bonita, Savannah called Tammy on her cell phone.

Tammy snapped it up on the first ring. "Those are bad, evil, nasty guys that you had us check out," she said without her customary sunshine-and-light "hello."

"Oh, we know," Savannah told her. "We just wanted you to find out *how* bad."

"Stay the heck away from them! That's how bad. One stalks and beats up women, and the second one makes the first guy look like a saint."

"Yes, we know. We're on our way right now to try to find the stalker dude in Luna Bonita. Got an address?"

Tammy rattled off the information as Savannah jotted it and directions on the back of one of Dirk's bank deposit receipts, which she'd found lying on the floorboard. She quickly ran out of room on the tiny sheet and had to write the rest on a discarded McDonald's bag.

"Someday you gotta clean out this car, boy," she mumbled as she scribbled.

"If I do, you won't have anything to write on," he shot back.

"This guy you're on your way to see," Tammy said, "is a felon. Served two sentences for assault on two differ-

ent women. Then there are all the times the police arrested him, but the females wouldn't press charges."

"How bad were his attacks?" Savannah asked.

"He's been violent for years. But the earlier accusa-
tions were for pushing, shoving, slapping . . . that kind
of thing. It was six years ago that he beat the crap out of
his ex-wife. Broke her jaw. He served a year for that.
He'd only been out six months when he messed up a
girlfriend really, really bad. She was in a coma for
weeks. He served two years for that. I can see here that
Amelia Northrop had an RO against him."

"Yes, he was stalking her."

"Oh no! Poor woman. And he was escalating." There
was a long, heavy pause on the other end before Tammy
added, "They always do."

"Yes, darlin', they do," Savannah agreed.

She hated to hear such pain in Tammy's voice. This
was a difficult topic for them both. Like many strong,
intelligent, loving women, Tammy had once found herself ensnared in an abusive relationship. She had finally
gotten out, but the price for her freedom had been terribly high. Neither Tammy nor Savannah could ever
forget how high.

"Want me to whack him upside the head or across
the chops one for you?" Savannah asked, trying to
lighten the mood of the moment. "Or, like Granny says,
I could jerk a knot in his tail."

"I like the sound of that one," came back the half-
playful, still half-sad reply.

"Then consider it done."

Savannah saw their exit ramp approaching and knew
she would soon have to be directing Dirk to Burt Ferris's residence. "I gotta go, sweet cheeks," she said.
"Thank you for that good work."

"Okay. No problem. But I have to go home and

throw some things into a suitcase, get ready to go out to the island with Ryan and John. I'll get back to my research once I'm there."

"Sounds good, kiddo. Bye-bye."

She hung up and turned to Dirk. "Would you mind terribly if I conducted this upcoming interview myself?"

He gave her a quick sideways glance, then snickered. "Can I watch?"

"Sure. You get a ringside seat."

"How many rounds you figure it'll go?"

"As many as it takes to get the job done."

Chapter 9

There were some lovely residential areas in Luna Bonita. Areas where flowers bloomed in well-kept yards; lawns were not only mowed but nicely edged. Houses were freshly painted. Most cars were parked in garages, and those that sat in driveways were clean and had all four tires.

Burt Ferris didn't live in one of those areas.

He lived on a street of deteriorating apartment buildings with broken windows, broken-down cars lining the driveways, and people with broken dreams sitting on stoops and curbs, swigging alcoholic beverages.

"Strange, ain't it?" she told Dirk as they passed one building after another, looking for number 163. "You never see folks sitting on street curbs suckin' on beer cans in good neighborhoods."

"That's 'cause they do their swilling inside closed doors," he replied. "And you don't see a lot of wrought-iron bars over the windows in good neighborhoods either."

Savannah glanced up. "Even on the second story. We may do well to get outta here alive."

"What are you talking about? We worked worst places than this in our day. With our eyes blindfolded and our hands tied behind our backs. We were badasses."

"And now?"

"You're still bad. I'm just an ass."

They looked at each other and grinned.

"I love you, Van," he said.

"I love you, too. You grew on me when I wasn't looking."

She saw some numbers on a building to her right. It looked like "193," but then she realized the "9" was a "6" that had fallen over.

"There it is," she said. "Wouldn't you know it. It'd be the worst one on the block."

"Well, of course. If we're going to spend our honeymoon slumming, might as well be for real."

They parked, and as Savannah got out of the car, she was nearly run over by a young girl on a bicycle.

"Oh, I'm sorry, ma'am," the girl said humbly, stopping and stepping off the bike. "Did I hurt you?"

"No, sugar. I'm fine. But you really shouldn't ride on the sidewalk."

"I don't most places," the child replied. "But there's bad holes in the street here. I fell in one the other day." She pointed to a badly skinned knee, which didn't appear to have received any first aid at all.

Savannah gave her a smile and a pat on the shoulder. "Don't worry about it then, punkin'. You ride on the sidewalk, if you need to. Just be careful and don't mow anybody down. 'Kay?"

The girl nodded, got back on her bike, and rode away. Savannah watched her, thinking of how she had once been much like that little girl. Poor and neglected, living in an area unsafe even for hardened criminals, let alone softhearted children.

"Tell me something," Dirk said as he walked over to her and laced his arm through hers, "why is it that you Southerners always call children by food names?"

"What? Food names?"

"Yeah . . . 'sugar,' 'honey bun,' 'dumplin',' 'sweet cakes,' 'punkin,' 'butter bean,' 'cow pie.' "

"I'd never call a child a 'cow pie.' "

"You call *me* a 'cow pie'!"

"That's different."

"One of these days, I'm gonna ask Granny to tell me what all these phrases mean that you've been using on me over the years."

"I wouldn't recommend that."

"Why not?"

Savannah gulped, then shrugged. "Um, let's just say Southernisms lose a lot in translation."

They reached the building and located apartment number 13, which was upstairs and on the far end.

"Guess he wasn't superstitious when he rented it," Savannah said as she checked her weapon, which was now strapped in its holster on her left side.

Dirk readied his as well; then he gave the door his loudest, most official, authoritative "police" knock.

It was a while before anyone answered, and then it was only a shout through the closed door.

"Yeah? Who are you, and what do you want?"

"San Carmelita *Police Department*. Open up!"

Savannah suppressed a chuckle. She couldn't help noticing that he had mumbled the "San Carmelita" part of his announcement and emphasized the "Police Department."

While California law would allow him to make an arrest if necessary, even outside the San Carmelita city limits, Amelia Northrop's murder wasn't officially his case. And it certainly wasn't hers. So their presence at ol' Burt's place of residence might be questionable at best.

But that sort of thing had never stopped them before. And it wasn't likely to now.

The door opened a crack with the chain on, and a guy whom Savannah could only classify as "weasely-lookin' " peeked out.

"What do you want?" he repeated.

"To talk to you," Dirk said. "Are you Burt Ferris?"

"Yeah. Why?"

"Open the door."

"I don't have to. Nothing's going on in here that needs cop attention. Huh, babe?" He turned around and nodded to someone behind him. "Tell 'em there's nothing they need to worry about going on in here."

"Nothing's going on," came a quavering female voice from inside. "Nothing at all."

Savannah felt like it was Christmas morning, and she had won the lottery and had gotten exactly what she wanted from Santa Claus—all at the same time.

This was going to be better than she'd even hoped.

"Open this door," Dirk said. "Now. Or I'm gonna kick it down. If you're standing behind it when I do, all the better."

The guy stood there, staring at Dirk—as best he could with one eye. He quickly scanned Dirk, taking in his height and bulk, head to toe. Then he glanced at the small, flimsy chain.

Finally he closed the door and they could hear the chain rattling as he removed it from its slot. They could also hear him barking some sort of order to the woman behind him.

A moment later, he opened it.

"Who called you guys?" he asked, looking and sounding severely annoyed. "There wasn't no reason for any-body to call you guys this time."

"This time?" Dirk asked. "You get a lot of visits from the boys in blue, huh?"

"I got nosy neighbors who've got nothing better to do than eavesdrop on other people's business and then call the police over nothing."

"Thank the good Lord in heaven for 'nosy' neighbors," Savannah said, trying to see past him. "And for people who care about others, and who pick up a phone and call the cops to get 'em some help when they need it most. I call those folks 'saints.' "

She glanced over Burt Ferris's naked chest and won-dered, not for the first time, why so many criminals went shirtless. Good guys ran around bare-chested, too, but she had noticed years ago that bad guys made a habit of it. Especially when they were up to no good.

"Step aside," Dirk said. "We need to come in." When Burt hesitated, Dirk added, "Unless you want to talk to us outside, where all your nosy neighbors will hear every word of it. Keep in mind, I talk loud."

"Yeah," Savannah added. "He's got one of those voices that really carries."

Burt glanced nervously back over his shoulder. "Yeah, well. Let's talk outside, but try to keep it down, would you? I don't need everybody knowing all my busi-ness."

"Whatever you say," Dirk told him. "Inside or out-side, we're definitely talking to your ol' lady. We're not leaving here without seeing her, so it's your call."

Burt let out a long sigh and stepped back into the apartment. Then he motioned them to enter.

As they walked in, Savannah gave the small studio a quick once-over, taking everything in with a glance.

The place was sparsely and poorly furnished. One small table and two chairs. A ragged pullout sofa bed. Two mismatched end tables, with a couple of mismatched lamps.

And yet, the apartment was neat and clean. As though someone had spent a lot of time making it as livable as possible.

Something told Savannah that someone wasn't Burt.

"All right," Burt said, "let's get this over and done with. I've got things to do, and there's gotta be something illegal going on in this town that you two could be tending to, instead of harassing innocent citizens like me."

Savannah looked him over and wondered how any woman could find him attractive. But then, he probably wore a shirt on most of his first dates. Might have combed his hair. And it was almost a lock that he would have pasted a smile on his face when he first met a potential bed partner, and not worn the surly smirk he was wearing now.

After years of observation, seeing the misery they brought into the lives of their victims, Savannah had formulated the hypothesis that loser abusers were often even better than normal guys at pouring on the charm, at least long enough to worm their way into a woman's life. She had also seen that once they were there, much like any other vermin infestation, it was next to impossible to get rid of them.

"Where's the woman?" she asked him. "Did you tell her to hide in the bathroom?"

He gave her a cold, threatening look, which she was pretty sure he would never have given Dirk. She would bet he saved it for women.

She had to admit, it probably worked very well for him, because he was particularly good at it.

So she stepped closer, invading his "space" and gave

him a look that was even colder and more threatening than the one he had generated.

"Do you really think you're just going to banish her to the toilet, and that's gonna be that?" she asked him. "Do you really think we're going to walk out of here without questioning her about what you've done to her?"

"She won't tell you nothin'," he said, practically spitting the words in her face.

"You're pretty good at keeping your women under control, aren't you, Burt?" she asked. "Most of them. You take pride in that. But then, there've been a couple who pressed charges against you and sent you away for a year here, a couple of years there."

His face flushed bright red and a dew of sweat suddenly appeared across his forehead.

"They did *not* press charges against me! They didn't!"

"Oh, so the state charged you? That's fine. Doesn't matter who did it, as long as it got done."

"I was innocent. Those women just got what they had coming to them. You don't know what they were like! They're the ones who should've been thrown in jail, not me!"

"Yeah, yeah, we've heard it all before," Dirk said as he walked over to him and pointed to one of the two folding chairs that sat across from each other at a battered card table. "Sit yourself down there, Mr. Ferris. While my partn—I mean, my wi—I mean, that lady there goes and has a talk with the woman in the bathroom, you and I are gonna have our own little chat."

"What about?"

"About yesterday morning. 'Cause we caught a glimpse of you, running around in some trees, right after you did a really awful thing. . . ."

Savannah left the men to their conversation and walked to the small door in the rear of the room.

She knocked softly. Then a second time, a bit harder, but there was no answer.

She glanced over at Burt and saw he was watching her as he talked with Dirk. He gave her a satisfied I-told-you-so look, which made her blood pressure rise a couple of notches.

She turned back to the door and said, "My name is Savannah, and I'm coming in now. Don't worry. I just want to talk to you. Everything's gonna be just fine."

She twisted the doorknob, praying the door would open. And it did.

Inside the small bathroom, she found a woman who looked like every other woman she had found over the years, hiding from her life and the intolerable situation she was in.

This woman wore a simple tee-shirt and jeans. But Savannah had found them in their various hiding places, wearing everything from designer evening gowns and priceless jewels to rags or, in a few cases, nothing at all. Domestic abuse crossed all social and economic lines.

Rich and poor, educated and uneducated, drug users and nonusers, drinkers and teetotalers, religious and nonreligious, straight and gay, male and female, they all wore one thing in common: a horrible, frightened look on their faces.

"It's okay, sugar," she told the woman. "I'm here to help you. Everything's going to get better for you, starting right now. I promise."

The woman stared back at her with eyes that were filled with hopelessness—something else these victims had in common that broke Savannah's heart and made her feel the intense need to pummel guys like Burt.

Savannah wriggled her way through the half-open door and into the small room. Closing it behind her, she turned to the woman. "Like I said, my name's Savannah," she told her, holding out her hand.

After a moment, the woman shook her hand and with a half-smile said, "I'm Georgia."

Savannah was taken aback. "You're kidding."

"No, really. That's my name."

"Well, I reckon that's some sorta sign that this was meant to be," Savannah said. "Were you born in Georgia?"

"No, but my momma was, and she always wanted to go back." Georgia grinned, and it occurred to Savannah that the expression seemed awkward for her, as though she didn't do it often.

"I don't have to ask," Georgia said, "if you were born there. I can tell by your accent. You sound like my mom."

"Good. 'Cause I want you to listen to me, just like you would your momma if she was standing here right now, okay?"

The fear crept back over Georgia's face, but she nodded.

Savannah looked down at the woman's hands and arms and saw what she somehow knew she would. The telltale signs of violence. Her wrists were red and so were her upper arms.

"Does he hit you every day, or just when he's not getting what he wants, the way he wants it, as fast as he wants it?"

"No! Not every day, he"—she gulped and looked away—"he doesn't mean to do it. He's out of work, and so am I, and we can't pay the bills. So he's under a lot of pressure."

"If he can't pay the bills, then you can't pay them either. So you must be under a lot of pressure, just like him."

"Yeah, I guess."

"But I'd bet dollars to donuts that *you* don't beat *him* up. Right?"

Georgia shrugged. "He was out looking for work this morning. When he got back, he saw that I hadn't cleaned up the place. You can't blame him for getting mad about that."

"It looked pretty clean to me. What was wrong with it?"

"He found a ball of dust in the corner by the bed. Burt's a very neat person. Real particular about where he lives and what he wears. He hates stuff like dust or dirt of any kind."

"He's a very neat person? Always picks up after himself, does he? He works his fingers to the bone vacuuming and dusting and scrubbing the commode?"

"Well, no."

"Let me tell you something about guys like your ol' Burt there. They're big on everything being neat and clean and perfect, as long as they've got somebody else to do the work. I've seen, time and again, that the minute it's on them to do the cleaning, they live like pigs."

Georgia bit her lower lip. "But I know he feels bad when he hurts me," she said. "Sometimes he buys me stuff . . . you know . . . afterward. He swears he won't ever do it again, but he's got a bad temper. His daddy had a bad temper. Sometimes, when I forget stuff or don't do things the right way, he just can't control himself."

Savannah glanced over the woman's face and throat. Not a bruise or mark of any kind.

"He hits you where it doesn't show, doesn't he." It wasn't a question. She already knew the answer.

Georgia nodded.

"Hmmm. Doesn't sound like some out-of-control nut job to me. Sounds pretty darned cold and calculated—like a guy who knows exactly what he's doing. I mean, how out-of-control could he be when he's being careful where he leaves the bruises?"

Georgia didn't reply, so Savannah gave her a moment to absorb the logic of her words.

"And let me guess," Savannah continued, "there've been times when he was a raging lunatic, hurting you and scaring the daylights out of you by threatening to do worse. But the second the cops knock on your door, he flips a switch and turns into Mr. Sunshine for the time that he's talking to them. In fact, the cops take one look at you, crying and all, and they think *he's* the sane one and you're the one who's bonkers. Right?"

Georgia just stared down at her bare feet.

"I don't know about you, but to me that doesn't sound like somebody who can't control himself. It sounds more like somebody who uses anger and acts of violence to get what he wants."

Georgia started to cry. "But he wouldn't just be mean deliberately. Why would he do that?"

"I just told you. He believes he's entitled to get whatever he wants from you. He gets off on the power it gives him to control you. That's more important to him than your happiness or your need to be safe."

"It can't be that simple."

"But it is, sugar. It's horrible how simple it is. He knows how bad he's hurting you, and he's choosing to do it anyway."

Savannah reached out and put her hands on the woman's shoulders. She felt her flinch at the touch.

"No!" She pushed Savannah's hands off her and backed away as much as she could in the tiny space. "Burt loves me. He doesn't realize how bad he makes me feel. And he can't help himself. It's because of his drinking, and his temper, and us having no money, and him seeing his daddy beat his momma, and—"

"And as long as you keep thinking that, as long as you keep making excuses for him, you're going to be his victim." Savannah took a deep breath. "Accept the truth, Georgia. He does it because he wants to. He does it because he can."

"But that's . . . that's just . . . cruel!"

"Yes. It certainly is. So, how long are you going to let him get away with it?"

When Georgia didn't answer, Savannah reached down and pulled the bottom of her own shirt up, revealing one of the terrible scars on her abdomen. "I know what I'm talking about."

Georgia gasped and stared. Finally she said, "Is that a gunshot wound?"

"Yes. It is. I have other ones, too."

"Who did that to you?"

"Somebody a lot like your Burt out there. Do you know he's been hurting women for years?"

No. She didn't know. Savannah could see by her shocked expression that it was the first Georgia had heard of it.

"Did he tell you he's served two sentences for assaulting women before you?"

"No."

"Well, he did. I reckon they must have left some dust bunnies in the corner, too."

Savannah lowered her blouse. "Okay, I've shown you mine. Now you show me yours."

Slowly Georgia pulled her shirt down from the neckline, revealing numerous dark, ugly bruises.

"He did that to me yesterday. I'd told him I was going on a diet, 'cause he hates how fat I am. But he found my candy bar wrapper in the garbage can. I'd forgotten to throw it out."

"What time yesterday did he do that to you?" Savannah asked, her mental wheels spinning.

"Yesterday morning."

"Are you absolutely sure it was in the morning?"

"I'm sure. I was polishing his shoes. I always polish his shoes in the morning, after I iron his shirt and his jeans. Burt likes to look sharp when he goes out drinking with his buddies at night."

Savannah reached for her arm and pulled her toward the door.

"Well, darlin', you've polished his shoes for the last time," she told her. "Where ol' Burt's going, he'll be wearing rubber slippers. If he figures they need a shine, maybe he can get his cellmates, Rocco the Rat or the Southside Stabber, to do it."

Chapter 10

"**W**e have good news and bad news," Savannah told Tammy on the phone as she and Dirk traveled from Luna Bonita toward the Pacific coast on Interstate 10. "First of all, Burt Ferris didn't kill Amelia. He was too busy beating up his girlfriend."

"Is that the good news or the bad?" Tammy asked.

"Both. We have to rule him out for Amelia's murder, but his girlfriend is pressing charges against him, and it'll be his third strike."

"Three times, he's out!" Tammy said.

"That's right."

"That is awesome!"

Savannah decided not to remind Tammy of all the conversations they'd had about the pros and cons of California's controversial three-strikes law, where three felonies sent the offender to prison for life.

"I can't pretend I'm not happy about that," Tammy said. "He won't abuse anybody else."

"Not girlfriends anyway. I don't know how he'll do with the other dudes in jail."

"Well, it just so happens, I'm at your house. While

Waycross and I are waiting for Granny to pack for the island, we've been doing some more research. We've got some news for you," Tammy said. "Don't know if it's good or bad, but it's interesting."

"Okay, let 'er rip, kiddo. I'm putting you on speaker-phone so Dirk can hear."

Savannah punched some buttons, then laid the phone on the Buick's dash.

"Hey, airhead," Dirk said.

"Hey, doody face," came the reply.

"Stop it!" Savannah nudged Dirk with her elbow. "Act your ages, you couple of pee-pee puddles. Tams, tell us your news."

After the giggling subsided on the other end, Tammy said, "I ran a check on William Northrop."

"Yes," Savannah replied. "And . . . ?"

"He's loaded."

"We knew that already," Dirk said as he passed a female driver, who was undeniably driving far too slow.

He gave her the obligatory glare as he went around her, but she didn't notice. She was too busy texting.

"Northrop's a land developer," Savannah said. "If a guy's gonna go around buying huge tracts of land, clearing them off, and building office complexes, strip malls, and luxury apartment buildings, he's gotta have at least a few shekels in his pocket."

They heard Tammy sigh. "Well, if you two are such smarty-pants," she said, "*you* tell *me* where Mr. William Northrop has been for the past two weeks. And think 'interesting.' "

Savannah took the bait. "Okay, Miss Tamitha Hart, font of all knowledge. Where?"

"The hospital."

"Hmmm." Savannah turned and looked at Dirk. "I suppose that could be *interesting*."

Dirk said, "What was he there for? Let me guess. Getting his tonsils taken out? A hangnail-ectomy?"

"No. It's better than that. *Way* better." She paused far longer than she needed to for effect.

Everything but the damned drumroll and twenty-one gun salute, Savannah thought as she waited and fantasized about holding Tammy up by the heels and shaking the information out of her.

"No, it wasn't hangnail surgery. No liposuction or Botox treatments," Tammy said finally. "Nothing fun like that. And he wasn't getting his tonsils taken out either." Another interminable pause, and then, "He was getting the *bullet* taken out."

" 'Bullet'?" Savannah and Dirk said in unison.

"That's right." Tammy sounded insufferably self-satisfied. "Someone shot him in the abdomen area. Nearly killed him."

"Oh, wow!" Savannah said. "No wonder you were so smug. That was actually worth your annoyingly long, pregnant pause that had me wanting to throttle you."

"He's still in the hospital?" Dirk asked.

"Nope. He was released day before yesterday."

"Do they know who shot him or why?" Savannah wanted to know.

"Awww, come on. I'm good, but I'm not *that* good! I know they haven't made any arrests for it. That's as far as I got."

"Ya did good, kid," Dirk told her.

Tammy giggled. "You know, I could be arrested for what I do for you guys. Hacking personal medical files like that."

"Shhh," Dirk said. "You can tell Savannah the nitty-gritty details, but not me. I'm still a law enforcement officer and—"

"And if they stretched him on a torture rack to get it

out of him," Savannah interjected, "he'd fold like a cheap lawn chair."

He shot her a dirty look. "I was thinking more along the lines of me flunking a lie detector test. Sheez."

"You guys are going by your house on your way to the island, aren't you?" Tammy asked.

"Yes," Savannah said. "I want to pick up a few things to take to the cottage. Why?"

"Because Granny just told me to tell you that she filled up a cooler with stuff from the refrigerator for you. It's on the table."

"Tell her, 'Thank you,' and give her a hug for me."

"Will do."

Up ahead, Savannah could see one of her favorite landmarks in the world, the McClure Tunnel.

"If that's all, puddin', we're gonna go for now," she told Tammy. "We're about an hour and change away from San Carmelita. I'll check back with you later, once we're on the island."

"Okay."

"Thank you for all your good work. Waycross too."

"I'll tell him you said so. And we'll see if we can figure out who shot Mr. Northrop."

"You do that. Toodle-oo."

Savannah hung up the phone, stuck it back in her purse, and got ready for a pleasure that never grew old for her, no matter how many times she experienced it.

"Here comes your tunnel, baby," Dirk said as the cement walls, asphalt roadway, and metal railings all fed into a dark passageway, leading to Paradise on earth.

"I love this," she said.

"I know you do," he replied. "That's why I always come this way instead of taking the 101."

They and their fellow interstate travelers were being funneled into Santa Monica's McClure Tunnel, a delicious gateway from inland California to the Pacific coastline.

Dirk honked halfway through for Savannah's benefit, as he always did. It made her feel about five years old, but in a good way.

"Is it just this tunnel that turns you on," he asked, "or will any tunnel do?"

A few seconds later, they emerged from the other end, and it was like plunging from the darkness into a pool of sunlight.

"It's this one," she said, drinking in the sight of the sparkling blue ocean to their left and the picturesque Santa Monica Pier. To their right, blue mountains edged the ocean, stretching far into the distance, dotted with mansions of every style imaginable.

"It's so special to me," she told him, "because this is where I first saw the ocean."

"The Pacific Ocean?"

"Any ocean. I came through that tunnel and saw this and I knew my spirit was at home. It was when I first came from Georgia to California . . . before I met you." She reached over and took his hand. "It took all the courage I could muster to leave everyone and everything I knew back there and move out here," she said. "But I had no choice. I just had to follow my dream. I'm so thankful I did."

He lifted her hand to his lips and kissed her fingers. "Me too, baby. Me too."

When Savannah and Dirk boarded the San Carmelita–Santa Tesla Ferry, Dirk and the hefty cooler he was carrying got a few weird looks from his fellow passengers.

But those weren't the looks that bothered Savannah.

"Did you get a load of that guy who checked our tickets?" Savannah said as Dirk stowed the cooler in the luggage compartment.

He pointed to a couple of empty seats nearby. "Yeah. Something tells me he wasn't just checking out the contents of the cooler when he told us to step aside and get inspected there."

They settled into the chairs, which were only a bit bigger and slightly less comfortable than airline seats. Savannah shoved her carry-on bag beneath her. Since it appeared their honeymoon was going to be a bit more practical and less romantic than she had expected, she figured she'd need a few more slacks and shirts and less of the beachwear she had waiting for her at the lightkeeper's cottage.

She leaned close to Dirk so their fellow passengers couldn't hear and whispered in his ear. "That other deckhand, the one standing behind the guy who checked the cooler—I'm pretty sure I saw him take our picture with his cell phone."

"Yeah, I saw that, too," Dirk replied. "And the two of them said something about us, once they'd let us on. People talk about me behind my back all the time. I know the signs."

Savannah chuckled. It was true. While she loved the curmudgeon sitting beside her, she had to admit that much of the rest of the world didn't. Dirk Coulter was an acquired taste. And where he was concerned, most people didn't bother to come back to the buffet for seconds.

Long ago, Granny Reid had taught Savannah to differentiate between someone's personality and their character. "Personality is what a body shows to the world," Gran said. "Salesmen have great personalities. They have to, or nobody'll buy what they've got to sell.

But not all of 'em will give you your money's worth. Not all of 'em have good character."

Granny had also told her grandchildren, "There are a lot of charming people out there with bad characters, and there are cranky people with hearts of gold. You can see a body's personality in a heartbeat. Might take years of seeing how they conduct their lives to know their character."

For years, Savannah had watched Dirk alienate most of the people around him with his impatience, his bluntness, and, at times, his downright rudeness. He was, without a doubt, the biggest grumbler, the crabbiest grouser, and all-around pain-in-the-butt curmudgeon she had ever known.

But while he didn't suffer fools gladly, Dirk had infinite patience with the few people he loved most in the world. And he was always kind and supportive of those who were trying their best to reach a mark, even when they fell short. He would gladly put his life on the line to save another person, simply because he considered it the right thing to do as a human being and because it was his duty as a cop.

Savannah loved him. Because—rotten personality aside—Dirk had good character. She knew she could count on him. And besides, salesmen with sparkling personalities were a dime a dozen.

"I'm gonna get sick again," he said as the ferry pulled away from the dock. "In a few minutes, I'm gonna be spittin' chunks over the side, just like I was on the trip before. Man, oh man—this bites."

"Try not to think about it, darlin'," she told him as she gave a sickly smile to the passengers sitting in their vicinity, who were all looking at Dirk with alarm and disgust.

He folded his arms across his belly and leaned forward. "Boy, that stew we had back at your house ain't gonna taste half as good comin' up as it did goin' down."

The couple sitting in front of them sprang to their feet and moved to seats that were much farther away.

"Uh-oh! That's it! I'm outta here." Dirk jumped up and headed for the back of the boat.

Savannah sat and considered her options. She could turn to everyone around her and say something like, "I don't actually know him. He just sorta followed me onto the boat." Or, "He's not usually like this. The rest of the time he's more like, um, Sean Connery or Cary Grant."

They kept staring at her. And it was going to be a long boat ride. She felt like she had to do something.

"Yeah, I know," she finally said to the woman sitting closest to her. "But if it was you who was sick, he's the kinda guy who'd hold your hair, pat you on the back, and then give you a stick of peppermint gum when it was all over with. Okay?"

The woman looked away. Eventually so did the rest of the passengers.

Savannah settled back in her seat and glanced down at the sparkling wedding ring on her finger. Once again, she contemplated the true meaning of love. It occurred to her that part of loving Dirk Coulter was going to be, for the rest of her life, telling the world that he was a much better guy than they thought he was.

As Savannah and Dirk turned the key to the lightkeeper's cottage and stepped inside, she said, "It feels like a year since we were here."

"Two years," he said, following her toward the back of the cottage, lugging the cooler with many a grunt and a groan.

"That was a first for me," he said, "carting food on a ferry and then in a taxi." He set it on the table with a grunt. "Last time I lifted a cooler that heavy, it had a dismembered body inside it."

"That was definitely more information than I needed right before dinner." She removed the cooler's lid and looked inside. "This one's full of amazing food, guaranteed, 'cause my blessed granny packed it."

"I'm sure that it is. You Reid gals live in perpetual fear that someone in your presence might actually suffer a hunger pang."

"Lucky you, that you're perpetually in the presence of a Reid gal."

"That's for sure."

Savannah put the perishables in the refrigerator while he popped himself a beer.

She held up a plastic cake carrier. "Granny's carrot cake, with cream cheese frosting."

"Did I say I minded carting that thing all the way here? No. I did not say I minded. Not one little bit."

"We need to call the gang," Savannah said as she peeled the top off the cake carrier. "I promised Tammy I would."

"No rush. Ryan and John can handle any problems she comes up with, and your grandma's feeding them, so they're all fine . . . uh . . . without us . . . for a little while. . . ."

His concentration lapsed as he watched her drag her forefinger across the top of the cake, then slowly, sensuously lick the frosting from her fingertip.

She noticed him watching her. "Oh, sorry. I'll cut

your piece from somewhere else when we have it tonight."

He swallowed hard. "Uh, yeah. Okay. Whatever."

Slowly she made another pass through the frosting and held up her finger. "Want some?"

Without a word, he hurried around the table, took her hand in his, and guided her finger to his mouth.

For what seemed like a very long, delicious time, he licked away every molecule of cream cheese.

By the time he was finished, she was leaning, weak-kneed, against the cupboard behind her.

The next thing she knew, their arms were wrapped tightly around each other. And they were kissing—as though they had just discovered a wonderful new pas-time—and sliding down onto the wooden floor.

"I'm sorry. Did you want to go upstairs first . . . get in the bed, where it's more comfortable?" he asked breathlessly as clothing began to come off and sail through the air.

"No!" she said. "No, I do not!"

"Oh, good! Me neither!"

Chapter 11

"I've never experienced afterglow on a kitchen floor before," Savannah said as she and Dirk lay side by side and stared up at the bottom of the table.

Dirk squinted and reached up to touch a small, dark spot on the underside of it. "Is that a piece of gum?"

"I think so. Leave it alone."

He turned onto his side, propped himself up onto one elbow, and looked down at her. "To be honest, till very recently, I haven't glowed all that much. Not anywhere. Not before, during, or after."

"Yeah, me either. Why you reckon that is?"

He twisted one of her dark curls around his forefinger and thought a few moments before answering. "From the time I met you, Van, I didn't really want anybody else. I mean, the opportunities were there, but I wasn't all that into it. I wanted you. And I didn't think I could ever have you, so . . . I was sorta stuck."

"Me too. Sometimes I wonder, if I hadn't had that close call, would we have just gone on like that forever?"

He leaned down and kissed her.

As he did, she had the distinct feeling it was more to

keep her from saying any more about that painful subject than it was for romance.

In some ways, she thought her near-death experience had hurt him even more than it had her. She seemed to be recovering from it emotionally faster than he was.

So she returned his kiss and let the subject go for the time being. Why cause him needless pain? What was past was past.

When he finally allowed her to come up for air, she said, "Are you hungry? Should we attack that fried chicken Granny sent?"

"You betcha! I—"

A loud, rapid knocking on the front door made them both jump.

They sat up abruptly, and Dirk smacked his head on the table.

"Who the hell is that?" he said, more than a little annoyed.

Savannah scrambled to collect her clothes, which were scattered to the four winds. "I don't know, but I can't imagine any of our gang would be rude enough just to drop by without phoning first."

"If it's any of them, I'm kicking 'em to the curb, no matter who it is. Except Granny, that is, of course."

He got his jeans on before she could wriggle into all of her female paraphernalia. After only two days of marriage, she had learned that he could shower and get completely dressed in less time than it took her to get the girls tucked neatly into her bra.

Apparently, there were some advantages to being male.

Another round of knocks sounded throughout the house.

"Hold on!" Dirk shouted. "We're coming, for Pete's sake! You don't have to break it down!"

Savannah had a sinking feeling as she followed him through the kitchen and the dining area and into the living room. She thought of that guy at the ferry dock, taking their pictures, and the little clandestine conversation he'd had with his fellow crewman after they'd passed by.

The third round of knocks reminded Savannah of someone else's style of knocking—Dirk's—when he wanted somebody to be aware of his authority as a cop.

As she passed the end table, where they had both placed their weapons when they'd entered, she grabbed the guns and shoved them under the sofa cushion.

Out of the corner of his eye, Dirk saw her. "Good idea," he muttered.

Then he strode to the door and yanked it open.

"What?" he barked, as loudly and as cranky as Savannah had ever heard him.

On the other side of the doorway stood a black suit. And the woman in it looked as crabby as he did.

"Chief La Cross," Dirk said. "What a pleasure to . . . Oh, hell, who am I kidding? No, it's not. What do you want?"

The chief took a step closer to the doorway. "I want to know why you're back on my island."

Savannah stepped forward to stand beside Dirk. Her hands were on her hips. "*Your* island?" she snapped. "Since when is it *your* island? I thought y'all were a property of the United States of America. Last I checked, folks were free to come and go here as they pleased, as long as they weren't breaking any laws."

"Which you two have done!" La Cross looked them both up and down with contempt in her dark eyes.

For some reason, the thought ran through Savannah's mind that Dirk wasn't wearing a shirt. And everybody knew what happened to guys who had their shirt off when law enforcement came calling at the door.

"You listen here!" Dirk said, his face getting redder by the moment. "My wife and I are just trying to enjoy our honeymoon, and—"

"That is not all you're doing here, and don't insult my intelligence by lying to me!" the chief shouted back.

Savannah decided it was time to defuse this situation with a bit of Southern charm, if at all possible, before she and Dirk both ended up on some sort of chain gang.

"Now, now, Chief La Cross," she said in her supersweet, patient voice. "What do you think we're doing here on Santa Tesla, if not enjoying our honeymoon?"

"You weren't here last night or earlier today. You went back to the mainland. While you were there, you defied my orders and did exactly what I told you not to do."

Savannah fought down her temper and stayed chocolate bonbon sweet—chocolate bonbons stuffed with cayenne pepper. "How, pray tell, did we do that?"

"You compromised a homicide investigation by leaking important information to the press," La Cross said. "Information I specifically asked you to keep to yourself."

"Oh!" Dirk said. "So, now it's a *homicide*. Last night on the news, it was an accidental drowning. We were wondering how you morons figure somebody could 'accidentally' get shot, numerous times, while they're out for a morning swim."

"A morning swim in a designer business suit, that is," Savannah said.

"Yeah, wearing fancy high heels and carrying a designer purse," Dirk added. "Someone blatantly lied to the press, Chief La Cross. Was it you who released that false statement?"

The chief's face flushed a shade darker, and Savannah saw her fists clench tightly at her sides. "You two have no idea what you're dealing with here, or how you've complicated an already difficult situation. I should arrest you both right now."

"On what charge?" Savannah wanted to know.

"Obstruction of justice, for one thing."

"What justice?" Dirk asked. "There's no justice here that we can see. You won't even admit the poor gal was murdered. How the hell are you gonna find out who killed her?"

Chief La Cross glanced right and then left, as though she suspected someone were standing nearby, eavesdropping.

Savannah thought how stupid that was, considering the nearest building was the gift shop—and that was two hundred yards away.

"I'm telling you," La Cross said, "that if I hear, one more time, that you two have been running around, talking about this case, I swear I will lock you up. You can believe me, or you can spend your honeymoon incarcerated. I don't care if you *are* a decorated police officer and a hotshot private detective."

She turned on her heel and marched away, back to a big, shiny black sedan parked in front of the cottage and the uniformed driver waiting behind the wheel.

As they watched her get into the car, Savannah reached for Dirk's hand. "I guess the television station manager gave her a call."

"Sure he did. Wouldn't you? I'll bet he told her off about the false information she gave him about his reporter."

"Edward looked a little on the wimpy side, but I got the idea he thought a lot of Amelia."

The sedan pulled away, stirring up a cloud of dust in its wake. Savannah and Dirk closed the door and went back inside.

"So, did she put the fear o' God in ya?" Dirk asked Savannah, with a playful wink.

"Oh, she made me reconsider my future plans. That's for sure. I was intending to sleep in tomorrow morning; but after her telling me I couldn't go talking to anybody about the case, I figure I'll get up bright and early and run over to Ryan and John's place. Now that I've talked to the lovely Chief La Cross, I'm determined to get crackin' as soon as possible."

Later, after a dinner of Granny's fried chicken and a long bubble bath in the oversized tub, Savannah and Dirk climbed onto the soft, feather bed mattress.

"Ah, this is heavenly," she said, "and if you don't think so, don't you say a word, 'cause nothing puts me in a worse mood than listening to your complaining."

"Me complain! Why, I'm as easygoing as they come. Go-with-the-Flow Coulter, that's what they call me."

"That's not what they call you," she said with a giggle as she pulled the quilt with its nautical designs up to her chin. "Believe me, I've heard what they call you, and that ain't it."

He laughed, reached over and tickled her under the chin. "Well, I don't give a hoot what they call me, as long as you call me sweet names."

"Like what?"

"Love of my life, lord of my castle, king of my—"

"Get real." She pinched him in the ribs. "You know, I

was thinking . . . I never told her you were a decorated police officer."

"And I never mentioned what a hotshot private detective you are."

"I am?"

"Sure."

"So, how did she know that?"

"Apparently, nasty ol' Chief La Cross has some investigation skills, after all."

"Good. Maybe she'll put them to good use and figure out who murdered Amelia Northrop."

"Wouldn't that be nice? Then we could get back to doing what's really important . . . finding out how many times a newlywed couple in their forties can do it without blowing a fuse."

They giggled and disappeared under the quilt.

A few minutes later, the clipper ships and sailboats on the quilt were rocking on the stormy sea of love.

True to her word, Savannah—and Dirk, because she gave him no choice—got an early start the next morning. It was barely past eight when the taxi pulled up to Ryan and John's borrowed vacation home and dropped them off.

"Woo-hoo," she said as they stood in the stone-paved driveway and took in the property, which looked more like a resort than a home. "This is awesome."

Instead of one large structure, the estate consisted of three separate A-frame cottages, on three different levels, joined by covered walkways. On a fourth, lower level, they could see an infinity pool, an oversized hot tub, and a cabana. The architecture had a Polynesian feel to it, with thatched roofs, bamboo fencing, lush tropical foliage, and carved stone and wood statues placed near waterfalls and fire pits.

"Must be nice, being Ryan and John, with friends in high places," she said.

This time, she meant it literally, because the estate was perched at the top of one of the island's highest peaks. From here they could see, literally, from one end of the island to the other.

Even their lighthouse looked small from such a distance.

And far, far away, across the glittering blue waters, just above the gray morning haze, she could see the faint outline of the California coastline.

"Harrumph," Dirk grumbled as he shoved his wallet back into his rear jeans pocket. "That was cold, hard cash down the toilet. Our golf cart could've made it up here."

Savannah scanned the distance between the distant light, then figured in the steep incline. They were at least fifteen hundred feet above sea level.

She turned back to him and said, "Boy, sometimes I think all your cups ain't in the cupboard."

He laughed. "You could be right." Nodding toward the nearest and largest building, he said, "Let's get this show on the road. I think I smell some of your granny's cinnamon rolls baking."

She sniffed the breeze and, sure enough, that delicious aroma was in the air. She'd know it anywhere.

"You're right. Let's hustle before they're all gone!"

Half an hour later, the entire Moonlight Magnolia Detective Agency was sitting at the edge of the infinity pool, enjoying the view and what remained of Granny's cinnamon rolls.

As Savannah lifted one of the soft, fragrant pastries to her mouth and bit into it, feeling the buttery frosting coat her upper lip, she thought, *I didn't have a chance in hell to be skinny.*

Yes, being born into a family of cooks like the Reids, she was cursed—or blessed, depending on one's point of view—with what Victorian women had lovingly termed their "silken layer." That thin layer of cushioning between the bones and skin gave them the beautiful, feminine softness so highly prized during that era.

When bombarded with media images that might cause her to feel insecure about her size, Savannah simply reminded herself that she wasn't fat. She'd simply been born in the wrong century. Silken layer? Heck, thanks to generations of tasty family cooking, she had a whole duvet!

"I've got Northrop's address," Tammy was saying as she sat on the edge of the cabana bed, her handheld device on her lap.

Savannah couldn't help noticing how lovely she looked—for a gal with no trace of a silken layer anywhere—in her white bikini and the gauzy aqua sarong she had tied low on her waist.

Savannah also couldn't help noticing that her brother was watching Tammy, taking in the view, like how the breeze lifted the skirt of her sarong, revealing perfectly toned and tanned legs.

Yes, Savannah thought, *"little" brother Waycross is a goner. That's all there is to it.*

"I'd be happy to have William Northrop's address," Savannah said, "because that's where we're headed next."

"Yeah," Dirk added. "Let's see how happy he is with the investigation the cops are doing of his wife's death."

"While you're at it," Ryan said, "maybe you can get some details about his own shooting."

Ryan was sitting on a chaise, several feet away, wearing sleek black swim trunks. Being a married woman now, Savannah was trying not to notice as he rubbed sunblock on his arms and legs.

Over the years, Savannah had never even tried to deny that Ryan looked like a Greek god, or that she had shamelessly lusted after him from the moment she had first set eyes on him.

But since she wasn't his type—not even in the most basic way—and since he had been devoted to John for many, many years now, she hadn't gone too far down that mental road. Why torture yourself, craving things you couldn't have . . . like a wild affair with a gay Adonis or eating a chocolate truffle from Lyon, France, every morning for breakfast?

Now that she had Dirk's ring on her finger, she was determined to do her best to stay off that path into fantasyland. After all, if Dirk could keep his eyes off Tammy's perfect little bod, she figured she should do the same with Ryan's.

"How can we help with your investigation, love?" John asked Savannah as he took a sip of his morning tea. "As charming as this setting may be, we're here to assist you, not spend our day bone-idle, dossing by the pool the entire time."

"There's one thing you can do," Dirk said. "You guys are the top o' the food chain when it comes to celebrity security."

Savannah smiled. Dirk had a way of boiling things down to one succinct and usually offensive phrase. In fact, Ryan and John were highly respected and extremely well-paid bodyguards, guarding some of the best known bodies in Hollywood. Having both been FBI agents in a previous life, they brought a great deal of investigation and surveillance expertise to the job.

They were always in high demand, and Savannah was enormously grateful that they assisted her anytime she asked and never accepted any form of compensation . . . except gifts from her kitchen, which she was more than happy to supply in abundance.

"Since you know everybody who's anybody in the bodyguard biz," Dirk was prattling on, "maybe you could find out if the Northrops hired any protection after William himself got shot."

Ryan nodded thoughtfully. "That's a good point. He can certainly afford that sort of thing. And if someone had made an attempt on my life like that, I'd be shopping around for some security."

"If they had security," John added, "the blokes surely didn't do an adequate job of it, considering what happened to that poor lass there on the beach."

The thought of Amelia Northrop lying in the sand, the life going out of her beautiful eyes, spurred Savannah to action.

"We need to get going," she said, standing and gathering up her cup and plate. "I can't wait to hear what Northrop's got to say about all this. I hate intruding on him in his time of grief, but that's the way it's gotta be."

Dirk stood, too. "I guess it's time to call that taxi service again. We're gonna spend a king's ransom gettin' around this island before all's said and done."

"Don't bother with that rubbish," John said, rising and reaching into the pocket of his linen slacks. "Our friend said we're more than welcome to use the three motorcars in the garage. We've no use for more than two."

He pulled out a set of keys and handed them to Dirk. When Dirk took them, he glanced down at the distinctive logo on the key chain. "Holy cow! A Jaguar?"

"You're trusting him with a Jag?" Savannah asked as she wondered whether she could snatch the keys from Dirk's hand while holding a cup and plate. She decided she couldn't. Taking the keys to a luxury vehicle from any male was a risky venture, at best.

"Not just any Jag," Ryan said. "A perfectly restored 1972 E-type coupe. Red. Black interior. Smokin' hot."

"I'm sure Dirk will show all due diligence while operating this wonderful piece of machinery," John said, his steely gray eyes boring into Dirk's. "Any sort of careless accident in our friend's fine vehicle could prove fatal."

Dirk chuckled. "If not at the scene, then later, huh?"

"Precisely." John turned to Savannah. "You should fare well on these roads. No lorries or jam sandwiches."

When John returned to his tea drinking, Dirk leaned down and whispered to Ryan, "Lorries? Jam sandwiches? You wanna translate that for us?"

"Trucks and highway patrolmen," Ryan replied, smoothing on more sunscreen. "What's the matter, Coulter? Don't you speak British?"

Dirk shook his head and sighed. "Hell, it's not enough I'm bilingual and speak Southern?"

As Savannah passed through the main cottage, heading for the garage and their newly acquired transportation, she found Granny lounging in the living room in a large wicker chair, her feet propped on an ottoman, her favorite reading material in her lap—the Bible and a supermarket tabloid magazine.

That combination had always puzzled Savannah.

They seemed like opposite ends of the reading spectrum in so many ways. But who was she to tell an octogenarian what to read? Granny considered both publications the absolute, gospel truth, and wasn't ever likely to believe differently.

Savannah glanced at the tabloid cover and found its headline most informative: MAJOR MOVIE STAR HAS ALIEN BABY.

To prove their story, the publishers splashed across the cover a picture of the greenish baby in the arms of its glamorous mother.

Yes, Savannah thought, *Granny's a complex, multifaceted woman.*

"We missed you at the meeting," Savannah said as she leaned over and kissed her grandmother on the top of her silver hair.

"I figured I'd done my do, supplyin' the rolls," Gran said, turning the page of the magazine. "I'll see if I can help Tammy on the computer later when she's lookin' up your bad guys for you. Yesterday, she taught me how to do something called 'browse.' You should try it yourself."

Savannah smiled lovingly down at her. "I'll have to do that sometime, Gran."

Granny flipped another page, squinting through her glasses at the print. "Yep. You can find out all sorts o' stuff on that-there Internet. They got directions to places, recipes, stories about everybody you ever heard tale of, all sorts of things."

"They do, at that."

"But you can't believe ever'thing you read on there. Some of it's made-up hogwash."

"Do tell?"

"Yessiree. Why, one article I run across said that the

North Pole's gonna plumb melt away one o' these days if we don't stop sprayin' too much o' that underarm-deodorant stuff."

"Hmmm."

"Now, who in their right mind would believe a bunch of hooey like that?" She turned the page and snapped to attention. "Hey! Look at this! They finally got a real honest-to-goodness picture of Bigfoot! Wanna see it?"

Chapter 12

As Savannah drove the Jaguar up yet another of Santa Tesla's steep-and-twisting hill roads, the automobile purred like a giant red panther hugging every curve. She shivered with delight, feeling the sexy surge of adrenaline race through her bloodstream.

Dirk, on the other hand, wasn't so happy.

He was sitting in the passenger seat, his arms crossed over his chest, a pout on his face. He hadn't said more than three sentences since they'd left. And those three sentences had been: "Give me back those keys, woman! Damn it, Savannah, I never got to drive a Jag before!" And . . . "If you don't give them back to me in the next five seconds, it's gonna put a serious damper on this honeymoon."

Reckon I'd best throw him an olive branch, she thought, *or this is gonna be a long, gloomy day.*

"I'll let you drive when we leave, okay?" she said. "Just help me find this address. We should be there soon."

Dead silence.

"Come on. Don't be a sourpuss. You got to drive the golf cart first."

"You can't compare a stupid golf cart with a 1972 Jaguar E-type!" he spat out, breaking his vow of silence. "And you nearly broke my hand jerking those keys outta it. That's gotta be the rudest thing you ever did to me, Savannah. And considering our rocky relationship, that's saying something."

"Okay," she muttered under her breath. "Just throw my olive branch in the wood chipper, would ya?"

She decided, then and there, that she wouldn't utter another word to him until Satan took up ice-skating. . . .

"Since when is our relationship rocky?" she snapped back. "This morning, I was the love of your life."

She had never been good at the "Silent Treatment." Mostly because it required being silent.

"That was before you broke my hand."

"Your hand isn't broken. A manly man like yourself doesn't break that easily. And stick your bottom lip in before I roll it up like a window shade."

She glanced down at the bit of paper in her lap and compared the number written on it to the brass numbers mounted on a stone mailbox beside some wrought-iron gates.

"This is it, 667 Vista Del Mar," she said.

"It's gated. Don't ram the Jag into the gate and blame the damage on me."

She looked up at the seven-foot wooden barrier, with its hammered-iron hardware. "I see the gates, Mr. Smarty-Pants. They're a little hard to miss. Sheez."

"You ran into the back of a donut shop one time."

"I was wearing weird new cowboy boots, and when I went for the brake, the edge of the sole hit the accelerator."

"So you said."

"I also told you a long time ago that I never wanted

to discuss that incident again—not for the rest of our natural lives."

"If you can snatch keys out of my hand, I can discuss donut shop rammings if I want to."

"Boy, you are getting on my last nerve."

She drove up to the gate's security access panel, rolled down her window, and pushed the intercom button.

"You pulled pretty close to that thing," Dirk said. "Don't scrape the side of the car when you pull away."

As she wondered how hard it would be to remove all traces of blood from Jaguar seats, the intercom buzzed and crackled. A woman's voice said, "Northrop residence. May I help you?"

"Yes, hello. My name is Savannah Reid. I'm with Detective Sergeant Dirk Coulter, and we'd like to have a word with Mr. Northrop."

There was a long, long wait, and Savannah was just getting ready to push the button again when the woman said, "I'm sorry, but Mr. Northrop isn't receiving visitors today."

"Please tell him it's extremely important," Savannah told her. "We need to speak to him about Mrs. Northrop . . . about his wife's . . . passing. He really, really needs to hear what we have to say."

Again, there was an insufferably long wait. Then the giant gates began to swing away from the Jaguar, opening wide.

"Hurry up," Dirk said, "before they close. You don't want them to close on the—"

"Dirk, darlin'," she said as she drove through the gates, "if you say one more word about this car or my driving, I swear, one of us is gonna be sleeping on the sofa tonight. And if that doesn't strike fear in your heart, let me tell you that I'll also eat the rest of that carrot cake all by myself." She shot him a stern look. "You know I can do it."

He mumbled something that sounded like, "That's for sure," but she wasn't certain, so she decided to let it drop. For now.

They went only a short distance before they saw the house—the strangest house Savannah had ever seen.

"It looks like a giant Rubik's Cube, only made of glass," she said as she stared at the building, looking right through it and out the other side. Every exterior wall was glass, floor to ceiling. And from what she could see, most of the interior walls, too.

Every room, every piece of furniture—all of which appeared to be white—was clearly on display for everyone to see.

"I guess the Northrops are those people you're always hearing about who shouldn't throw stones," she added.

"No kidding. Can you picture yourself living in something like that?"

"Not on your life. You can see everything right now, in the daytime. It'd be way worse at night."

"So much for running around in the buff," he mused, "and there'd be nothing left to the imagination when you made love. Even worse when nature called."

"Okay," she said, turning off the key and handing it to him. "Don't say I never gave you nothin'."

"Gee, you're too generous."

"So, are we buddies again?"

"I wanna drive it the whole rest of the day."

She leaned over and puckered up. "Every other trip. That's the rule."

He gave her a quick peck, then glanced at the house. "If we can see in, they can see out. We might lose some credibility if they catch us smooching."

"Point taken."

They got out of the car and walked up to the front door, which was, of course, also glass.

They watched as a woman wearing a white dress appeared from somewhere in the back of the house and hurried to the door to greet them.

She was a dignified, middle-aged lady, with long brown hair and very large brown eyes. She had a slight accent, which sounded German, when she said, "Hello. Won't you come inside?"

She ushered them into the living room and gestured toward a large white leather sectional sofa. "Please have a seat and make yourself comfortable. Mr. Northrop will be with you in a moment. May I get you some refreshment? Something cold to drink perhaps?"

"No, thank you," Savannah said. "We're fine."

But Savannah wasn't fine at all, she decided as the maid left them and walked toward the rear of the house. In fact, she was really dreading this conversation.

It was never easy to speak with those who had recently lost someone close to them. That difficulty was compounded if the loss had been a result of violence. Then, to that terrible mix, was the additional misery that William Northrop himself had recently been a victim of an attack.

Savannah knew all too well what that was like.

But being aware of all these sad factors was little preparation for the emotional jolt she felt when Northrop descended the stairs and stood before them.

He was a tall, thin man, perhaps in his midforties, with hair that had once been dark but was now silver on the sides. It was cut in a gentleman's conservative style, which made Savannah think of high-ranking politicians' hairstyles.

He was wearing black silk pajamas, leather slippers, and a robe of thick, luxurious charcoal cashmere—the exact evening attire she'd imagined that Ryan Stone wore . . . that is, before she'd become a married woman and sworn off such fantasies.

He could have stepped directly from his exotic glass house straight onto the glossy cover of any men's fashion magazine. Except for his eyes.

They were an unusual shade of pale gray that Savannah had never seen before. But that wasn't what startled her.

What she found unsettling was how terribly red and swollen they looked. If the eyes were the windows of the soul, this man's soul had been destroyed.

When he and Savannah looked at each other, she felt a chill sweep over her.

She could recall a few times—but only a very few—when, for a moment, she might have felt as empty and completely joyless as this man did. But, thankfully, those periods had been brief. Her world had righted itself and life was good again.

But as she looked into William Northrop's eyes, it occurred to Savannah that the damage to this man's life was too great for him ever to recover fully. The wound to his soul appeared totally devastating and permanent.

She held out her hand to him. "Mr. Northrop," she said, "my name is Savannah Reid. This is Detective Sergeant Dirk Coulter. We're so very sorry for your loss."

"Thank you," he said, his verbal response as weak as his handshake. "I was told you might be coming. Won't you sit down?" He motioned to the white leather sofa.

Savannah and Dirk sat as directed.

Northrop walked over to a chrome chair. He slowly, carefully, and stiffly sank into it. One of his hands was clasped against his belly, on his right side just below his waist.

Savannah knew the routine. She, herself, had moved exactly that way while recuperating from her wounds. As she watched him, it was as though she could feel every searing pain in her own body all over again.

"It'll get better with time," she told him, thinking how lame and trite the words sounded. "The physical pain, at any rate," she added in an attempt to be completely honest.

"So my doctors tell me," Northrop replied.

Dirk cleared his throat. "Excuse me, sir, but a moment ago, you said you were told we might be coming around. May I ask who told you that?"

"Charlotte La Cross. Or, I guess I should say, Chief La Cross. It's hard to call her by her title when we've been friends for so many years."

Oh, great, Savannah thought. *He's bosom buddies with Dragon Lady. Just what we need.*

"Did she mention that my wife and I saw your wife . . . saw what happened to her?" Dirk asked.

Northrop grimaced and put his hand quickly to his belly. "Yes. She said you were eyewitnesses."

"We were," Savannah added. "I'm sorry to say."

"I'm sorry for you that you had to see it." Northrop closed his eyes for a moment. Savannah wondered what he might be envisioning behind his lids. "But for Amelia's sake, I'm glad you were there."

He took a deep breath and struggled for his next words. "I don't think I could have stood it if I'd heard she died alone. I'm glad you were with her when she . . ."

Savannah nodded. "If it's any comfort to you, I believe she passed peacefully . . . under the circumstances. She didn't appear to be in pain or in a lot of distress."

A sob caught in his throat and he passed his hand

over his eyes. "Thank you for that. I was wondering, but I couldn't ask."

"I understand. And there's one other thing," Savannah added, "it may give you comfort to know that her last words were about you."

"Really? What did she say?"

Savannah decided not to tell him that she had been asking the woman for the name of the person who had killed her. Or that she had denied it was him. "Just your name. She spoke it several times."

"I don't know if that makes me feel better or worse," Northrop said. "I should have been there to protect her."

"You can't protect somebody from bullets," Dirk said.

A heavy silence hung in the air for a moment.

Dirk cleared his throat. "Hopefully, your good buddy Charlotte mentioned that your wife didn't die by drowning, like they said on the evening news."

"Yes, she told me what really happened."

"Well, it was your friend," Dirk said, "or somebody from her department, who released that false story to the media. Why do you think she's done something like that?"

"To protect me."

Savannah wasn't sure how she'd expected him to reply. But that wasn't what she was anticipating. "Protect you? How?"

At that moment, the maid appeared with a crystal tumbler filled with water, along with a bottle of pills. "I'm sorry, Mr. Northrop," she said. "I don't want to interrupt, but it's time for your medicine. The doctor said it was important for you to take it when—"

"It's okay. Thank you," Northrop said as he put a pill into his mouth and washed it down with the water.

He waited until the maid was well out of earshot before he answered Savannah's question. "Charlotte told me that she's sure you're attributing evil motives to her actions, and you shouldn't do that. Her intentions are honorable."

"I don't know what kind of law books she uses, but in my book there's nothing honorable about covering up a murder," Dirk said with his usual degree of tact.

Savannah gave Northrop what she hoped was a sympathetic, conciliatory smile, though she had to agree with Dirk. Some things you just didn't lie about. And a homicide was one of them.

"Perhaps," she said sweetly, "you can explain what you mean by that."

"It's complicated," Northrop said.

"Why don't you just spell it out and us dummies'll try to follow along," Dirk replied.

"What happened to me," Northrop began, "and, of course, what happened to poor Amelia . . . those are only two chapters in a long, difficult saga."

"Then why don't you start with chapter one," Savannah said.

"It started a couple of years ago when I came up with the idea of building a casino-hotel complex here on the island. Tourism is the lifeblood of Santa Tesla, but it's been steadily declining in the past decade."

With some effort, he stood and slowly walked over to an elegant accent table, which had pictures displayed on it. He picked up one of himself and Amelia and looked at it as he continued. "Amelia and I loved this place, ever since we honeymooned here five years ago. And we wanted to help the island and its people, if we could."

"You thought a gambling joint would elevate the standard of living?" Dirk asked .

Savannah cringed and gave him a reproving frown.

"You'd be surprised how much revenue a casino can bring to an area," Northrop replied. "It would save this island's economy. Something has to be done. The full-time residents are leaving in droves. They love it here, but if they can't keep a roof over their heads or feed their families, they can't stay."

"What does all this have to do with what happened to you and Amelia?" Savannah asked.

"Building the casino isn't without opposition here on the island," Northrop replied as he replaced the photo on the table.

"Imagine that." Dirk gave a little sniff. "Some people complaining that it'll bring in organized crime and political corruption, breed more prostitution and gambling addictions, more broken homes, stuff like that?"

Northrop fixed him with a long, pointed stare before he replied in quite an even tone. "Yes, some have mentioned those things in passing. But, actually, our biggest opposition is from some environmental groups that object to us developing the land—no matter what we intend to build."

"What's their major complaint?" Savannah asked.

"They're terribly concerned that we might disrupt a couple of species that are endangered, or whatever. They're all up in arms about something called the island fox and some special jaybirds and flowers called silver lotuses."

"And the groups trying to protect those animals seem stupid to you?" Dirk asked. He always sided with the animals. People, Dirk didn't like so much; but when it came to protecting critters, he was rabid.

"It seems to me," Northrop said, looking annoyed, "that once we brought out the bulldozers, the foxes and birds would simply move to another part of the island.

And if the environmentalists are all that worried about the lotus plants, we could dig them up and transplant them anywhere they suggest."

"How upset are these environmentalists?" Savannah asked.

"Enough to threaten me."

"What did they threaten to do to you?" Dirk asked, all ears.

"They said that if I broke ground on the project, they would see to it that I paid the 'ultimate price.' " He looked back at the picture on the table. "Now I have."

"So you've broken ground on the casino property?" Savannah asked.

Northrop nodded. "Seventeen days ago."

Something clicked in Savannah's head, something that Tammy had said. "When were you shot?"

"Sixteen days ago."

"How did it happen?"

Northrop walked back to his chair and sat down. If possible, he even looked more exhausted than when he had first come down the stairs. "We had gone out to dinner at the Lobster Bisque. That's our favorite little seafood hut, down in the harbor. We walked back to our car, which was parked in a lot behind the restaurant. I was opening Amelia's passenger door and this guy walked up to us. He was wearing a white shirt and black pants, like what the waiters in the restaurant wore. So, at first, I thought maybe Amelia had left her doggy bag, like she always did. We frequently had waiters chase us to our car with her leftovers."

He paused, steeled himself, and continued. "But when he lifted his hand, he wasn't holding a bag. It was a gun. The next thing I knew, he'd shot me."

"What happened then?" Dirk asked.

"At first, I didn't even realize I was hurt. It was more like a weird bad dream."

Savannah nodded, remembering. "Yes. It's sort of surreal. Until the pain kicks in. That jerks you back to reality, fast and furious."

"True. I didn't know how bad it was until Amelia saw the front of my shirt, and she started screaming. She shoved me into the car and drove me to the hospital."

"You have a hospital on this island?" Dirk asked.

"It's more like a clinic. But they saved my life. Once the casino's up and running, I'm going to build them a new facility to say, 'Thank you.' "

"How long were you in the hospital . . . er . . . clinic?" Savannah asked.

"Two weeks. Amelia came to see me every day, and that was quite a sacrifice for her, what with her long LA commute. She was a devoted wife."

"So they released you the day before she was, you know . . . ?" Dirk made an inane wave of his hand.

Savannah had noticed years ago, that Dirk had a difficult time saying the hardest words and often left blanks in his sentences when discussing heartbreaking subjects. Especially when talking to the families of the recently deceased.

"Yes. I was with her less than twenty-four hours after I left the hospital before . . ."

Savannah noted that Northrop had difficulty with those words, too. But she couldn't blame him. What was worse than having a loved one die? Having them taken from you with murder.

She couldn't imagine a torment more hellish than that.

So she was particularly gentle when she asked her next question. "Mr. Northrop, as difficult as this must be, could you please tell us everything you remember about that morning?"

"I've already told Charlotte everything, but if you think it might help find whoever did this to Amelia, I'll do it."

"It might," Savannah said. "Both Detective Coulter and myself have quite a bit of experience investigating homicides. Not that we'll do any better than your friend Chief La Cross, but"—she glanced over at Dirk and saw the grimace on his face—"but we'll certainly try."

"Since we saw it happen right in front of us," Dirk added, "we've sorta got an investment in the outcome."

Northrop thought for a moment; then he said, "It was really just a regular morning. Amelia got up and fixed us some coffee. She brought me one of my favorite muffins and a bowl of yogurt and served me in bed. She got dressed for work and made sure that our maid knew which meds I was supposed to take and when. Then she kissed me good-bye, and—"

His voice caught and it was a while before he could continue. "I told her I loved her and thanked her for helping me through such an awful time. Then she left. That was the last time I ever saw her."

"How did you find out what happened to her?" Dirk asked.

"Charlotte came by and broke the news to me. She was very upset. She and Amelia were very close."

Savannah thought back on Charlotte La Cross's mood at the scene and didn't recall her appearing particularly distraught. But then, people register anguish differently.

"What did La Cross say to you?" Dirk asked. "Did she tell you your wife had been shot, or did she give you that load of crap that she told the television station?"

"She told me the truth. Just as we had when I was

shot, we agreed it might be best for all concerned not to be forthcoming with all the details."

"How would that benefit anyone?" Savannah asked.

Northrop looked down, toying with the sash on his robe. "We've broken ground on the casino, but we had a few investors drop out because of those environmentalists. Until others are on board and fully committed, we can't have that sort of negative publicity."

For the first time since they had arrived, Savannah had an unsympathetic thought about William Northrop. At the moment, hearing what he had just said, she thought he seemed more like a coldhearted bastard than a loving, grieving husband.

"Negative publicity?" Dirk snapped. Apparently, he was seeing Northrop the same way. "You refer to the facts of your wife's murder as 'negative publicity'?"

Northrop's pale complexion flushed red with anger. "It's not like we were going to bury it forever! Charlotte is investigating the crime exactly the same way she would whether all the information had been released or not. Why does it matter?"

"Someone might have information," Savannah said. "Someone could have seen something important, maybe even the killer fleeing the scene. But if the public just thinks it was an accidental drowning. . . . Do you see my point?"

"Yes, but my investors will be making their decisions in the next twenty-four hours. By then, the autopsy will be done on Amelia, and Charlotte can announce the coroner's findings. About the bullets and all."

Dirk leaned back and crossed his arms over his chest. "It couldn't be that your chief of police wants to hide the fact that she's had two people shot—one of them dead—in the past two weeks, in this little island paradise of hers?"

"That might have played a part in her decision, too," Northrop replied. "But whatever her reasons, everything that Charlotte does is for the island. She loves it, and so do I. So did Amelia. She would want us to do what's best for Santa Tesla and its inhabitants."

Dirk stood. Savannah could tell he'd had enough. "What's the name of that environmental group, the one that threatened you?" he asked.

"They call themselves the Island Protection League."

Dirk pulled out his notebook and scribbled in it. "What's the head honcho's name, the one who threatened you?"

"The death threats were anonymous, of course. But the woman in charge is Dr. June Glenn. She has an office down in the harbor, next to the coast guard station."

Savannah stood, too, and held out her hand to Northrop. With some difficulty, he rose and took it between both of his. This time, his handshake was stronger, and his skin felt warmer and less clammy than before.

"We're going to do all we can to help you," she said, "in honor of your wife's memory. No one should have their life taken from them like that. The person responsible has to pay."

"Thank you, Ms. Reid. I truly appreciate your efforts."

Dirk, however, was less gracious. He shook Northrop's hand, but it was a quick, curt gesture. "We'll try not to generate any of that 'negative publicity' while we're doing it," he added as he headed toward the door. "God forbid you don't get that fine establishment built and the people of Santa Tesla have to keep eating macaroni and cheese three times a day."

Savannah watched her beloved new husband walk out the door. She turned back to Northrop and tried to think of something she could say to make such an awkward exit a little more gracious.

But she couldn't think of a darned thing.

"Bye," she said, and then followed after Dirk.

Chapter 13

"Sorry, babe," Dirk said as they walked from Northrop's door back to the Jaguar, "but I couldn't handle being around that guy a minute longer. That stuff he was saying made me wanna punch his lights out."

When he opened her car door for her, Savannah thought of what Northrop had said about getting shot as he was opening Amelia's door for her. She couldn't help feeling a pang of sympathy for him.

"Oh, I don't know. He doesn't seem like such a bad sort, overall," she said as she got in. "I can see he's broken up about Amelia—in spite of the other stuff he said."

Dirk closed her door, walked around, and got into the driver's seat. As he started up the powerful engine, he said, "You're just feeling sorry for him because he got shot, like you did. It's clouding your judgment."

Savannah's temper flared. To suggest that she wasn't being objective was insulting. It was a particularly infuriating insult because, in her heart, she knew it was true.

Those were always the biggest piss-offs. The ones you knew were dead on.

"It's not just that," she snapped back. "He's also a newly made widower. When I look at him, I can't help thinking how I'd feel if, God forbid, anything happened to you."

Dirk turned the Jag around in the driveway and headed for the gates. "That's an emotional thing, too. You're all goo-goo because you're a newlywed, so that sorta thing gets to you quicker."

She shot him a dirty look. "Well, with you talking like that, I'm getting less goo-goo by the minute."

He reached over and put his hand on her knee. "I'm just saying you can't let your sweet, compassionate, emotional side get in the way here. You have to evaluate every person and every situation logically at a time like this."

"What's your oh-so-logical evaluation of the situation and that guy back there?"

The gates parted in front of them, and Dirk wasted no time getting past them.

"Northrop's a guy with an expensive bathrobe and an expensive, weird glass house, who's covering up what happened to him and his wife—a couple of crimes that are as serious as they get—all for the sake of turning a buck."

"You think that's all the casino complex is to him? A way to make money?"

"Of course it is. Don't tell me you believed all that BS about how concerned he is about the island and its poor, struggling inhabitants."

"He might care about them."

"William Northrop's a hotshot developer who's at the top of his game. He's got money to burn on stupid-

looking houses that aren't even practical for human beings to live in. He sure as hell didn't get where he's at by
sacrificing to serve the suffering masses. He's in it for
the money."

Savannah had a feeling he was right, but she was too
far into the argument to abandon it now. "I think he
cared about his wife."

"I didn't say he didn't. I just said he's acting like a
jerk for covering up what happened to her, no matter
how he rationalizes it."

"That's true."

He gave her a quick, sideways glance—his expression
that of total astonishment. "Are you saying I'm right?"

"About that? Yeah."

He grinned. "Are you telling me I just won an argument with you?"

"You keep this up, I won't be telling you anything,
because I won't be speaking to you."

"Holy cow! I just won an argument with you! I've
known you for how many years and that's never happened before! It must be because we're married now!
We should've gotten married a long time ago!"

"So, where you do want to go now? What's the next
step?"

He laughed. "That's it. Change the subject."

As he guided the Jag slowly around the hairpin
curves, Savannah took advantage of the view of the harbor below. The morning fog had burned away and the
water was a spectacular shade of sapphire blue, which
was her favorite color. Since she'd been a child, people
had told her that her eyes were that color. Sometimes
she wondered if that was part of why she had always had
an affinity for the sea.

She decided to think about that instead of the crowing, highly annoying guy in the driver's seat next to her.

"Well, what do you think we should do next?" he asked, much to her relief.

"We have two possible suspects. We should follow up on one of them, then the other. Who do you want to do first?"

"This conservation group is right here on the island," he said. "That terrorist behind the knockoff watches and purses . . . didn't the TV station guy say he's somewhere in the LA area, waiting to go to trial?"

"Yes. Maybe Tammy can find out where exactly."

Dirk turned the Jag down the hill, heading for the harbor. "Northrop said that conservation lady, June Glenn, has an office down by the coast guard's headquarters. Why don't we go talk to her?"

"Good idea."

They drove a little way in silence. Then Savannah said, "You're right about Northrop being a jerk. We'll keep an eye on him, too."

"You never trust the spouses."

She reached over and patted his hand that was resting on the Jaguar's gear shift. "I trust mine," she said softly.

"That's all that matters to me."

Finding the office of the Island Protection League was a bit of a challenge for Savannah and Dirk, even though it was, just as William Northrop had said, located next door to the coast guard station on the harbor front.

What he had neglected to mention was that the league's front door wasn't visible from the street. One had to duck between the station and Coconut Jane's Tavern, walk down a narrow passageway, which wasn't even three feet wide, to the rear of Jane's building to find the small door, with peeling blue paint, that bore the IPL sign painted haphazardly by an amateur hand.

"Fancy digs," Dirk said. "Hell, my trailer looks way better than this. Bet it's a dump inside, too."

Savannah shot him a look and thought of the way he'd handled the interview with Northrop. On a good day, Dirk's basic personality leaned toward "morose." Sometimes he ventured over into "cranky." But when he was in "downright cantankerous" territory, she preferred to conduct her interviews without him.

"I've got an idea," she said. "Why don't you let me talk to this Dr. Glenn gal and you go next door to the coast guard?"

"Why would I wanna do that?"

"They might have logs or manifests or whatever you call 'em from the ferries that go back and forth to the mainland. It might prove interesting to see who was coming and going around the days the Northrops were shot. You'd do better with, you know, the guys than I would."

He nodded thoughtfully. "That's a very good idea. I'll do that. You take care of the lady doctor, and I'll deal with the rowdy sailors."

She smiled. To get Dirk to do something, all she had to do was appeal to his inner Knight in Shining Armor. It was one of the more endearing facets of his complex psyche.

"Thank you, darlin'," she said, giving him the benefit of a deep-dimpled smile.

"Anything for my lady" was the reply before he disappeared down the narrow walkway.

She breathed a small sigh of relief, turned to the battered old door, and knocked lightly.

"Come in," said a soft voice from within. "The door's open."

Savannah turned the knob and pushed. At first, the door stuck in its warped frame. But with a bit more effort, it swung open.

She stepped inside what turned out to be a very small office. One desk, two folding metal chairs, and a wastepaper basket were all the Island Protection League appeared to own in the world.

The walls had probably been white at one time but were now a dingy gray. Their only adornment was a poster of a sea lion touching noses with her adorable pup.

But the lady sitting behind the desk, who stood to greet Savannah, was the exact opposite of her lackluster surroundings.

Savannah figured the woman was around fifty, an elegant, blond woman, with graceful bearing and intelligent green eyes that met Savannah's with a scrutiny that would have made a more timid soul uneasy.

She was wearing a royal blue suit, a cream blouse made of crepe de chine, accented with a blue-and-black scarf twisted loosely around her neck. Her only jewelry was a pair of small, gold hoop earrings.

As she walked around the desk, Savannah noticed how well the perfectly tailored suit showed off her figure. Savannah also decided that she'd be glad to have a shapely pair of legs like that at any age, but especially at fifty.

"I'm June Glenn," she said, offering her hand. "How may I help you?"

Savannah returned the firm, confident handshake and answered, "My name is Savannah Reid. I'd like to talk to you a few minutes, if you have some spare time."

Dr. Glenn chuckled and motioned for Savannah to sit on one of the folding chairs. "Time, Ms. Reid, is probably the one thing I have the least of." She glanced at her watch. "I have an appointment in fifteen minutes, but until then, you have my full attention. What's on your mind?"

"William Northrop," Savannah said bluntly.

Savannah had decided that if she only had fifteen minutes, there was no time to pussyfoot around. She might as well get down to business.

She noticed that the woman's warm, friendly green eyes went a bit cold at the mention of Northrop's name.

"What about him?" Dr. Glenn asked.

"I understand that you and your organization have, shall we say, differences with him."

"He's determined to destroy this island; we're determined to save it. Yes, I suppose you could say we have differences."

"Would you tell me more about that?" Savannah asked.

The green eyes swept over her, evaluating. "Perhaps. First I'd like to know who you are—besides your name—and why you want to know about this."

Savannah drew a deep breath; then she said, "I'm a private detective from San Carmelita. My new husband and I were here on Santa Tesla, honeymooning, when we saw a woman shot and killed."

"Amelia Northrop."

It wasn't a question, Savannah noticed.

"Yes. Amelia Northrop. So you know it wasn't an accidental drowning."

June Glenn smiled, just a little. "I make it my business to know most of what happens on this island. It's been my home for many years."

"Then you may also know what happened to William Northrop two weeks before that."

"He was also shot."

"That's right. I spoke to him about it less than an hour ago."

The doctor's cell phone on her desk buzzed. She reached down, picked it up, and looked at the caller ID. Then she turned it off.

"Did he tell you that I shot him?" she asked.

Savannah was a bit taken aback by her bluntness, but she welcomed it. If everyone she interviewed was this straightforward, her job would be far easier.

"He didn't accuse you personally. But when asked who his enemies are, who might want to do him harm, he named your organization."

"My organization." Dr. Glenn looked around the shabby office and shook her head. "My organization consists of exactly what you see here, plus two drawers in my desk at home, four volunteers, a beat-up SUV, and a few boxes of equipment in my garage. We're woefully underfunded. We hardly have the resources to oppose someone like Northrop and his multimillion-dollar company. I can't imagine why he would name us as a threat."

Savannah gave her a pointed look of her own. "Bullets don't cost that much."

"I didn't shoot him. When it comes to violence against the person of William Northrop, I'm afraid the height of my ambition is to slap him. And that's only in my most reckless fantasies."

"Why is that?" Savannah asked, knowing the answer but interested in hearing this lady's side of the controversy.

"Because he's a soulless mercenary who would destroy this island for monetary gain. If he has his way, he'll build a monstrous complex on some of the most pristine, beautiful beaches in Southern California."

She glanced up at the picture of the sea lions on the

wall. "There are animals and plants here on Santa Tesla that aren't found anywhere else on earth. But Northrop couldn't care less. The islands along this area of the California coast are essential to many species of waterfowl, not to mention the seals and sea lions. But Northrop figures he needs a casino more than they need a place to breed and raise their young. It's unconscionable. And we'll do anything to stop him."

"Anything?"

"Short of killing him? Yes."

"Did you send him death threats?"

"Death threats?" Dr. Glenn looked genuinely shocked. "We most certainly did not."

Savannah thought for a moment. She believed that the gracious woman in front of her was speaking the truth, as she knew it. But how often does a person completely know those around her?

"Among your volunteers," Savannah said, "is there anyone whose outlook might be a bit more, say, militant than yours?"

"Absolutely not."

"Anyone you might have had to dismiss for that sort of thing?"

"No. We carefully screen everyone who wants to join the league. We're determined not to have anyone like that besmirching and undermining our cause with violence."

"Okay. Please think carefully. Is there anyone you can think of who might have wanted to join your organization, but he or she was refused on those grounds?"

Dr. Glenn thought only a moment before her eyes widened and a horrified look crossed her face. "Oh no!" she said.

"What is it?"

"There was a man last year . . ."

"And?"

"He came to us from another group, an organization in the San Fernando Valley. They did a lot of illegal things to bring attention to their cause. They vandalized and stole property. They threatened researchers at laboratories, and they were suspected of bombing a major research facility in Anaheim."

"What's his name?"

Dr. Glenn hesitated. "I don't want to cause him any problems if he's an innocent person."

Savannah gave her a long, searching look. "Dr. Glenn, if you wouldn't allow this man into your organization, you must have had a pretty good reason."

"Actually, I didn't have a solid reason," she said. "I just had an instinctive distrust of the man. I rely on my hunches. They're usually accurate."

"Mine too. And if you had a sense this man was a problem, that's enough for me to conduct a discreet investigation of him. Don't worry. It won't come back to you or your organization."

Dr. Glenn thought it over for what seemed like forever to Savannah. Finally she said, "Okay. His name is Hank Jordan."

"Does he live here on Santa Tesla?"

"Part-time, I believe. If I remember correctly, he said he works as a handyman at one of the motels on the other side of the island."

"Do you recall which one?"

"No, I'm sorry."

Savannah stood to leave. Once more she looked around the office and its sparse furnishings. Something told her that this was one charitable organization that spent every available cent on the work at hand, and not on anything frivolous . . . like a comfortable chair for its president.

She glanced up at the picture of the mother sea lion and its baby, and she decided that she liked Dr. June Glenn. A lot.

"Thank you for the good work you're doing here," she said. "Some friends of mine gave my husband and me a honeymoon stay at the lighthouse. The next time I go up in the light, I'll look down on those beautiful beaches and think of you keeping them that way."

Dr. Glenn stood, too. She smiled and nodded. "And I thank you for the work you're doing. It was terrible what happened to Amelia, and what happened to William, too, for that matter. I hope you catch the person or persons who did it. Threats and violence are no way to get what you want in this world."

Savannah sighed, thinking of all the abusers she had arrested when she'd been a police officer. They were individuals who believed that threats and violence were *exactly* the way to get what they wanted.

"I wish everyone lived by your code, Dr. Glenn," she said. "There'd be a lot less pain and misery in this sad ol' world of ours."

Chapter 14

Savannah and Dirk dropped by the "vacation compound," where the rest of the gang was hanging out, expecting to find them all lounging beside the magnificent pool. They couldn't imagine anybody resisting that temptation.

But when they got out of the Jaguar and walked down to the pool area, they found no one at all swimming, sunning, or bubbling in the hot tub.

So they headed up to the house.

When they walked into the kitchen, they saw Tammy and Waycross huddled together at the table. Their heads were nearly touching as they laughed and talked. Both were working away at their computers. Sheets of paper were spread out around them—bits and pieces of information that the two of them had collected, relating to their numerous suspects.

"Hey, just look at those younguns," Savannah whispered to Dirk. "Ain't they sweet?"

"They are," Dirk replied. "An airhead and a carrot-top. They're perfect for each other."

"Shhh," Savannah said, poking him with her elbow.

"You've gotta stop calling her that. She's smarter than three of you and one of me all rolled up together."

"Three of me and one of you?"

"Yeah."

"I'm not sure, but I think I was just insulted."

"Maybe you could locate two more of you and the three of you could decide."

Tammy spotted them and said, "Hey, you honeymoon lovebirds! What are you doing back here again?"

Dirk walked over to her and tugged on a strand of her hair. "We wanted to find out what you two dug up for us and to give you another shopping list."

" 'Shopping list'?" Waycross asked.

"A list of stuff we want you to find out for us."

Waycross's ruddy face lit up with a big smile. "You betcha. This spyin' on folks and finding out all their dirty laundry's fun! Of course, we do the same thing back home, too, but we don't get paid for it."

Savannah walked up behind him and put her hands on her brother's shoulders. When did this little freckle-faced, curly-headed kid, who had been so dear to her heart, become a man? She could distinctly recall wrestling with him in Granny's backyard . . . and winning, too.

Feeling the rounded hardness of his muscles under her palms, she knew such victories were forever in the past. Now she was "Big Sis" in name only.

Dirk walked to the other side of the table and sat down. Savannah joined him.

"So, what've y'all got for us there?" Savannah asked them, nodding toward the mess of strewn papers.

Waycross reached for some that were closest to him and shoved them across the table to her. "This stuff is about your designer purse knockoff guy."

"Not just purses," Tammy said. "Watches, scarves,

wallets, you name it. They were even selling fake perfume that had carcinogens in it! Can you imagine? He's got an army of fly-by-night vendors who unload tons of it in Los Angeles and New York City. It's very big business."

"Yeah, we found Amelia's report on the Internet and watched it," Waycross said.

In a sad tone, Tammy added, "She was a really pretty lady. Had a passion for what she did, too. You could see it all over her. She was really enjoying exposing that guy."

"Yeah, well," Dirk said, "it might've gotten her killed. I'm fairly sure that'd come under the category of 'Not Worth It.' "

"You said yesterday that Xenos is out on bail. Do you know where he's staying until his trial?" Savannah asked.

"Of course I do." Tammy reached for another piece of paper and gave it to Savannah. "There's his home address in Malibu."

"Malibu, huh?" Dirk said. "Who'd think fake Chanels and Rolexes would sell well enough to buy a place in Malibu?"

"Some people wanna look like caviar on a bologna budget." Savannah folded the paper and stuck it in her pocket. "They think they're just buying a purse to impress their girlfriends, but a lot of that money's going to organized crime. In Xenos's case, some of it's finding its way to the Middle East and anti-American terrorist groups."

"So much for a cute, little, victimless crime," Dirk said. "Personally, you couldn't give me one of those knockoff girlie purses."

"How about a fake Rolex?" Waycross asked him, a grin on his freckled face.

Dirk hesitated, thinking it over. Then he glanced at Savannah and Tammy, who were giving him a don't-you-dare look. "Nope," he said. "You couldn't give me one of those crummy things. No way. I'd rather be dragged across an anthill. Killer ants! Naked!"

"*Eeew.*" Tammy wrinkled her nose. "There's a visual I could've done without!"

"What sort of record does this Xenos guy have?" Savannah wanted to know.

Waycross gathered up a stack of papers. "Let's just say, if we taped these-here papers together, our good buddy would have hisself a rap sheet a lot longer than your arm."

"Assaults galore," Tammy said. "He's been arrested twice for murder, but he never went to trial for those. He's served a total of seven years."

"Lovely," Savannah said. That was just what she wanted, to chase down and question some terrorist-funding thug on her honeymoon. *Or any other time, for that matter*, she thought.

"Maybe we won't even have to look for him," she said, thinking aloud. "With any luck, it'll be this crazy conservationist."

"Conservationist?" Tammy was all ears.

"That's right," Dirk said. "We need to talk to a dude named . . ." He turned to Savannah. "What was it, Van?"

"Hank Jordan. From what I heard, he's a handyman for a motel on the other side of the island. He's been involved in animal protection groups that use violence to make their points."

Tammy started clicking away on her computer. "I love animals as much as the next person," she said, "and more than some. But I never understood the people who do that awful stuff in the name of compassion.

Don't they see how they're undermining their own cause?"

"Reckon some folks can't see the nose stuck right there on the front of their faces," said Waycross.

Tammy laughed uproariously.

Savannah smiled and shot a look at Dirk, who rolled his eyes.

Waycross had made a halfway-good funny, but it wasn't all *that* funny. Unless, of course, the Love Bug had nipped you behind the right ear.

"Let's see who can find 'im first," Waycross challenged Tammy as his own fingers started to pound away on his keyboard. He grinned across the table at Savannah. "She done taught me all of her tricks, and now it's gonna come back to bite 'er."

"You don't know them all, buddy boy," Tammy said. "I could still show you a thing or . . . Oh! Wait! I've got him!"

"Dang it!" Waycross closed his computer with a snap. "She's just too good for me."

Oh, Lord, Savannah thought. *Do we sound as sappy as that? Heaven forbid.*

"Well? Where's he at?" Savannah asked Tammy.

"The Island Lagoon. Just like you said, on the other side of the island. Although, I'm looking at a picture of it here on a travel advisory site, and I don't see an oversized mud puddle, let alone a lagoon."

Waycross leaned across her shoulder and stared at her screen. "There it is."

"Where?"

"In the logo. It's one of the *O*'s."

Tammy squinted at the screen. "That's a pretty bad logo."

Waycross nodded. "And a pretty bad motel, too. Me

and Tammy could go check it out for you, if you want us to."

"Why, Brother Waycross," Savannah said, her drawl thick, "are you suggesting that you'd like to take my pretty young assistant to a seedy motel?"

Instantly Waycross turned as red as his curls. "No! Of course not! I'd never take Miss Tammy here to no nasty motel! I mean, I wouldn't take her to . . . I mean . . . shoot. You know what I mean."

Tammy reached over and patted him on the shoulder. "I know exactly what you mean, and so do they. Don't let them tease you. Once they get started, they don't know when to quit."

"Tell me about it! You oughta growed up having her for a big sister! It was awful! She was bossy and kept after me all the time to do right. She was worse than Granny!"

"You got me back, putting that frog in my underwear drawer."

He snickered. "Yeah. That was a good 'un. It was worth that trip behind the henhouse with Granny and her hickory switch."

They heard the sound of voices coming from the living-room area, and footsteps. Ryan and John had returned.

They walked into the kitchen, greeted all sitting at the table, then raided the refrigerator.

John began assembling ingredients from the cupboard and refrigerator, including a cucumber, some mint, ginger ale, and a bottle of some sort of alcohol from the bar. "Anyone for a Pimm's?" he offered.

"Is it booze?" Tammy asked.

He smiled. "Most assuredly."

"Then no. We're working," she replied with utmost seriousness.

"So you teetotalers won't go for a beer either?" Ryan asked as he pulled one out for himself.

"No way. Dulls the senses," Tammy said. "But I'll take one of those herbal teas. They have ginseng. It helps me think clearly."

"By all means, get her two," Dirk whispered, low enough for only Savannah to hear.

Savannah kicked him under the table.

Ryan reached inside the refrigerator for the bottle of tea. "You got it, Tammy. Anybody else?"

"A Coke for me," Waycross said. "Make it a Dr Pepper, if you've got one handy."

Still bent over, his head inside the refrigerator, Ryan looked around the door, bewildered. "Say what?"

Savannah translated. "Down where we come from, 'Coke' is sorta a generic term for all soft drinks. You gotta specify which one you want."

"O-o-o-kay." Ryan closed the door. "I'm fairly certain that I speak better Mandarin than I do Southern. I feel like I need one of those pocket translators when I'm with the Reid clan."

Ryan distributed the beverages, then popped his beer and took a long swig.

"Since when do you drink beer?" Savannah asked, watching him. "You're more of a wine-sorta guy."

Ryan pointed to Dirk. "Your hubby there wore off on me."

Dirk grinned and shrugged. "What can I say? It was that hot day him and me were fixin' the faucet on the back of your house. I offered him one, and that's all it took."

John walked up with his drink—an unusual-looking cocktail, with a spear of cucumber for a stirrer.

"What the heck is that?" Savannah asked.

" 'Tis a Pimm's, love. Would you like to try it?"

"She's working," Tammy interjected, just as Savannah had held out her hand to John.

Savannah pulled it back. "I guess not. I'm afraid I may have overtrained my assistant here."

"Well, *I'm* not working, and neither is his nibs there." John nodded toward Ryan as he pulled up a chair and sat down at the table. "Though we certainly gave it the old heave-ho."

Everyone looked to Ryan for clarification. "We checked around, like you asked, and found that your friend William Northrop hasn't hired any protection of any kind. At least not for the past year. So we asked him if he wanted to hire us as bodyguards. It seemed like a reasonable proposition, considering all that's gone on around him lately."

"Wait a minute . . . you two actually went to see Northrop?" Savannah said, more than a little surprised.

"Knocked him up about half eleven," John said.

Again, they looked to Ryan.

"Dropped by his house at eleven-thirty. Presented our case to him. He said, 'No,' in no uncertain terms."

"Actually," John said, "a few of the terms he used when addressing us were distinctly rude."

Dirk cleared his throat. "I didn't know you boys were that hard up for work. Things a little lean in the bodyguard biz right now?"

"Not at all," John replied. "We just wanted to get inside—infiltrate, if you will—and find out whatever we could about him."

"It's just as well," Ryan said. "I didn't feel so great about the plan anyway. I've never offered to protect someone with the express purpose of spying on him."

"True," Savannah said. "I'm pretty sure that's on the

list of 'Bodyguard No-Nos.' Don't spy on your client and try to collect damning evidence against him."

"Here," Tammy said, "I've got directions for you to the motel where that weirdo is."

"What motel?" Ryan asked.

John set down his Pimm's. "What weirdo?"

"A dude on the other side of the island," Dirk replied, "who thinks it's okay to bomb laboratories. Stuff like that."

"We're headed over to rattle his cage a bit," Savannah told them.

"You want some backup?" Ryan asked.

"I don't think he's *that* weird, but thanks for the offer," Savannah replied.

She heard the sound of shuffling, scurrying feet behind her and turned, knowing whose footsteps it was. That was a beloved sound—one she'd known since childhood.

"Granny," she said as her grandmother walked into the kitchen, shopping bags in each arm. "I thought you were in one of those cottages taking a nap."

In an instant, Ryan and John slid their alcoholic beverages beneath the edge of the table. Gran was hell on "demon rum." She felt pretty much the same way about beer, wine, margaritas, and daiquiris—even though she had been known to order a Shirley Temple served in a pineapple, with a little paper umbrella, when she was out of town. She would splurge and order one of those concoctions when she wasn't in any danger of being spotted by her minister's wife.

Well trained by Gran and Savannah, respectively, Waycross and Dirk jumped up to relieve Gran of her burden. They set the sacks on the counter and returned to the table.

Immediately Gran dug in and started taking out grocery items and putting them in the refrigerator and inside the cupboards. "Can you believe," she said indignantly, "that there's nary a box o' grits on this entire island? I know, 'cause I had that taxi driver take me to all six grocery stores before I finally gave up the search."

"You were out running errands in a cab?" Ryan asked. "You should have asked one of us to drive you."

"That's okay," she said. "I made good friends with my driver. He was a nice feller. Named Jesus, but pronounced it 'Hay-soos.' Reckon you gotta be a decent person if you've got a name like that."

"I thought you were out by the pool reading your paper," Waycross told her.

"And I thought you were out taking a stroll somewhere in the neighborhood," Tammy added.

"No time for that rigmarole when the kitchen's got no grits in it," Gran replied. "That's not all I did either. Wait'll you see what I've got for you."

"The fixin's for cornbread?" Savannah guessed.

"Oh, way better than that."

Her groceries put away, Granny hurried over to the table and pulled her cell phone out of her purse.

She was grinning so broadly that Savannah knew her surprise was going to be something of consequence. Gran had lived too long to get excited or ruffled over trivialities.

"Whatcha got there, Gran?" Dirk asked as she held the phone between him and Savannah so they could see the small screen.

"Just some pictures I took."

Savannah leaned over and squinted at the phone, half-expecting to see a touristy picture of seagulls or boats in the harbor. But it was of a car. A large black sedan. With someone in it.

"How do I send this thing to you so you can see it there on your computer?" Gran asked Tammy.

Tammy reached for the phone. "May I?"

"Sure." Gran placed it in her hand.

Tammy's thumbs flew over the tiny keyboard.

They heard a couple of beeps and a catchy five-note tune. Then Tammy handed it back to Gran.

Tammy turned back to her computer, brought up a new window, and clicked. There was Gran's picture on the screen, large enough to see all the details.

"It's that contrary chief of police, La Cross," Savannah said. "I'd know her sour puss anywhere."

"Yep. I saw her and remembered what you said about her. Figured it was her," Gran replied, toying with her phone again.

"You spotted the chief and knew it was her, based on what little I told you about her?" Savannah asked, incredulous.

She was starting to think maybe she'd received some sort of "detecting gene" from the Reid side of the family.

"Partly that," Gran said, "but it was also what she was doing at the time I took that picture."

Everyone looked at the picture again. This time, Savannah saw that Chief La Cross had something in her hand.

"What's that she's holdin' there?" Waycross asked, pointing to the screen.

Tammy cropped the area of the photo around the chief's hand and zoomed in on it.

"Yes, it's definitely a phone," Tammy said, "but she's not talking on it."

"She's taking a picture," Dirk added.

Gran chuckled and looked terribly pleased with herself. "She most certainly is. Wait'll you see this other one."

Having located picture number two, she handed the phone to Tammy, who repeated her process of sending it to the computer.

A moment later, they were studying the second one.

But it didn't take Savannah long to figure out what she was seeing.

Chief Charlotte La Cross was still snapping pictures. And from this angle, Granny had captured the subject of her surveillance.

There was the coast guard station. There was Coconut Jane's Tavern, in all of its shabby glory. And there, turning to go down the narrow passageway between the two buildings, were Savannah and Dirk.

"Holy sh . . . !" Dirk started to say. Then he shot a quick look at Granny.

"Yeah, that's about what I thought, too, when I saw what she was up to," Gran said. "If I'd had a frying pan in reach, I'd have been tempted to give her a good skillet smackin'."

Tammy nodded, a serious look on her face. "Savannah told us about that, Gran. She says you're known far and wide in Georgia for being deadly with cooking utensils."

"Ain't no big thang," Gran replied, puffing out her chest a bit. "I just beat the tar outta one of my no-good neighbors after he beat the tar outta his wife and children. After that, my reputation was solidified for all eternity."

But Savannah wasn't listening to their chitter-chatter about past kitchen gadget glory. She was staring at that picture and feeling her blood pressure soar by the moment.

When she turned and looked at Dirk, Savannah

could tell by the dark expression on his face that he was feeling the same way.

"I've had about enough of this," she said to him, keeping her voice low and even, so as not to alarm the others. The last thing she wanted was for Gran to be worried sick that she was getting ready to confront the island's *capitan* of law enforcement.

"Yeah. Me too," Dirk replied.

Quietly they stood and gathered up their papers. Savannah picked up her purse. Dirk grabbed the Jaguar's keys.

"We need to get going," Savannah said in her best pseudocasual voice. "We've got a handyman to talk to. Maybe we'll pick up some lunch somewhere, relax a little, and pretend we're actually newlyweds on a romantic island honeymoon."

Gran fixed them with a long, concerned look.

Uh-oh, Savannah thought. *Here comes the grandma speech about being careful, about watching yourself and not letting your temper get the best of you, about showing good Christian charity to all your fellow men, women, beasts, and fowl alike.*

Gran put her hands on her hips. Her lower lip protruded just a bit. "Well, lan's sakes," she said in a slightly huffy tone. "You'd think, after what I just showed ya, that y'all would have more important things to do than that romantic-lunch nonsense."

"I beg your pardon, Gran?" Dirk said. "What are you—"

"If I were you," Gran replied with a lift of her chin, "I'd hunt down that nosy chief of police and ask her what in tarnation she thinks she's doin', takin' pictures of innocent people on the street, who're just goin' about their business. Tell her I said to get some business of her own and mind *it*!"

Savannah smiled. "Yes, we'll schedule that in, too."

"Good. You might wanna do it before lunch. You gotta keep your priorities in order, girl. I always taught you that."

As she and Dirk were leaving the room, Gran called out, "If she gives you any lip, you tell her to watch herself. I may not be able to find any grits on this-here backwards island, but I'll just betcha I could lay my hands on a cast-iron skillet!"

Chapter 15

"You're really lucky to have a grandmother like Granny Reid," Dirk told Savannah as they headed up steep hills where no structures had been built, and very little except scrub brush grew.

"Truer words were never spoken," Savannah replied. "The court taking the nine of us kids away from our parents and giving us to Gran, that was the best thing that ever happened to us."

"You don't talk much about that," Dirk said, giving her a cautious, sideways glance. "It has to be pretty bad before the courts will actually take kids away permanently and change custody of them to their grandparents."

"It was bad," Savannah said. "With my ol' man being a trucker and always on the road, and my mom's butt glued to a bar stool, nine kids can get in a heap of trouble. We were no exception."

"Did you play with matches and burn the neighborhood down?"

"Just one pine forest, east of town."

"I was kidding."

"I'm not. Then there was the time that Waycross and

Marietta squirted glue in all the door frames of the school on Friday night. On Monday morning, when everybody showed up, well . . . you can imagine."

Dirk laughed. "We won't share that one with Tammy."

"But some incidents weren't so funny. Our mom thought it was just fine if her kids entertained themselves at night in the alley behind the tavern, while she was inside drinking. I don't know how much time you've spent playing behind bars, but there're a lot of broken bottles behind most of them."

Savannah turned her head to the right and stared out the window, remembering all too well. She was seeing the magnificent, sunlit scenery of a Pacific island, but recalling a dark, chilly Georgia night. "Vidalia was running from Marietta, playing tag or whatever, when she slipped and sliced her leg wide open. It was about a six-inch gash."

"Holy cow!"

"Yeah. I ran in the bar and dragged Shirley off her stool. She tried to drive us all to the hospital, which was forty miles away. But she was way too sloshed to operate a vehicle. So we all wound up wrecked in a ditch, and Vidalia gushin' blood like Niagara Falls."

Savannah stopped and drew a deep, regrouping breath. "That's the way the cops found us. Shirley sitting on the edge of the road, bawling. Me in the back of the wrecked car, with Vidalia and the rest of the kids, trying to stop the bleeding with an old grease rag."

"And that was the last straw for the authorities?"

"One of several. They checked out the state of the house, did an investigation like they'd done many times before. Finally they agreed that the welfare of the children was as important as the rights of their parents to maintain custody."

"Sounds like it wasn't a minute too soon."

"It was years too late. But better late than never."

"I notice you always call her 'Shirley' and not 'Mom.'"

"She insisted on it when I was a kid. When I got to be an adult, I chose to just continue."

They drove along in companionable silence for a while. Then Savannah decided to broach a topic that she'd always figured was off-limits with Dirk, and she assumed that because he had never opened up about it on his own.

"What did you call your mom?" she said, her voice gentle and soft.

It took him a long time to reply. "Nothing. I never knew her."

"Oh." Savannah swallowed. She figured his relationship with his family had been rocky. Maybe *very* rocky. But she hadn't expected that. "So you were adopted when you were a baby?"

"No. I was raised in an orphanage till I was thirteen. The pretty, blond, blue-eyed kids got adopted. The ones who knew how to turn on the 'cuteness act' and be charming when the prospective parents made the rounds. That just wasn't me."

Savannah reached over and put her hand on his forearm. "I'm so sorry, sweetie. That must've been plumb awful!"

He chuckled, but there was no humor in the sound. "Felt a bit like being the ugly dog at the pound."

"Oh, honey."

"It's all right. I got along."

Savannah fought back the tears as she thought of him there, being passed over year after year.

"What happened when you were thirteen?" she asked.

"I got adopted. This couple came around, looking at

all the kids. I'd already had my growth spurt and was the size of most grown men. The guy didn't ask me a single question, just picked me out, 'cause I was the biggest. A few days later, when they took me home with them, I found out right away why they'd adopted me."

"Why was that?" Savannah asked, afraid of the answer.

"He had a small, one-man construction business. He needed some free labor, picking up the junk on sites after he'd finished working, loading and unloading lumber off his truck, crap like that."

This time, Savannah couldn't stop the flow of tears. Her heart ached for that little boy in a man's body, finally getting adopted, only to realize that he hadn't been chosen for himself, and would never be truly loved for who he was.

"How about your adopted mother?" she asked, dabbing beneath her eyes with the hem of her sleeve.

"She had problems of her own, dealing with him. He made her pretty miserable, so she just sorta moped around the house, getting through each day. Kept a low profile, you know?"

Yes, Savannah knew the type all too well. Invisible women, afraid to show who they were to the world because their man would object. So many lights hidden under so many bushels.

"You don't have any idea who your biological parents were, then?"

"No. The guy who adopted me said my mom was a hooker. She didn't even know who my dad was."

Savannah's jaw clenched and so did her fist. "Your adopted dad was a real piece of work, telling a kid something like that."

Dirk reached over and patted the top of her head.

"Don't let it bum you out, babe. I stopped letting it bother me a long time ago. Johnny Cash said, 'Close the door on the past. Don't let it have any of your energy, or any of your time, or any of your space.' And you know what a great guy he was!"

Savannah laughed, in spite of her sadness. Dirk's heroes were Johnny Cash, Elvis Presley, and Ben "Pa" Cartwright. She decided he could have chosen far worse, for sure.

"Is he still alive, this so-called 'adoptive dad' of yours?"

"No."

"And his wife?"

"They're both gone. They'd also adopted a girl, before me. She was a lot older than I was. She did quite a bit of the cooking and cleaning. She and I hardly ever spoke a word to each other, but I guess she's the closest thing I ever had to a sister."

"Do you two talk?"

"She used to live in Twin Oaks, till she got married. Soon after that, she and her husband moved to Chicago. We haven't stayed in touch. I think she'd just as soon forget her whole childhood, me included. And I can't blame her."

"I'm sorry, darlin'," Savannah said. "Thank you for telling me all that. I know it's not easy, talking about stuff from the past. Stuff that hurts."

"You're my wife now. You've got a right to know." He turned and winked at her. "Now be honest, you've suspected more than once that Dirk Coulter was a real bastard."

She looked into his eyes and saw the pain that belied the stupid joke. "I'm married to Mr. Dirk Coulter," she said in her most indignant version of a Southern drawl.

"And as his wife, I'll ask you to keep a civil tongue in your head when you discuss him with me. He's a fine gentleman, no matter what his parentage. And I'm proud to say, he rose above his raisin'."

Suddenly Dirk slowed the Jaguar down and looked the other way, finding something terribly important to watch to his left. She heard him sniff a time or two. When he turned his full attention back to the road ahead, she could see his eyes were filled with tears.

"I love you, Savannah," he said.

"I love you, too, darlin'. And I wouldn't take a million bucks for you, no matter what's written on your birth certificate."

A few minutes later, Savannah and Dirk arrived at the Island Lagoon Motel.

Just as Tammy had described it, the place was lagoon-free. In fact, it had no landscaping at all. The one-story, ten-unit no-tell motel had all the charm of a long, rusty cracker tin with windows.

"I've made better buildings than this with Tinkertoys and Lincoln Logs," Dirk said as he pulled the Jaguar into one of the parking spaces in the pothole-ridden parking lot.

"It makes that fleabag motel where we spent our honeymoon night look like the Taj Mahal," she replied.

They got out of the car and walked to the lobby. The room was no larger than ten by ten feet and had dark, fake walnut paneling of a style and quality that Savannah had only seen in the basements of her childhood friends back in Georgia.

In front of the counter was a display rack, featuring brochures from the myriad attractions in California, from Alcatraz to Disneyland, and on down to the San

Diego Zoo Safari Park. The pamphlets were the only bright spot in the room.

Behind the counter stood a woman who looked like she had never been anywhere but that one spot. Not even in front of the counter, let alone to Alcatraz or San Diego. She looked tired—of her job, to be sure, and maybe even of her life.

"Yeah?" she asked.

While Savannah hesitated, wondering exactly how to answer such a complex question, the woman sighed, leaned forward on the counter, and said, "Thirty bucks an hour. You go over the hour, even five minutes, it's another thirty. Got it?"

"Yeah," Savannah replied, "but we don't want a room. We want to talk to Hank."

"He's busy."

Dirk stepped up to the counter and leaned on it, which put him and Miss Hospitality nearly eye to eye. "We're busy, too," he said. "And we can see that you're just working your fingers to the bone back there on . . . well . . . whatever it is you do." He reached into his pocket, pulled out a twenty-dollar bill, and placed it on the counter. "So this might help pay for your time."

"My time's worth more than that."

"It'll take you five seconds to tell us where Hank's at," Dirk said. "Let's see now, that's"—he did the math in his head—"over fourteen thousand dollars an hour for your valuable time. I'll bet you never made that kind of money before in your life."

She reached for the twenty, but Dirk put his finger on it.

"He's cleaning room eight," she said.

"I thought he was the handyman here," Savannah said. "Not a maid."

"Hank does it all." She reached down again for the bill. This time, Dirk released it. She nabbed it and shoved it into her jeans pocket.

As Savannah and Dirk walked out of the lobby, back into the parking lot, and headed for the rooms, Savannah said, "What do you call a guy who cleans a motel room or house or whatever?"

"I don't know, but you can't call him a 'maid.' A male 'maid' just ain't natural."

"Then what would you call him?"

"A 'cleaner-upper'? Hell, I don't know."

"If he'd clean my house for me, I'd call him 'lover boy.' "

"I'll keep that in mind."

They found Hank Jordan in room eight, as promised. The door was open and even before they entered, they could see him inside, yanking the sheets off a bed.

He looked about as thrilled with his life career choice as the gal at the desk. In his early fifties, generously enhanced around the midsection, a mop of long, dirty hair pulled back into a greasy ponytail, he peered at them from behind glasses that had blotches of something that looked like green paint on the lenses.

Savannah noticed it matched the blotches of green paint on his black sweatshirt. At least he was accessory coordinated.

"Is your name Hank?" Dirk asked him as he and Savannah stepped into the room.

"Maybe it is, but maybe it ain't" was the reply.

Dirk turned to Savannah. "Don't you just hate it when their mothers don't teach them their names before they start school?"

"It's pitiful," she said. "Plumb pity-full."

She turned back to Hank, who had just finished

putting fresh sheets on the bed and was in the process of picking the bedspread up off the filthy, stained carpet and putting it back on the bed.

"Y'all don't put clean bedspreads on, too, when you change the sheets?" she asked.

He smirked, and she could see he was missing a front tooth. "The smile of a quarrelsome man," Granny would say.

"You're kidding, right?" he replied. "We don't put on clean bedspreads every time, and neither do the five-star hotels in the real world."

"*Ewww. Gross.*" She had to make a mental effort to put that disturbing bit of information aside and contemplate it later—if she dared.

Hank threw a couple of pillows onto the bed; then he grabbed a squirt bottle and a dingy rag off the floor and headed for the bathroom.

Dirk followed after him, his badge in hand. "I'm a cop," he said, "and I've gotta ask you a couple of questions about something that happened here on the island two days ago."

"I didn't see anything or do anything," Hank replied as he gave the sink what Savannah called "a lick and a promise" with the dirty rag.

"You need to take this seriously," Dirk said, using his deepest, most officious voice. "A very bad crime was committed."

"Not by me," Hank replied.

"Well, let's don't act like you're above it," Dirk snapped. "I've looked at your record and you ain't spotless. Sorta like that sink you just kinda cleaned there."

"I did some stuff, back in my day. But nothin' lately." He grinned again. "Nothing the statute of limitations hasn't run out on."

"Where were you day before yesterday, in the morning?"

"Was that when it happened?"

"When what happened?"

"The bad crime you think I might've done."

Dirk's eyes narrowed. "Hank, my man, I'm gettin' sick and tired of you real quick here. Now—day before yesterday, midmorning—where the hell were you? Spit it out, or you'll be missing both of your front teeth."

"I was in jail."

Savannah and Dirk stared at him, silently, for a moment.

"'In jail'?" Savannah repeated. "And you had the gall to tell us just now that you've been clean for years."

"I have. Just 'cause I was in jail doesn't mean I was guilty of anything. You know that."

"Why were you in there?"

"The chief of police herself was questioning me. I've been real popular with you cops this week. She seemed to think I had something to do with somebody or the other getting shot. But I didn't. And I couldn't have done whatever else you think I did."

He turned away from them and gave the lid of the toilet the same brief swipe as he'd offered the sink.

"Just ask Chief La Cross if you don't believe me. She knows I was there from eight o'clock in the morning till one in the afternoon."

He picked up the drinking glass on the counter and, with the same rag that he had just used on the sink and the toilet, he wiped out the inside of the glass, then set it back down.

"Oh no! That does it!" Savannah said, suddenly rushing out of the room. Once outside, she leaned against the side of the building and took some long, deep breaths. "*I'm gonna be sick*," she said to herself, "*and I'm*

sure as shootin' never staying in a motel again. Not for the rest
of my born days!"

"Why do I feel a bit like Daniel walking into the
lion's den?" Savannah asked Dirk as they got out of the
Jaguar and walked up to the modest stucco building
bearing the sign SANTA TESLA POLICE DEPARTMENT.

"Me too." He slipped his arm around her waist and
gave her a little hug. "This may not go down in history
as the smartest thing we ever did together."

"Do you think she meant it about arresting us and
putting us in separate cells?"

"Something tells me she's just mean enough to do it."

"Well, she ain't got the corner on 'mean,' so she'd
better watch out. Sneaking around, taking pictures of
us like that, when we didn't know it! She's got a lot of
gall, if you ask me."

Dirk chuckled. "How many times, Miss Private Detective, have you done the exact same thing?"

Savannah thought it over for a second, then sniffed.
"That's different. It's all in the line of duty. A necessary
evil. Stuff like that."

"But mostly, what makes it okay is that *you* do it. It's
not all right when *she* does it."

She scowled up at him. "I have to tell you, I'm not
happy with this new trend we're developing here, this
business of you winning arguments. We've gotta nip it
in the bud before it gets outta hand."

"Don't confuse you with the facts?"

"Something like that."

They reached the building, and Dirk opened the
door. She entered to find the tiniest reception area she
had ever seen in any police station. Unlike some of the
hardcore facilities Savannah had worked in during her

career, this place looked like it was set up to handle maybe one jaywalker a year.

As she flashed back on Dr. Glenn's minuscule office, it occurred to Savannah that, here on this island, if a building wasn't a place created for luring in tourists, not a lot of money or effort was spent on its construction or décor.

Maybe what William Northrop had said was true. Perhaps Santa Tesla Island's inhabitants were poor and in need of some form of economic stimulus.

Was a casino complex the answer? She decided to leave that up to wiser minds than her own. For right now, she had a killer to catch and a police chief to confront.

She turned and saw a tiny desk and, behind it, a sight that made her skin crawl. Turning to Dirk, she whispered, "Oh no! Look at that! It's Kenny's evil twin!"

Dirk took one look and said, "Oh, man. This is freaky." He hummed a couple of bars from the *Twilight Zone* theme song.

At the morgue in San Carmelita, Savannah had experienced far more than her share of unpleasant encounters with a boorish buffoon named Kenny Bates. From the minute Kenny had laid eyes on Savannah, he had been hopelessly, pathetically in lust with her. Unfortunately, he never bothered to conceal the fact every time she walked through the morgue doors.

From the too-small uniform on a too-rotund body to the bad toupee, this guy was Kenny to a tee.

He nodded to Dirk, but his eyes lingered on Savannah. And more specifically, her bustline.

"Yeah? What can I do you for?" he asked; then he snickered at his own tired joke.

"Not for a million dollars and the Hope Diamond,"

Savannah replied, giving him a cold stare—which he missed entirely because he was still soaking in the view.

"Hey, over here!" Dirk snapped his fingers. "You wanna put your eyeballs back in their sockets and take care o' business here, guy?"

Kenny's clone shook his head slightly, as if coming out of some sort of fantasy—the details of which Savannah hoped never to know.

"We need to talk to Chief La Cross," Dirk told him. "Now."

"She ain't here" was the professional response. He turned back to Savannah. "But you can talk to me anytime you want to, pretty lady."

"Oh, Lord, just kill me now," Savannah whispered. "Or, better yet, kill *him*, if you ain't too busy workin' out that world hunger problem."

"That pretty lady is my wife," Dirk said. "So you'd better spend the rest of our little conversation here looking into *my* eyes. Otherwise, one or both of yours are gonna be black. Got it?"

The guy appeared to grasp Dirk's meaning because, with effort, he turned and looked straight at him. "I told you the chief's not here."

"Yes, and I heard you," Dirk said.

"Then what else do you want from me?"

"I've got one more question for you. Listen close now, 'cause it's a toughie. Where is she?"

"I don't have to tell you that."

Savannah stepped closer to him, the expression on her face deeply unfriendly. "No, you don't have to. But whether you do or not, we'll find her. When we do, I'm going to complain to her, long and hard, about how you practically stared a hole through the front of my blouse and were quite unprofessional with me."

"But—but . . . I . . ."

"Something tells me that my complaint won't be the first one she's ever gotten about you. I'll just bet that your job's hanging on by a thread right now. If you get fired, with your abundance of charm and the bad economy around here, you'd be lucky to get work as a dogcatcher."

The passion in his eyes flickered; then it died a quick death. He gave her a nasty look, then turned to Dirk. "She's having lunch at the Lobster Bisque down on the water in the harbor," he said. "Now, why don't you two leave and let me get back to my work here. I'm a busy man."

Savannah glanced at the video game on the computer. "Yeah, get back to all that protecting and serving. Make the world a safer place."

As Dirk and Savannah walked out of the station and headed for the Jaguar, she said to him, "That was so spooky. I guess we all *do* have a double somewhere in the world."

When Dirk opened Savannah's car door, she said, "Maybe they were identical twins separated at birth."

"Would you blame the parents? Who could stand to raise two of those?"

"Hey," she said, pausing with one foot in the Jag, "I just thought of something. The chief's at the Lobster Bisque. I knew that sounded familiar."

He thought for a moment. "Oh yeah, isn't that the place that Northrop said was his favorite restaurant, too?"

"I'm sure it is."

They looked at each other, weighing any significance.

"Probably doesn't mean a thing," she finally said.

"How many really great restaurants could there be on this little island? It's probably ninety percent of the population's favorite eatery."

"True. Besides . . . La Cross? Ugh." He shuddered.

"Yeah. I agree."

Chapter 16

Savannah and Dirk stood on the sidewalk and looked across the street at the Lobster Bisque, a simple but charming seaside establishment. It looked as though it had once been a nice house, someone's vacation cottage. Now with its exterior painted an icy white and with deep blue umbrellas shading its outdoor tables, the place looked most inviting.

Apparently, a lot of Santa Teslans thought so, too, because not a single table was vacant.

But it wasn't the ambiance of the place or even the capacity crowd that captured Savannah's and Dirk's attention. It was the table to their far right, in the rear, by some planted palms—the table least visible from the street.

It was the table where Chief of Police Charlotte La Cross and William Northrop were sharing lunch and a couple of cocktails.

"Well, well, well," Dirk said, grinning at Savannah. "I wouldn't say for sure that they're up to no good, but you have to admit this is an interesting little rendezvous."

"This is going to be fun. Just watch." Savannah took her phone from her purse and crossed the street. Her spine was pool stick straight, her stride determined.

Dirk followed close behind her as they darted between the pedestrians, bicycles, motor scooters, and omnipresent golf carts. He stayed right behind her as she wove her way among the tables.

She stopped a few feet from La Cross's table and pointed the camera of her cell phone directly at the chief and her luncheon companion.

At first, the two diners failed to notice, so absorbed were they in their conversation, food, and drinks. But the instant La Cross glanced up and recognized Savannah and Dirk, the cozy, happy expression fell off her face.

Savannah could almost imagine that she heard it plop into her umbrella-adorned pink cocktail.

"What the hell do you think you're doing there?" La Cross snapped as she jumped to her feet, knocking her chair over backward in the process. It fell to the floor with a tremendous clatter, which caught everyone's attention.

Suddenly the busy, bustling, noisy restaurant was as silent as a well-tended library. The crowd sat, wide-eyed and all ears, taking in what was going on at their neighbors' table.

"Who, me?" Savannah asked, checking the picture on her phone, smiling, and then pushing the camera button again.

"Stop that!" Chief La Cross rushed around the table and tried to grab the phone from Savannah's hand.

"Stop what?" Savannah quickly shoved the camera down the front of her blouse and into her bra. "I was just taking some pictures of people who were minding their own business. People who didn't know they were having their pictures taken. Nothing illegal about that. Right?"

Savannah quirked one eyebrow and gave her an unpleasant, bitter smile. "But then, it isn't nearly as bad as taking pictures of a couple on their honeymoon—an unsuspecting guy and gal who're just hanging out, minding their own business around, say . . . Coconut Jane's Tavern or maybe somewhere nearby there."

La Cross looked like she had just been caught stealing an expensive diamond ring in a jewelry store. She also seemed to notice she was making a scene as she glanced around the restaurant and realized that her fellow islanders were watching this highly entertaining exchange with rapt attention.

"It's not like this is a romantic lunch," Savannah said, waving a hand toward William Northrop, who was leaning back in his chair, almost as if trying to hide behind the potted palm. "Is it, Chief La Cross? You aren't having a cuddly lunch with a man who's only been widowed a little over forty-eight hours, are you?"

"You leave!" La Cross whispered, leaning so close to Savannah that Savannah could smell the alcohol and fruit juice on her breath. "Get out of here this minute. I'll deal with you two later."

"No, you can deal with us right now," Dirk said. "We want to know if you take pictures of all the residents who live here on the island without their knowledge or permission. Without them knowing it."

At several of the tables, people turned to each other and began to whisper furiously. "Or is it just the tourists you spy on?" he added for a bit of extra spice. "People who visit your island like us . . . like these folks sitting around here, just trying to have a nice meal?"

The whispers around them suddenly turned into an

uproar. Several guests pushed away their plates and motioned for the waiter to bring their checks. Others got
out their own cell phones and began snapping pictures
of Dirk and Savannah and Northrop. And even more of
Chief La Cross, whose face was turning more crimson
by the second.

Even her eyeballs looked red. For a moment, Savannah wondered, if a police chief had a stroke while argu-
ing with you, would that be murder or manslaughter?

"We have one thing to ask you and then we'll leave,"
Savannah told her. "A simple yes or no will suffice."

When La Cross didn't reply—just stood there breath-
ing heavy, her nostrils flaring—Savannah continued.
"Was Hank Jordan at your station house when Amelia
Northrop was murdered?"

It seemed to take forever, but eventually the chief
gave Savannah the slightest nod.

"Thank you," Savannah said. "One more thing, as we
bid you a good day. Do not take any more pictures of
me or my husband. We aren't the bad guys here."

Savannah glanced over at William Northrop, who
still looked like he wanted to climb into the palm tree
next to him and hide. He hadn't said a word, and somehow, Savannah didn't respect him much for not even
bothering to get out of his chair and stand up for his
dear old buddy Charlotte.

"Now *he* might be your bad guy," Savannah said,
pointing at Northrop. "For all we know, you might be
questioning him right now. But if you want to question
us any further, I'd suggest you invite us out to lunch,
too. Maybe buy us a couple of fancy cocktails, and we'll
sit at a table and giggle together, like y'all are doing
there. But either way, stop spying on us, and let us enjoy
our honeymoon in peace."

She and Dirk turned and left, following the same pathway through the tables of people, who now looked far less peaceful than when they had entered.

But none more so than William Northrop and Chief of Police Charlotte La Cross.

La Cross slowly returned to her seat; then she sat down so quickly that it looked like her legs had collapsed beneath her. She gave Northrop one quick, dirty look, then began to chugalug her drink.

He waded into his salad with a vengeance, not looking at any of the other diners, who were openly staring at them.

When Savannah and Dirk got back into the Jaguar, they turned to look and saw that La Cross was glaring at them with an intensity that would have sent shivers through Savannah if she hadn't been so mad herself.

"When it comes right down to it, she didn't do anything all that awful," Dirk said as he started the car and pulled out into traffic.

"She violated our privacy," Savannah shot back.

"Something that we do to other people almost every day of our careers."

"But—but . . ."

"Come on. It's me. You can be honest with me."

"No, I can't," she replied with a sigh. "Because to get real with you, I'd have to fess up to myself first. And I'm not ready to do that, thank you very much."

"How about if I tell you why you're so mad at her?"

"Okay, Mr. Smarty Farty, lay it on me. The cold, hard truth. Smack me right between the eyes with it."

"It's easy. You're mad at her for the same reason I am. She was able to surveil us without us even knowing it. We're pissed at her 'cause she beat us at our own game."

He nudged her with his elbow. "How's that, babe? Was I even close?"

She smiled in spite of herself. "You've gotten smarter since you became a married man."

"I know."

"Well, I don't like it."

"If this ain't the most beautiful place on earth, I don't know what is," Gran said as she stood in front of the lightkeeper's cottage with the rest of the gang and looked up at the tower.

Silhouetted against the deepening evening sky, with its brilliant coral-and-turquoise glow, the structure had an almost ethereal beauty about it.

"What do you reckon it is," Savannah asked, her arm around her grandmother's shoulders, "that makes that shape so appealing to the human eye?"

The moment the words were out of her mouth, Savannah realized she had just opened the door for a flood of stupid, adolescent jokes. She looked around the Moonlight Magnolia gang seated in a circle of beach chairs in front of the cottage and saw far too many males for the opportunity for "bawdy" to just slip by.

"The first one who says something nasty and ruins this precious moment is gonna get his jaw smacked," Granny said, still gazing up at the tower.

Waycross grinned. Dirk snickered. Ryan and John looked at each other and covered the lower portions of their faces with their hands.

Savannah sighed, envying Gran. How lovely would it be to have that kind of power?

She'd only have to wait another forty years to know.

"It was really generous of you two inviting us all over for dinner like that," Ryan said.

"We don't mind you guys that much," Dirk replied, then took a long drink from his bottle of root beer—a concession to Granny being present.

John lifted his cup of evening tea. "Kinder words were never spoken."

"Not by Dirk-o," Tammy muttered, sipping from her own sparkling mineral water, enhanced by lemon and lime slices.

Waycross was watching her as she swirled her finger-tip in the drink, and Savannah noticed that he had a slightly sad look on his face tonight.

Perpetually the nosy big sister, Savannah couldn't help wondering what that was all about. Being terminally codependent, as well, she couldn't resist spinning her mental wheels about how she might be able to fix it . . . once she found out what it was.

"Actually, we had an ulterior motive for having y'all over for dinner," she said.

"Uh-oh, here it comes." Tammy laughed. "Somebody invites you to their house during their honeymoon, you have to know they're after something."

She looked anything but annoyed. Savannah chuckled to herself. This gang loved nothing more than to be "used" in an investigation. In fact, they lived for it.

Dirk downed the last gulp of his root beer. "Ordinarily, I wouldn't request backup," he said.

"Being a strong, tough, virile man possessing super-natural powers, and all that," Ryan interjected.

"Exactly. But this Xenos dude, he's got a really nasty record, and—"

"Say no more. We're in." Ryan turned to John. "It's been a while since we went after a guy like that. It'll knock the rust off, huh?"

John lifted his teacup in a toast. "Most certainly. It'll be a pleasure."

"Don't be so sure about that," Savannah said. "Since he's got a trail of nasty assaults and some unsolved murders in his past, I doubt we're going to find him pleasant company."

Tammy reached for her handheld device, which was never far away. Savannah and Dirk had given it to her for her last birthday; now it was like an extra appendage. "I've been researching him and found where he'd posted a bunch of messages on a boxing gym's blog. Apparently, he works out there every afternoon at two, without fail. It's in the southern end of Malibu, near Santa Monica. And it's on the same block as his house."

"I'll bet he walks there," Savannah said. "It'd be pretty stupid, even in Southern California, to drive less than a block."

"That'd be a good time to nab him," Granny added.

"We might luck out, and he'd even be alone," said Ryan.

Tammy nodded. "That's what I was thinking." She turned off her device and looked down, a bit of a woebegone look on her face. "So you four are going to go to Malibu tomorrow and interrogate our terrorist fashion counterfeiter. I guess Gran and Waycross and I can hang out here and wait to hear how it goes."

"No way," Savannah said. "Do you really think we're gonna do something as dangerous as that and just let you guys cool your heels here by a pool? Nice try."

Tammy beamed. "Really? Wow! What do you want us to do?"

Savannah's brain froze. Of course, they weren't going to put three "civilians" in the midst of the action, when the situation was as dicey as this one might turn out to be. But she had to think of something. It wasn't fair to ask the others to do all the dry research work and leave them out of the juicier stuff.

She looked over at Dirk. He gave a slight shrug and shook his head. He couldn't think of anything either.

Suddenly Ryan chimed in. "We need you three to man the audio-surveillance recorders."

A wave of gratitude washed over Savannah. She flashed him a brilliant smile. "Yes!" she said. "We'll want to record the whole thing, just in case he says something incriminating."

"You mean you'll be wearin' microphones under your clothes or somethin'?" Waycross asked, nearly as excited as Tammy.

"Sure they will," Granny replied, looking most authoritative with her nose slightly elevated. "Don't you ever watch television, grandson? They call it 'bein' wired' "

"We'll take our surveillance van," Ryan said. "It's got everything we need. You'll be parked on the street, watching the whole thing out the window."

Tammy rubbed her hands together with glee. "That's so cool! I can hardly wait for tomorrow! It feels like Christmas Eve."

Savannah laughed and looked up at the light tower. The beam had just turned on and was beginning its nightly rotations.

"If you guys are gonna go up there and look around, you'd better do it now," she said. "Daylight's about gone."

Ryan glanced over at Tammy and Waycross. "John and I, we've had a long day. We'll go up another time."

"Me too," Gran said. "Not that I'm too old or nothin' like that, but I'm just not in the mood right now. Somebody else go."

Tammy turned to Waycross. Her pretty face was glow-ing with excitement. "I want to. I've never been up in a lighthouse before. Do you want to come with me?"

Savannah was surprised to see Waycross hesitate.

A beautiful lighthouse, with a gorgeous girl whom he was obviously very attracted to . . . it seemed like an op-portunity he would jump at.

"Yeah, sure," he said, "if you want to."

He rose and held out his hand, helping her up from the low-seated beach chair. But once she was standing, he quickly released her hand.

Together—but not as together as Savannah would have liked—they left the group, walked to the tower, and disappeared inside.

"Hmmm," Savannah said under her breath. "What's up with him?"

She looked around and saw her own puzzlement re-flected on the faces of everyone else present.

Granny shook her head and sighed. "Sooner or later, me and that boy are gonna have to sit ourselves down and have a *long* talk."

Chapter 17

"I can see why you love this place, Savannah girl," Granny said as Dirk drove the three of them south, along Pacific Coast Highway through Malibu. "I swear, when the good Lord was makin' the big ol' world, he must've spent some extra time on this part."

Savannah turned to her grandmother, who was sitting in the backseat, right behind Dirk. "That's true, Gran. I agree. I look at those sparkling waters every day of my life, and yet, I never get over it."

"Get a gander at those houses," Gran said as they passed one dramatic and luxurious beach home after another. Every style was represented, from ultramodern to Italian villas to Tudor mansions.

Although the houses were getting closer and closer together, the farther south they went, Savannah couldn't help thinking that the price of one of those places and the tiny footprint of beach that it was built on would be enough money for her and Dirk to retire in style for the rest of their lives, and then some.

Malibu was a unique community, even in the Los Angeles area where "abnormal" was the "norm."

TWENTY-SEVEN MILES OF SCENIC BEAUTY, the sign said when you entered the town. And that accurately described the layout of the community. The Pacific Coast Highway hugged the coastline, and the houses and businesses of Malibu lined either side of the PCH.

Some exquisite estates sat on the hillsides, overlooking the rest of the town, and some of the canyons had luxury residences tucked away inside, but the vast majority of Malibu residents lived on the beach or right across the highway from it.

Almost everyone had a breathtaking view of the ocean.

"If you ever got blessed with more money than you knew what to do with," Gran said, "would you buy one of these houses?"

Savannah thought she probably would not, considering all of the natural disasters the town of Malibu was famous for. It seemed every few months there were either raging brush fires sweeping over the hills above the highway, or there were storms with pounding surf attacking the coastline. And then there were the spring rains that brought massive mudslides.

It wasn't unusual for the same areas that had been endangered by ever-spreading flames during fire season to then be slip-sliding down the hills during the torrential rainfall. Contrary to a popular song title, it did rain in Southern California.

In fact, Savannah thought as they rode along, *in March, the rain pours like a tall cow whizzing on a flat rock.*

But, like the mouse and the cotton ball metaphor, Savannah decided not to share that particular thought with Gran. Granny Reid wasn't much on terms or sayings that had any sexual references or mentions of bodily functions. Unless, of course, she herself was highly irritated—then all bets were off.

More than once, Savannah had heard her grandmother use "polite profanity" after spilling milk on the
kitchen floor or other such calamities. "Shoot f're,
thunderation," and "Heavens to Betsy Bug" were some
of her fallbacks when times were tough or mishaps
highly annoying.

"No, Gran," she said. "When I hit the lotto, I'll just
add a west wing to the house I've got and invite you to
come live with us."

"You play the lottery? Why, that's gamblin', girl."

"Just a figure of speech, Gran. I wouldn't dream of it."

Savannah glanced over at Dirk, expecting him to
have a sheepish look on his face. Unlike her, he seldom
passed up the opportunity to plunk down a dollar for a
dream.

But, instead, she saw that his expression was grim as
he focused on the road ahead. He had been unusually
quiet during the drive down. And she knew why.

"You okay?" she asked him.

He nodded, but it wasn't his most convincing nod.

"You sure?"

"I'll just be glad when this is over."

"Me too."

She glanced at the address numbers on some of the
buildings and realized they would be there soon. "Have
you got any particular plan," she asked, "about how
you'd like to see this go down?"

"You know how our plans usually work out. We plan
all day long how it's gonna go, and then the perps never
do what you think they're going to do. You mow
through Plan A to Plan J in five seconds. So, what's the
point?"

Granny piped up from the backseat. "You just fly by
the seat of your pants. A man who trusts his own gut

feelings and common sense to get him through moment to moment—I like that."

Savannah's cell phone rang. "It's Tammy," she told them as she answered.

"You're on speaker, darlin'," she said. "What's up?"

"We're about there, huh?" Tammy asked.

"Yes. I noticed. Just a few more blocks."

"As soon as we get parked, you're going to send Granny back to us, right?"

Gran did a little tsk-tsk in the back. "Those younguns are nervous and want an old lady with 'em for protection. That's pretty funny."

Savannah knew that Tammy was far more concerned about Gran being safe in the van with her and Waycross than the other way around. But, of course, it would take a braver soul than she to mention that to Gran.

"That's right, Granny," Tammy said, always kind. "We'd just feel better if you were with us."

Savannah glanced down at her watch. "Okay. It's one-thirty. He doesn't usually go to the gym until two. So we've got plenty of time to get in place and check the audio equipment."

"Maybe go over our plan?" Tammy suggested.

"Um, Dirk figures we'll just play this one by ear."

Even as she was saying the words, Savannah felt a bit uneasy. This particular mission felt wrong somehow, and more than a little troublesome to her.

She wasn't sure why.

They'd taken down many a bad guy in their day—career criminals galore and even a couple of serial killers. But only a foolish law enforcement officer would take someone like Ian Xenos lightly.

She'd looked at his picture earlier on Tammy's computer, and something had sent a chill through her. It

wasn't his muscular body that bothered her. She and
Dirk had taken down a lot of muscle-bound knuckleheads in their day. Those fellows and their muscles hit
the ground just as quickly and as hard as anybody else.

No, it was the expression on Ian Xenos's face that instinctively set her nerves on edge. Or, more accurately,
it was the *non*expression. "Flat affect," the shrinks called
it. The few experiences she'd had dealing with individuals with that dead look in their eyes had been unpleasant, to be sure. Some had even been terrifying. It kept
her awake at night when she thought of the horrible
acts that were committed by those who felt no empathy
whatsoever for their fellow man.

"There's the gym up there on the right," Tammy
said. "The big orange sign. I recognize the logo."

Savannah looked at the large orange circle with the
cartoon bulldog in the center, standing on his rear legs,
his front paws up and gloved. His jagged teeth were displayed in an ugly snarl.

"Nice," she said. "Kinda gives you that warm, fuzzy
feeling."

"His house should be right down there, also on the
right," Tammy told them.

Dirk pulled over into the first available parking spot.
"You guys go on down, get the next one," he said. "We'll
approach him when he's exactly halfway between home
and the gym. We don't want his buddies in either place
to feel they have to come rescue him."

"Especially if they look anything like that-there bulldog in the sign," Granny said.

Parked on the side of the road in front of an ice
cream store, they watched as Ryan and John's big white
surveillance van passed them, then pulled into a parking spot about sixty feet away.

"Okay, Gran," Savannah said as she opened the door.

"Let's go get you in the van with those young people so you can keep an eye on 'em."

"That's why I'm here," Gran said proudly. "To make sure everything goes okay with you younguns."

Savannah watched as her eighty-year-old–plus grandmother strode off toward the van, ready to do battle, if necessary, to protect her loved ones.

She hoped that someday, maybe, if she tried really hard, she might turn out to be just like her.

The waiting was the hardest part. Always.

Savannah truly believed that with some luck, the good Lord's help, and all the courage you could scrounge up from deep inside, there was nothing much a body couldn't do when they set their mind to it.

But waiting to do it, when all you wanted to do was just get it over and done with, that was the toughest part.

Dirk, Gran, Ryan, John, Waycross, Tammy, and Savannah were all crowded into the van, watching for Ian Xenos to stick his ugly mug out of his house. Even though it was a roomy and quite luxurious van, with all those bodies and all the equipment, it was pretty darned crowded.

Contrary to his previous inclination not to formulate a solid game plan, Dirk was running down his latest ideas. To Ryan and John, he said, "We don't wanna all pounce on him like an army. Let me and Savannah go out first. You'll be listening and watching. If it looks like we need you, come on out and join in."

"Gotcha," Ryan said.

"Tammy and Gran . . . I want you here in the van, getting everything on tape. Waycross, you're here, too, filming with the camera, like we showed you."

Waycross nodded vigorously, his red curls bobbing. "Understood."

"Then understand this, too. Under no circumstances will any one of you three get out of this van." Dirk turned a stern look on Granny. "That means no running into the affray with a skillet in your hand. Got it?"

She gave him a curt nod.

Savannah's mental wheels were spinning. She had a plan of her own, which she didn't think was going to sit well with Dirk, but she decided to bounce it off him anyway. "I'd like to go up to him first. Alone," she said. When Dirk started shaking his head, she added, "Just hear me out, dadgum it. I might be able to just have a civil conversation with him, and wouldn't that be better than a brawl right here on Pacific Coast Highway?"

Dirk paused to think it over, so she kept talking. "Let's get out right now. You act like you're going into that convenience store, and I'll hang around by the phone booth, like I'm waiting for a call. Then when he comes out, I'll try to talk to him, and you'll be right there if I need you."

"Do what you think is best, old boy," John told Dirk, "but I tend to agree with her. Too many chefs spoil the broth, and all that."

Dirk sighed. "We'll try it your way. But if he starts anything . . ."

Savannah reached for the van door. "Let's go."

Their timing was perfect. No sooner had they taken their agreed-upon positions than the front door of the house opened and Ian Xenos strode out. He was the size of a grizzly bear and was wearing a skimpy black tank top, which was cut very low in the front with enormous armholes. It was intended, no doubt, to show off every one of his muscles that he had so carefully developed.

He had a deep, deep tan, with a suspiciously orange tint to it. His head was shaved bald, and his scalp was tattooed with a set of bright red horns. Around his neck was more ink—a vine of thorns dripping crimson blood down onto his shoulders and chest.

Subtle, she thought. *The jury's just gonna love that at your trial, you badass nitwit.*

But, of course, any good defense lawyer would insist that he grow some hair before his next court appearance. And dressed in a nice suit, a white shirt, and a conservative tie, no one would guess that in his natural state he looked like the son of Lucifer.

When he passed by her, he gave her a quick once-over. Although he didn't make eye contact or smile at her, she could tell he liked what he saw.

So he appreciated a full-figured gal.

Proof that nobody was all bad.

She fell into step beside him. In her sweetest Dixie drawl, she said, "Excuse me, sir. You look like you're in a bit of a hurry, but could you spare a minute for me? I'd sure appreciate it."

Out of the corner of her eye, she could see Dirk coming up behind him, hanging back, not getting too close, but close enough.

Xenos stopped, gave her another, longer, lustier look, and said, "Yeah. What's shakin', sugar?"

To her shock, he had a Southern accent that made her sound like a Yankee!

Why, wonders never cease! she thought. *Who'd have thought Ian Xenos was a good ol' boy?*

"I know you, don't I?" she said. "I'm just sure I've seen your picture in the newspaper."

He frowned. "Yeah, I reckon you might've. So what?"

"Oh, I know who you are! They say your company

sells those fake purses that me and my girlfriends buy all the time."

He frowned a bit less, so she continued. "I gotta tell you, I think you got a bum deal. That gal on TV, that reporter, it was obvious she had it in for you from the start."

Now he was looking surprised, and more than a little pleased. Something told Savannah that running into women on the street with burgeoning breasts, who sympathized with his cause, wasn't something that happened to ol' Ian every day.

But he liked it.

"Well, thank you, sugar," he said in a deep voice that was just crawling with "smarmy"—Southern accent notwithstanding.

"I don't think she was objective at all about her reporting," Savannah continued, laying it on thicker than she could spread Granny's preserves on a biscuit, and twice as sweet. "Her saying you're tied into those terrorist fellas, that your group sends them money so's they can do their jihad terror business over here. I don't believe that hooey for a minute. I can just tell by looking at you that you're a fine American. And I can tell by your sweet Southern drawl that you were born in the land o' cotton like myself."

All of her sunshine and light were proving pointless. Because the moment she had mentioned the terrorists, his eyes had glazed over with that flat, shark look. Just like his mug shot on the Internet.

"Who are you?" he asked. Suddenly his voice was like a jug of lemonade with no sugar in it at all.

"Just a concerned citizen," she said. "I don't like to see innocent people get railroaded by the media. That gal was just trying to build her career by pulling you down." She batted her eyes at him and lowered her voice a bit. "You must've been pretty happy to hear 'bout somebody takin' care of her for you, huh? Without her testimony, it's gonna be pretty hard for the prosecutor to make his case against you."

Something snapped inside old Ian; Savannah saw it happen in his eyes. A flash of temper like hot lightning, then nothing. With a chillingly blank expression on his face, he reached out and shoved her, very hard, on the chest. She stumbled backward a couple of steps before regaining her balance.

"Get out of my way, you stinkin' cu—"

He was only able to get the first bit of the filthy word out of his mouth before Dirk tackled him from the back, landing on him in an explosion of fury. They both fell, facedown toward the sidewalk, and landed with a terrible thud.

The violence of nearly five hundred pounds of male rage hitting the ground in front of her impressed even Savannah, who thought she had seen it all.

Ian Xenos was an enormous man, and Dirk was a big boy himself. The fight definitely qualified as a heavyweight bout.

Dirk was on the top when they landed. But it only took a couple of seconds for Xenos to reverse the situation. He managed to roll Dirk off, then flip onto his back, grab Dirk, and then the wrestling-punching began in earnest.

Fists, arms, legs, and feet were flying so furiously that Savannah couldn't even find an opening where she could join in and add some licks of her own.

She thought of pulling her weapon, but she'd be as likely to shoot Dirk as Ian. Besides, she'd never shot an unarmed person; and from what she could see, Ian had no weapon. Except for his fists and feet, which he was using quite skillfully.

Suddenly he was on top of Dirk, pounding away. Savannah saw her opening. She jumped on his back, placing her arms around his neck in a choke hold.

At least she had fully intended for it to be a choke hold, but Xenos didn't appear to be choking. In fact, as he and Dirk traded slug for slug, Xenos didn't even seem to notice he had a large woman hanging around his neck and down his back.

That was a fact Savannah found most annoying—and more than a little frightening.

She'd never been astride a man who felt more like a bull than a human being.

She couldn't believe it when she felt him rising with her still holding on for dear life, trying her best to throttle him—or at least letting him know she was there.

With strength that seemed superhuman, considering that he had an amply endowed woman on his back, Ian managed to get to his feet. Still dangling behind him, Savannah threw her legs around his waist and squeezed until her thighs felt like they were on fire.

Once, he reached over his shoulder and slapped at her head, much as she would have done to a pesky fly that was irritating her.

For a second, she considered sinking her teeth into his neck muscles, but she decided instead to lower her right leg slightly and dig her heel into his crotch.

He let out a yelp of pain . . . and kicked at Dirk.

Dirk grabbed his leg and yanked it out from under him.

All three landed in a kicking, punching, squeezing, grappling free-for-all.

Savannah lost her choke hold and grabbed onto a limb. At first, she thought it was his leg because of the size of it. Then, to her dismay, she realized it was his arm.

With one half-twist, Xeon freed it and smacked Savannah on the side of the head so hard that she saw stars.

Dirk retaliated with a brutal punch to the left side of the guy's face, but it had no effect at all.

For a split second her eyes met Dirk's and she could see he was as confused as she was about what to do next. They had wrestled bigger guys, and some perps under the influence of drugs that had given them extraordinary strength.

She couldn't imagine what Ian Xenos was on.

"Get . . . his . . . legs . . . ," Dirk gasped as he tried to climb onto the upper part of Xeon's body and pin him.

Savannah maneuvered herself downward until she was straddling Xenos's lower body, but she could tell it would only be a matter of seconds until he escaped that hold, too.

Suddenly they had help. She heard Ryan yell, "Help Savannah with his legs!" A second later, John was behind her, sitting across Xenos's calves . . . or trying to, and getting kicked hard in the process.

She could see past Dirk, who was across his shoulders, to Ryan, who was trying to help Dirk get a cuff on one wrist.

It wasn't working. They were both getting badly punched in the process.

"Stop fighting, damn it!" Dirk shouted. "We're gonna have to hurt you!"

Yeah, right! Savannah thought as Xenos's foot caught John squarely in the crotch.

John doubled over, face-first, onto the sidewalk, holding himself in a manner most uncharacteristic of the dignified Brit.

In Savannah's peripheral vision, she saw a fuzzy redhead. A moment later, Waycross threw himself down onto Xenos's lower legs, the position just vacated by the incapacitated John.

Savannah did a quick count in her head. Five against one. And as Xenos landed more blows than he received, she realized it was they who were "outnumbered."

Ryan had given up on trying to get a cuff on him, and she was grateful for that. When a guy was fighting like Xenos, the last thing he needed was a metal cuff on one wrist to use as a weapon.

No sooner had the thought crossed her mind that she was grateful Xenos had no weapon, than she saw him jerk his hand free of Ryan's and snatch at Dirk's Smith and Wesson strapped to his side.

"Dirk, gun!" she yelled.

She grabbed at Xenos's hand and missed.

He had his hand on Dirk's gun!

A second later, she heard a loud *pop*. Then a strange, crackling sound.

Xenos let out a scream, like that of a tortured animal! She felt his body beneath her buck wildly.

What the hell? she thought. *Has he been shot? Is he having some sort of seizure?*

Five seconds later, he stopped and lay still, groaning. And, most important, not fighting.

Savannah looked over her right shoulder and saw Granny standing there beside them, looking down the barrel of a gun.

It took Savannah's brain a couple more seconds to register the wires leading from the gun to Xenos's thigh and the metal prongs sticking in his flesh.

"You lay still," Granny roared, "you mangy rattlesnake, or I'll zap you again, I will!"

Standing right behind Granny was Tammy, a deeply satisfied look on her face.

"Don't hit him again, Gran," Dirk said. "Unless he acts up."

Dirk looked down at the stunned Xenos. He slapped him lightly on the cheeks, bringing him around. "Come on, dude," he said. "All we were gonna do is ask you a question. Then you had to go push my lady. What's the matter with you?"

"What do you idiots want?" Xenos asked feebly, coming around.

"Simple," Dirk told him. "To know where you were two mornings ago."

Xenos thought for a moment. "What? Two days ago? You mean Sunday morning?"

"Yeah."

"That's easy. I was in the hospital with my wife, from seven till two in the afternoon. She was having a baby."

A deadly silence descended on the group. Savannah could practically hear her fingernails growing.

She looked from one to the other of the exhausted, bleeding, and bruised Moonlight Magnolia members and saw the same look of horror and shock on their faces that she was feeling.

They had gone through all this for nothing?

She watched as though in slow motion as Tammy suddenly produced her handheld device and began to type on it.

"Um . . . was it a boy or a girl, Mr. Xenos?" Tammy asked, barely squeaking out the words.

"A girl, Antonette Rose, seven pounds two ounces. . . . Not that it's any of your damned business."

Tammy's thumbs flew over the keyboard. They waited and watched her breathlessly.

As she studied the small screen in front of her, a look of dismay washed over her face. She glanced from one of them to the other; then she nodded.

Dirk turned to Savannah, who looked at Waycross, and John, who had just managed to rise off the sidewalk. They all turned to Ryan, who looked like he'd prefer to be absolutely anywhere but leaning over Ian Xenos, pinning his arms to the ground.

Finally, after about ten years, Dirk reached down and put his hands tightly over Xenos's ears.

To Savannah, he whispered, "Did you tell him your name?"

"No," she whispered back.

In an equally low voice, Ryan said to Dirk, "We didn't hear you announce yourself before you jumped him. Did you?"

"No."

Dirk cleared his throat, looked around to see how many spectators had gathered, but there were few bystanders and none of them nearby.

"Okay," he said. "Here's the plan. I'm gonna count to three. On three, we turn him loose." They all turned to see how far it was to the van. "And we run like hell!"

Chapter 18

"**O**kay, so that wasn't a shining moment in the history of the Moonlight Magnolia Detective Agency," Savannah said. It wasn't easy to speak while holding a small plastic bag filled with ice cubes against her swollen lip.

Her two honest-to-goodness ice packs had gone to John and Dirk. They needed them worse than she, Ryan, or Waycross did.

Dirk kept moving his from his eye, which was getting blacker by the minute, to his swelling jaw, to the knuckles of his right hand.

Poor John was sitting on his pack, the very picture of abject suffering and humiliation. The other men in the room kept shooting him looks of sympathy.

Watching them, Savannah felt a certain male-bonding thing going on. She suspected that even though she and the other women felt bad for him, you actually had to own a set of the equipment to grasp the full gravity of his situation.

Ryan also had a simple bag of ice, which he was applying to his knee. He'd stumbled and fallen while hightailing it back to the van.

Waycross was smearing antibiotic cream on his skinned shin as Tammy sat on the floor, looking up at him with a woeful expression filled with affection and deep concern.

Gran was lounging in Savannah's easy chair, quietly reading her Bible and ignoring them all.

"Not a 'shining moment'? Is that what you said?" Dirk barked. "That was the absolute pits! We were the frickin' three stooges out there!"

"Five," Ryan said. "Five stooges, and we couldn't even put a dent in that guy."

John nodded. "Something tells me that *he* isn't sitting on an ice pack, frosting *his* naughty bits tonight."

Waycross snickered. "Makes me shudder just thinkin' where we'd be if Gran hadn't showed up in the nick o' time with that stun gun."

"That's easy," Gran chimed in. "You'd still be tryin' to hog-tie that ugly yahoo. Lord o' mercy, I've seen Brahman bulls easier to corral than that 'un."

"That's for sure," Dirk agreed.

"And him with them devil horn things tattooed on his head." Gran shook her head. "A boy raised in Dixie oughta know better than that. Nearly makes me ashamed to be Southern. If I'd had a good, long hickory switch with me, he'd be in need of an ice pack, I'll tell ya."

"That's true," Savannah said. "Gran and a green saplin' switch can turn most any evildoer around."

Granny giggled. "Make 'im dance a jig anyway."

"I saw the stun gun there in the van," Tammy said, "but I didn't know how to use it."

"A gun's a gun," Gran said. "You take off the safety, if it's got one. You aim and pull the trigger. But I guess anybody who never had to hunt down their supper might not know that."

"Um, no." Tammy looked down at her hands, which were folded demurely in her lap. "I feel bad," she said. "I always check people's social network pages. I don't know why I didn't with him. If I had, I'd have seen that picture of his wife and baby, and him standing there, next to them, wearing green surgical scrubs. He'd posted every fifteen minutes or so while she was in labor. It was obvious he was right there with her every minute. I'm really sorry, guys."

"Oh, come on, kiddo," Dirk said. "Even a whiz kid like you can't nail everything all the time."

"I'll make it up to you. I promise," she said.

Savannah saw Waycross reach over as though he was going to lay his hand on Tammy's shoulder. Then he withdrew it—a sad look on his face.

Savannah couldn't help wondering what was up with him and that situation.

"Anyway," Dirk said, wriggling one of his front teeth, "if it's all the same to you-all, I'd just as soon never speak of this indignity again."

Everyone nodded solemnly.

"What indignity is that?" Marietta asked as she sashayed down the stairs in skintight, tiger-striped leggings and a sparkling black blouse cut down to the equator.

"Never you mind," Savannah said.

Marietta strolled into the living room, teetering on heels suitable for pole dancing. She glanced around, taking in the various injuries. "Land sakes! Y'all look like you tangled with the business end of a momma bear."

"A papa bear's more like it. You should probably keep your observations to yourself, Miss Mari," Savannah said. "This ain't the time, and we are *so* not in the mood."

"I ain't got time anyway. I got a date to go on."

It occurred to Savannah to ask Marietta if she had ever met the fellow she was about to go out with. But since she wanted to sleep tonight and not dream about serial killers who murdered dingbat floozies wearing tiger-striped pants, she decided not to inquire.

As soon as Marietta left the room, she had to ask, "Gran, I'm surprised you didn't say anything about the way she was dressed. You're slippin'."

Gran casually licked her finger and turned another page of her Bible. "Nope. I ain't slipped. I just gave up on that sister of yours. The day I caught 'er wearing her brassiere on the outside, over her shirt. Yessiree, Bob. That was the straw that broke the camel's back."

A while later, Savannah went into the kitchen to make a pot of hot coffee. Since they'd used up all the ice cubes, iced tea was out of the question. She found Waycross standing at the sink, washing a mug, but she could tell by the faraway look in his eyes that he was thinking about anything but what he was doing.

She walked up and laid her hand on his back. "Hey, Big Red, whatcha up to?"

" 'Bout six-three" was his standard reply.

Waycross was proud of his height, and Savannah didn't blame him. Poor kids from McGill, Georgia, had a tough time finding things to be proud of.

"I was proud of you today," she said, "jumping in headfirst to help like that."

He gave her a little smile. "Looked like somebody needed to."

"Pretty sorry sight, huh?"

"One I'll never forget."

"If you live to be a hundred and one?"

"Somethin' like that."

She reached across the counter and got the coffee canister. "It's probably none of my business, but . . ."

He chuckled. "That's what you always say when you're about to ask me somethin' that's none of your business."

"Do you mind my nosiness?"

"No. If I don't wanna tell you, I don't."

"Fair enough." Savannah stuck a coffee filter into the machine's basket. "I'm a wee bit curious about how things are going between you and Tammy."

"Wee bit curious?" He laughed. "Since when is my big sister a 'wee bit' anything, let alone curious? More like you're *burnin' up* with curiosity."

"Well, put me outta my misery, boy. Spill it."

He turned his back to her and slowly placed the mug into the cupboard. "Spill what?"

"You like her."

"So?"

"She likes you, too. A lot. I can tell."

"That's 'cause she don't know me."

Savannah caught her breath. She didn't know what she'd been expecting, but it wasn't that. "Waycross Reid, what the heck are you talking about? You're one of the finest people in this world."

When he turned to face her, she wondered if those were tears she saw in his eyes. "She doesn't know what she'd be getting with me," he said.

She reached over, grabbed his hand, and squeezed it. "Well, I know, sure as shootin' what she'd be getting, and that's the best any girl could hope for."

"But look at her. She's so beautiful, like a princess or something. And look at me."

"I *am* looking at you. You're a hunk and a half."

"Aw, you're just saying that 'cause you're my sister."

"That doesn't mean it's not true. I have good taste in men, and, babycakes, you're a catch!"

"No, don't tell me that." He walked away from her and over to the refrigerator, where he stood, looking down at his shoes. "She doesn't know who I am."

She set the filter and coffee on the counter and walked over to him. With her hands on his shoulders, she forced him to turn around and face her.

"So you tell me. Who are you?"

Yes, those were definitely tears in his eyes, she realized. She couldn't recall the last time she had seen him cry. Maybe when he had been six years old.

"I'm—I'm Macon Reid Sr.'s son. I'm Shirley Reid's son. You know who they are. He never saw a truck stop hooker he didn't want. She never saw a bottle of beer she didn't want."

Savannah opened her mouth to argue with him; then she closed it. How could you argue with the truth?

"That's who I'm made of, Savannah," he said. "I'm half of him and half of her."

She reached up and put her hands on either side of his face. "Oh, sweetie, that kinda thing doesn't matter one little bit."

"I didn't think so either, till I met her. I just wish to God I could give her somebody better than me."

"Stop it, Waycross." She gave him a little shake. "You may be Macon and Shirley's son, but you've got Grandpa's and Granny's blood running through your veins, too. That's something to be mighty proud of. Don't you forget it."

He reached up and pulled her hands down from his cheeks. He kissed one, then the other, then released them. "Thank you, sis," he said.

Then he walked away, leaving her standing alone in the kitchen with a heavy, aching heart.

Heavy, because she, too, felt the weight of the dark legacy their troubled parents had left to all nine of their children. And aching because she knew her brother had heard her words with his ears, but she could tell by the sadness in his eyes, the truth she had spoken to him hadn't made it all the way down to his heart.

When Savannah got into bed and cuddled up next to Dirk, she groaned. Touching him hurt. Touching the sheets hurt. The kitties snuggling up against her hurt.

"You all right, Van?" he asked, sliding his arm around her.

"*Oww!* Yes. Just feeling the aftereffects."

"Tell me about it. I ache in places I didn't think I had places." He hugged her closer, but extra gently. "While all that fighting was going down, I was worried about you. A tussle like that was the last thing you needed—what with you still healing and all."

It had been over six months since she had been shot, and the doctors had pronounced her "healed." But she realized that for her husband, she would always be fragile merchandise. While that warmed her heart, it made her feel fragile—which, in her mind, was a kissing cousin to being weak.

She wasn't about to think of herself that way, and she'd be damned before she'd let anyone else think that either.

Especially her husband.

"I'm not a china doll, darlin'," she said as gently as she could. "I got through the worst already. If that didn't break me, ain't nothin' gonna."

He was quiet for a long time. She could only hear

him breathing in the darkness and wished she could see his face.

Then, to her relief, she heard him chuckle.

"You certainly didn't look like no china doll hangin' on that monster's neck. You were squeezin' the daylights outta him, and he was turning as purple as Marietta's underwear."

"He was?" She couldn't help being pleased to hear it. "It felt like he didn't know I was even there."

"Oh, he knew. I'd like to think he's got a few sore spots himself tonight."

"Whether he does or not, at least a few of those blows you landed on his face had to leave some marks. I figure the bruises will be just about right, all spread out and supercolorful, come time for him to go to trial."

They both laughed and pulled the sheet up around their necks.

"Boy, this is some killer honeymoon we're havin' here, huh, babe?" he said. "We went through hell and back just to get married, and now all this. It's like we're cursed or doomed or something."

"Naw, we're just getting all the bad stuff out of the way so we can live happily ever after like all the people in the fairy tales. Could be worse. Nobody's eaten any poisoned apples or had to fight any dragons or whatever . . . except Xenos, that is."

"Tell you what," Dirk said. "Once this is all over and the case is solved, and we're back home here for good, let's plan another honeymoon. Maybe Hawaii or Vegas or something like that."

"Once this is over and we're back home, we have to get you moved in, boy. Call me old-fashioned, but I always figured my husband would live in the same house with me."

He ran his fingers through her hair; then he gently

massaged her temple. "What are we gonna do with my sofa?" he asked.

"You mean the old school bus seat?"

"And my entertainment center?"

"Those plastic milk crates full of VHS tapes?"

"Not to mention my decorations."

"No, let's don't mention them. I guess you mean that rusty tin Harley-Davidson sign on your door?"

"Hey, I must have a million dollars' worth of Harley stuff. That junk's worth a fortune!"

Savannah felt Cleopatra wriggling her way up between them, and Diamante wrapping herself around her ankles.

"Let's just go to sleep," she told him. "I can only slay one monster per day, and Xenos maxed me out. We can tackle that problem another time."

Apparently, Dirk felt the same way, because he never answered her. He'd already begun to snore.

Chapter 19

Savannah, Dirk, Ryan, John, and Gran found a corner on the ferry where they could all sit together and chat in relative privacy. They gave Dirk the seat closest to the railing, just in case.

"I feel funny leaving Tammy and Waycross back there at home with nobody to chaperone them, 'cept Marietta," Granny said as she sat, her arms crossed over her chest, her silver hair blowing in the sea breeze as they sped over the water toward the island. "You can tell they've got a shine for each other, and it's invitin' the devil's mischief, leavin' them alone together like that."

"They won't have time to get in trouble," Savannah told her. "I had a talk with both of them first thing this morning, and I can guarantee you they'll be too busy to be making mischief . . . the devil's or anybody else's, for that matter."

"What are they doing?" Dirk wanted to know.

"Using their talents for good," she replied slyly. "Beyond that, my lips are sealed."

Savannah looked around the little group, all of

whom were holding cups of steaming coffee, except for Gran, who had opted for hot chocolate.

Dirk's black eye was quite dramatic, both in color and in swelling. Ryan was sitting with his leg up on the seat across from him. And poor John had opted to stand for the entirety of the trip.

The aftermath of battle.

"So, what's next on our agenda?" Ryan asked, massaging his hurt knee. "After all we've been through with this case, I'm determined we're going to close it. Nobody's causing this much misery to me and the ones I love and not paying for it."

"I wholeheartedly agree," John said, grimacing as he shifted from one leg to the other. "I've never believed in capital punishment before, but once this killer's caught, I'm going to see to it he's hanged, drawn, and quartered."

"What? No stretching on the rack first?" Savannah asked.

"That too." He thought for a moment, then added, "And his head mounted on a pike at the city's gates."

Savannah laughed. "Kick a compassionate liberal right where he lives and watch how quickly his politics change."

"No man's liberal or compassionate when it comes to that region of his body," Ryan said. "Now, seriously, how are we going to get this killer?"

Dirk rubbed his sore jaw. "The bottom line is we have no idea who he is. So far, all we've got for our troubles is an ever-lengthening list of people who it ain't."

"Or *she*," Savannah interjected. "Always remember, there are evil, nasty women in this world, too."

Granny gave a wicked little cackle. "That's for sure. And some of us know how to use a gun."

*   *   *

Having parted ways with Ryan, John, and Granny, who were returning to their vacation compound, Savannah and Dirk drove back to the lighthouse. Their plan was to walk on the beach, maybe go to the harbor and grab some lunch, rest their brains for a moment, and then, refreshed, attack the case.

But they had no sooner unlocked the door and stepped inside the lightkeeper's cottage than Savannah's phone rang.

"Hello, sweet Tamitha," she said as she tossed her purse onto the kitchen table. "Long time, no see." She glanced at her watch. "At least three hours."

"I know" was the sheepish response. "I try to leave you alone, but . . . ."

"What's up?"

"I thought you'd like to know that I hacked into Amelia Northrop's checking-account records."

Savannah shook her head and looked over at Dirk, who was getting a glass of water, but listening intently. "I don't know how you do that."

"It's surprisingly easy. Look at somebody's social network pages, find out the names of their kids or pets. If their password isn't one of those, it's probably their birthday . . . or one of their kids' birthdays, or their pets'. Then, one by one, you start checking the banks."

"It scares me how smart you are, and how dumb other people can be. So, did you find anything interesting?"

"Nothing unusual. She had her bills on AutoPay, same stuff every month. Some travel expenses for work. The only big-ticket item she'd had recently was a check for six thousand four hundred and fifty-two dollars to an Opal Parson."

"Who's that?"

"An interior decorator, there on the island."

"Oh." Savannah could practically hear her own bubble of expectation pop. "That's hardly sinister."

"That's what I thought, too. But it was written the day before her husband got shot."

"Probably pure coincidence."

"Probably, but I thought I should tell you. Are you back on the island yet?"

"Just walked in the door of the cottage." She looked over and saw Dirk waving his hand. "Dirk says 'hi.' "

"Actually, I was asking you to get rid of her," he mumbled under his breath.

Savannah nodded. "How's stuff there?"

"Stuff's great!" Tammy giggled. "That was a great idea you had, 'cause—"

"I gotta go. Thanks for, you know, everything."

"No problem. Glad to do it. *All* of it."

There were peals of giggles on the other end as Tammy hung up.

Savannah shook her head, laughing. "For just five minutes of my life, I'd like to be as cheerful as she is all the time."

"She's an airhead. It's easy for her to be chipper. She don't know no better."

A knock at the back door made them both jump. As Savannah went to answer it, she steeled herself that it could be Chief La Cross.

"Or the killer," whispered a quiet little voice. *"You wouldn't be the first witness who—"*

"Oh, shut up," she told it.

But she subconsciously reached under her arm and touched the Beretta in her holster. She glanced over her shoulder and saw Dirk was right behind her; his hand was on his weapon as well.

However, when she opened the door, it was Betty

Sue's smiling face that she saw. In her hands, the shop-keeper held a basket spilling over with freshly cut flow-ers, baked goods, and a bottle of wine.

"What's all this?" Savannah asked, opening the door and ushering her inside.

"Oh, it's nothing much. I heard you two weren't hav-ing a very nice honeymoon, and we can't have that!"

Betty Sue set the basket on the kitchen counter and turned to them. "Holy crap!" she said. "What happened to you two?"

Savannah put her hand to her swollen, bruised lip. Okay, so much for the merits of cover-up makeup.

"Uh, we sorta fell into a meat grinder," Dirk grum-bled.

"No kidding. I'd hate to see what the other guys look like."

Savannah felt no need to set any records straight by informing Betty Sue that it was only one guy, and the last time they'd seen him, he looked a heck of a lot bet-ter than they did.

"Thank you for this basket," Savannah said, rummag-ing through the goodies and finding all sorts of wonderful treats, many of which contained chocolate—Savannah's number one standard of quality. "You're a sweetheart to think of us."

Betty Sue lowered her voice and glanced around, as though expecting some sort of eavesdropping gremlins to appear inside the kitchen. "I heard you're trying to find out what happened to Amelia Northrop. And I re-member that friend of yours who rented this place for you, he said you're a cop and a private investigator."

"Guilty as charged," Dirk replied as he pulled out a cellophane-wrapped chocolate chip muffin and began to unwrap it.

"Do you know who did it yet?" Betty Sue asked. "Does

that have anything to do with the fact that your faces are all beat to hell and back?"

How lovely, Savannah thought. *Another nice little memory to tuck away in the mental honeymoon album. Being told that you look like you've been beaten "to hell and back."*

"Well, we certainly didn't do it to each other," Savannah said, "and that's all that matters."

Betty Sue glanced at her watch. "I gotta get back to the shop. You two enjoy your basket and, hopefully, the rest of your stay with us."

"Thank you, ma'am," Dirk said. "I'm sure we will."

Savannah walked Betty Sue to the door. Just as she was stepping outside, Savannah asked, "By the way, do you know a woman named Opal Parson?"

"Sure. Opal lives just a block away from me on Schooner Drive. She's got a big, wonderful house, sort of Victorian-ish, not like my little sea shack. But then, Opal can afford it. She's a successful interior decorator you know."

"Yes, so I heard."

Betty Sue paused halfway down the steps and looked around once again, as though checking for snoopers. "Don't tell anybody I told you, but you and Opal have more in common than you might think."

"Oh?" Savannah considered her own modest decorator skills and figured Betty Sue was mistaken.

"Yeah. When she's not decorating, she's got herself another little business on the side. Opal's a private detective."

"Really?" The hamster in Savannah's mental wheel started running like crazy.

"Yes. She's got herself a specialty, you might say."

Savannah could almost taste the sweet answer before Betty delivered it.

Betty Sue waggled one eyebrow and whispered, "Between you and me, she's real good at catching spouses who cheat."

Fortunately, Schooner Drive was short and had only one big Victorian-style house on it. Then there was the other clue that it was Opal's home—the large gilt, hand-carved sign in the yard: OPAL'S INTERIORS.

As Savannah pulled the Jaguar over to the side of the road and parked in front of the house, she told Dirk, "I think you should let me take the lead on this one. You know, it being a woman and all."

He was already sulking from having to give her a turn behind the wheel, so he wasn't thrilled with this new insult added to injury.

"Yeah, that worked out really great with Xenos," he snapped.

"Don't you *dare* throw that up to me, buddy boy!" she tossed back. "I was doing fine with him until—"

"Until he called you a filthy name and shoved you?"

"Until you felt the need to land on him like a ton of bricks!"

They both sat there forever, glaring at each other, nostrils flaring, breathing hard, until Savannah broke the stalemate. "Maybe in an effort to preserve domestic tranquility, we should never bring up Ian Xenos again."

"Good idea." He opened his door. "Let's get going."

"I do the talking."

"Yeah, yeah. Whatever."

They walked up to the arched door, which was carved mahogany, and knocked with the brass knocker. Though the sound echoed inside the house, no one answered.

"I think I hear something around back," Savannah said.

Dirk listened for a moment, and the sound of some sort of machine became even louder.

"I hear it, too. Let's go."

They walked around the house to the rear and followed the sound to a large garage shaped like a barn. Looking inside the open doors, they could see it had been converted to a workshop.

Inside, wearing stained jeans and a tee-shirt bearing a Victorian house as a logo on the front, was a slender woman with dark brown, short, curly hair. She was wearing an industrial-grade dust mask and was working over the top of an oak table with an electric sander. Dust was flying everywhere.

"Excuse me," Savannah said. Not surprisingly, the woman didn't hear her and continued to sand. "Hey! Excuse me!" she shouted.

This time, the woman heard. She turned off her sander and set it on a nearby workhorse table.

"Hi," she said as she walked over to greet them, wiping her dusty palms on her jeans.

Savannah held out her hand. "I'm Savannah Reid. This is my husband, Detective Sergeant Dirk Coulter."

At the mention of Dirk's rank, an expression of fear flickered across the woman's face, but she smiled nervously and shook their hands. "I'm Opal Parson. Sorry for the mess." She waved an arm, indicating the cluttered workroom, filled with half-done projects. "But contrary to popular opinion, interior decorating isn't always glamorous. In fact, it seldom is."

"I'm sure the end result is worth all the drudgery," Savannah said. "I wish I knew how to do what you do." She pointed to a gorgeous claw-foot armoire, which was half-restored. "Like knowing how to rescue a lovely thing like that. It must be fulfilling."

"It is. It's most satisfying." She looked from Savannah to Dirk. For a long, uncomfortable moment, no one said anything, and slowly the fake, friendly smile disappeared from her face. "But you didn't come here to talk about restoring furniture, did you?"

"No, Ms. Parson, we didn't," Savannah said.

Suddenly she looked tired, defeated. "I was wondering when someone was going to come question me. Figured it was just a matter of time." She tossed her mask down onto the table. "Let's get out of here," she said. "If I'm going to do this, I need some fresh air."

Opal led Savannah and Dirk up a small hill behind her house to a charming gazebo. Inside, she invited them to sit in comfortable wicker chairs. She sat across from them in the same type of chair, but she looked quite uncomfortable.

"Go ahead," Opal said, brushing some stray curls out of her eyes. "Tell me why you're here."

"It's about Amelia Northrop," Savannah told her.

"Like I didn't already know that." Opal sighed.

"You did some work for her."

"Yes. I did."

"I'm assuming you didn't decorate that big glass box of theirs," Dirk chimed in.

Savannah shot him a be-quiet look.

"No, I did not decorate that monstrosity, I'm happy to say."

Savannah drew a deep breath. "So the work you did for Amelia came under the heading of 'Unfaithful Spouse Investigation'?"

Opal looked down at her hands, which were folded in her lap. They were trembling. "I'm very uneasy about this," she said. Her voice was shaking as badly as her hands. "Normally, I'm very conscientious when it comes to client confidentiality. I pride myself on being highly discreet."

"I understand," Savannah replied. "Being a PI myself, I feel the same way."

"I have always believed that confidentiality extends even after a client's death."

Savannah was starting to get worried about where this might be headed. "Normally, I would agree," she said. "I suppose it would depend upon the circumstances."

"I'm afraid the circumstances of this case require me to break that rule." Opal closed her eyes as though feeling some sort of internal stab of pain. "Because I'm afraid that I may have inadvertently done something that led to a tragedy."

"Tell us about it," Dirk coaxed gently. "You'll feel better if you do."

"Oh, I don't know. I think it's going to take a lot more than that to make me feel better, but here goes."

She sat back in her chair and crossed her arms over her chest. Her voice became a flat monotone as she told them her story.

"Amelia Northrop came to me, here at my house. In fact, we sat right here in this gazebo while she poured her heart out to me. She had a strong suspicion that her husband, William, was being unfaithful to her. She had suspected it for some time and wanted to know for sure, once and for all.

"Frequently people come to me because they actually want to catch their cheating mate. They want out of

the marriage, and they're looking for a good reason to
leave.

"But Amelia wasn't like that. I think she truly wanted
to hear me report back to her that she was mistaken,
that he was as good a husband as she had hoped he
was."

"Let me guess," Dirk said, "he was a rat fink."

She nodded. "He was. No doubt about it. I had the
pictures, the video, and the audio recordings. She demanded to see and listen to everything I had. She was
devastated."

"I can imagine," Savannah said, thinking of the beautiful woman whose bright smile and bubbly personality
lit up the television screen every night at 11:00.

Thousands of men gazed at that beauty every night
and wanted her. And yet, for the man who had her, she
wasn't enough.

"I've been doing this for years, but I think her grief
was the deepest I've ever seen. She felt so terribly betrayed. And she was angry. Horribly angry.

"I couldn't console her. She left here, sobbing hys-
terically. I remember worrying if she would even be
able to drive, considering her state of mind."

"Did you hear anything more from her?" Savannah
asked.

"No. The next night, I was delivering a sofa, which I
had reupholstered, to a client, and that's when I'd
heard that William Northrop was in the hospital. That
he'd been shot."

"Do you think she did it?" Savannah asked.

"Well, yes. It certainly occurred to me that she might
have. I mean, what are the odds?"

Savannah looked over at Dirk and saw he was as intrigued by this news as she was.

"I suppose it might have been a coincidence," Savannah said, testing her.

"No." Opal shook her head. "You didn't see her eyes. I'm telling you, when Amelia Northrop left here that day, she looked like a woman who had completely lost her mind."

"That was the last time you saw her or communicated with her in any way?"

"Yes. After he was shot, I tried to phone her. Left her several messages. But she wouldn't return my calls. I was so relieved to hear that Mr. Northrop had survived his injuries. I was surprised when someone told me he had gone home from the hospital and she was still with him, nursing him even."

She wiped her hand over her eyes, as though trying not to see the haunting images inside her mind. "Then, just when I thought I was mistaken about the whole thing, just when I thought we were in the clear, I heard she was . . . that she'd been . . ."

Opal's voice broke, and she started to cry. Savannah got up from her chair, walked over to her and knelt beside her.

Taking the woman's hand, she patted it and said, "It's okay. It's all right. Whatever happened, you didn't cause it."

Opal choked in her tears and squeezed Savannah's fingers in a grip so tight it hurt. "I just don't know what to think now. I don't know what happened. I can't go to the Santa Tesla police with my information. It would just get me in that much more trouble."

"No, I don't believe it would," Savannah said. "From what you just told us, I can't think of any law you've broken. You didn't cause William Northrop to cheat on his wife. She came to you for a service, and you rendered it according to her desires. You didn't shoot anybody. I think you're okay."

"No, you don't understand," Opal told her, tears streaming down through the dust on her cheeks. "I can't go to the cops because the other woman, the one William Northrop was seeing, is Chief La Cross."

Chapter 20

"When did you *just know* the other woman was gonna be La Cross," Dirk asked as they drove away from Opal Parson's home.

"The minute Betty Sue told me Opal specialized in cheater catching," Savannah replied smugly.

"You did not."

"Did too. You saw the way she was looking at him across the table there at the Lobster Bisque. Goo-goo eyes all the way. I can't believe you missed it."

He shuddered. "I didn't consider it a real possibility. I mean, did you see that woman? I hate to say it, but she's one unattractive chick, and she's got a lousy personality, to boot. You wouldn't catch me within a ten-mile radius of her, if I could help it."

" 'Unattractive chick'?" Savannah shook her head. "Boy, you could use some enlightenment classes."

He laughed. "If you haven't been able to change me in all these years, do you really think classes are gonna help?"

"Good point."

They had arrived at the Santa Tesla police station, and Dirk found a parking spot for the Jaguar.

As they got out and went inside the building, Savannah couldn't help wondering when they'd be able to leave again. If things went badly with Chief La Cross, they might be looking at cement and iron bars for quite a while.

"Ryan and John are up to date on all this, right?" Dirk asked, his hand protectively on her waist. "They know that if we don't come up for air in an hour or so—"

"They'll be calling the FBI, the coast guard, the cavalry, and Batman and Robin."

"Good. And Granny'll take care of the cats if—"

"Shush! I'm nervous enough without you catastrophizing."

"And Granny'll bring us food if—"

She slapped him on the back of the head.

He laughed. "Okay, okay. Just making sure all bases are covered."

They entered the front door, and—just as Savannah had dreaded—there was her nemesis again. Or at least his carbon copy.

He lit up at the sight of her.

"No!" she said. "Do not even start with me. If you do, I swear, I'll snatch that ugly rug thing off your head and ram it down your throat."

The lust faded from his eyes as he donned a distinctly "pissy" look.

"We need to talk to the chief," Dirk said, "and don't give us any crap about her not being here. We saw that big black sedan of hers in the parking lot."

"We're not leaving until we talk to her," Savannah added.

The desk attendant reluctantly picked up his phone

and punched a couple of numbers. "Yes, Chief," he said. "You got a couple out here insisting they wanna see you." He glanced them over, head to toe, taking in their attire and general appearance. "Yeah, ratty-lookin' big guy in a beat-up bomber jacket. Tall, husky girl, dark hair. It's them. Okay."

Dirk looked down at his jacket. "'Beat-up'? What are you talking about, 'beat-up'?"

"'Husky'?" Savannah said. "Catch up on the latest PC terms, boy. It's full-figured or plus-sized these days. Sheez!"

The receptionist gave her a curt wave toward the hallway behind him. "Second door on the right."

"By the way," she said as they passed his desk, "you are follicle-free and comb unencumbered. And nobody gives a hoot. So take that dead-squirrel skin off your head and enjoy the fresh air and sunshine on your head for a change."

As they walked down the hall toward the chief's office, Dirk nudged her. "Did you mean what you said back there? Is it true that nobody cares if a guy's bald or not?"

Savannah stifled a grin. She knew Dirk was deadly serious about this topic. What he had on top was thinning year by year, and she wouldn't be surprised to find out that he literally counted the hairs on a regular basis.

"No one cares, but the guy. And he shouldn't," she said. "Really. Believe me. Women couldn't care less about that."

He smiled. "Good to know."

"But stop grinnin' like a goat chewin' bumblebees. You can't be in a good mood when we're fixing to do battle."

"That's true." He put on his best Clint Eastwood

scowl and knocked, a bit harder than necessary, on the door with CHIEF CHARLOTTE LA CROSS lettered in gold on the textured glass.

"Come in" was the less-than-friendly reply.

They entered the office and found it as austere as the woman in black who was seated behind a desk that was equally black. Savannah wondered if anyone had ever mentioned to Charlotte La Cross that a splash of color in one's surroundings or in a body's wardrobe could do wonders for depression and a sour disposition.

And Chief La Cross looked like she was feeling even more tart than usual.

"What do you two want?" she snapped as she rifled through a stack of papers on her desk without making eye contact with them. "Say what you've got to say and then get the hell out of my office. I'm busy."

"Yes, you do look busy, shuffling your papers around like that," Savannah said. "In fact, you look about as busy as a cat coverin' up crap on a marble floor. Is that what you're doing, Chief? Making sure all the crap's covered?"

"It's not possible, you know," Dirk told her. "There's always something you miss. And then you get caught."

Chief La Cross threw the papers down and glared at them. "I asked you what you want. You'd better say and then leave. I've had quite enough of you two, especially after that fiasco in the restaurant. I should have arrested you both then and there for disturbing the peace."

"Yeah. You probably should have," Dirk said. "Then we wouldn't have found out what we did."

"Though we did suspect it already," Savannah added.

Although La Cross hadn't invited them to sit down, they each took a chair on either side of her desk. Dirk leaned back in his, put his hands behind his head, and laced his fingers together. Savannah casually crossed one leg over the other, resting her ankle on her knee.

"So you been knockin' boots with ol' William for how long now?" Savannah asked. "And poor Amelia found out about it. We hear she didn't take it very well."

Under her tropical tan, the chief turned a few shades paler. "William and I are old friends. Nothing more."

Savannah dropped the fake smile and fixed her with her strongest blue-laser stare. "Don't insult us by lying to us," she said. "We've been put through the mill on this case of yours, trying to do the right thing by the victim. The case you should be solving, except that . . . Oh, right, you may not want to solve it, because as it turns out, you're one of the principals involved."

The wind seemed to go out of the chief's sails. She sighed, put her elbows on her desk, and rested her head in her hands. "You talked to Opal Parson," she said with a tone that sounded to Savannah like exhausted resignation.

"Yes, we did," Dirk said.

Savannah added, "You had to know we would, sooner or later."

"I was hoping for later."

"Why?" Savannah asked. "Why stall? What's the advantage of buying time?"

"I was hoping to solve Amelia's murder."

"Solve it or get away with it?" Savannah shot back.

La Cross lifted her head. "Watch yourself. No matter what you think you've found out, you're still in my office, my jurisdiction. You'd better never forget that."

"Are you telling us you didn't kill your boyfriend's wife?" Dirk asked, his tone as testy as hers.

"I most certainly am telling you that. I'm trying to find out who did."

"If you're telling the truth, and you really didn't do

it," Savannah said, "I don't think you have to look far to find the culprit. Just roll over in your sleep and you'll run flat dab into him."

Chief La Cross jumped up from her chair. For a second, Savannah thought the police chief was going to attack her.

The thought also occurred to her that she had never—even during the darkest days of her law enforcement career—had the bullpucky beaten out of her two days in a row. It wasn't a new record that she cared to set.

Instead, La Cross walked over to her window and stood, her back to them for a long time.

Finally, still looking out, she said, "William didn't kill Amelia. If you'll recall, he was shot himself. Badly. He very nearly died."

"Who says it was the same shooter?" Dirk asked. "Could've been two different guys."

"Same gun," La Cross said. "I recovered casings at both scenes. They were the same. We were also able to compare the slugs removed from William and from Amelia. We examined them under a microscope, and the lans and grooves line up. They were a perfect match. They were fired from the same weapon."

The chief turned around to face them, a bitterly smug look on her face. "Yeah, yeah, we aren't complete schmucks around here. We know a few cop tricks. We watch *CSI*, too."

"Well," Savannah said, "we have three people in this little love triangle. You're telling me it wasn't William or Amelia, because they both got shot by the same gun. I guess that leaves you. Did you pop William because—when push came to shove—he refused to leave his wife for you? Then, when you screwed up the hit on him and he recovered, you reconsidered and decided to take her out instead?"

"You think you have it all figured out, don't you?" La Cross said, her tone acidic, her dark eyes fathomless. "Well, figure this out. Someone took a shot at me, too. Only, fortunately for me, they missed."

Dirk sat up straight in his chair. "When?"

"The same day William was hit. I was walking out of my house and a shot came from a passing car. Missed me by inches. It struck the palm tree next to my front door. If you don't believe me, I'll take you to my house right now and you can examine the hole it left."

"Did you recover the slug and casing?" Savannah asked.

"Not the casing. I searched the road for it, but it probably landed in the shooter's car. I managed to dig the slug out of the tree without damaging it too badly."

"And?" Savannah could feel her pulse rate quickening. "Was it a match for the others?"

"Absolutely. No doubt about it."

Savannah stared into those black eyes, weighing the sincerity she saw there. Or lack of it. Of course, Savannah knew the woman could be lying.

Contrary to popular belief, with some people it was really hard to tell, even for a seasoned professional.

"Did you get a look at the driver?" Dirk asked.

"No. The vehicle had dark, tinted windows."

"Description?" Savannah said.

"A black Jeep, maybe ten years old. Rusty. In bad shape."

Dirk dug out his notepad and started to scribble. "Plate?"

"California, blue on white. First four—4NPC. I didn't get the rest. I was too busy pulling my own weapon and hiding behind my shrubs."

"Do you have any lead on that tag?" Savannah asked. "Any idea at all whose vehicle it is?"

"Obviously not, or I'd have the owner in my jail cell."

"There can't be too many vehicles on this island, let alone a lot of Jeeps," she said. "How hard can it be to find it?"

"With cars going back and forth on the ferries every day, you'd be surprised how hard it is. Besides, the shooter wouldn't be the first criminal to use stolen plates when they commit a crime."

"True." Savannah stood, and Dirk rose with her.

He tucked his notebook back inside his jacket pocket.

"If we help you catch this killer," he said, "there's something I want from you. In fact, I demand it."

"What's that?" La Cross asked suspiciously.

"I want a heartfelt apology from you. My wife is shapely, not husky. And this bomber jacket of mine is a classic."

"I agree. Your wife is a lovely woman," she said grudgingly.

He scowled. "And my jacket?"

"If you help me catch the killer, we'll talk about that jacket."

As Savannah slid between the sheets and pulled the quilt up around her, she glanced over at her cell phone on the night table to see if she'd gotten any calls while in the bathtub.

"Fluff Head didn't call," Dirk told her as he got in beside her. "And you know what they say about how a watched phone never rings."

"I thought it was a watched pot that never boils."

"Same principle."

She grimaced as he tossed one leg over hers, rubbing a tender spot on her shin—residual battle damage from the no-longer-mentioned "Xenos Affair."

"You really have to stop calling her stuff like that. It's rude and stupid, when you consider she does stuff to help us solve these cases that we could never do ourselves. Like run this partial plate number."

"Ryan and John are helping her."

"Yeah, because you and I couldn't even talk their lingo, let alone get results. You need to show your superiors proper respect, meadow muffin."

"And speaking of showing respect, why do I get a feeling that little term of endearment isn't all that reverential?"

She snickered and tickled his ribs until he wriggled and slapped her hand away. " 'Cause you're a cynical ol' curmudgeon," she told him.

"Hey! Why is it wrong for me to call Tammy a 'fluff head,' but you can call me a 'curmudgeon'?"

"Because in your case, it's true, where Tammy—"

Her phone began to play "You Are My Sunshine."

"Where Tammy is calling me right now." She reached for the phone and flipped it open. "Hey, baby-cakes. What's happenin'?"

"It's not too late, is it?" came the voice on the other end.

"Not for you. Got good news for me?"

"I have news. Whether it's good or not . . . that's up to you."

"Lay it on me."

"I got a possible on that plate." She drew a deep breath. "Those first four characters you gave me don't suggest it's a vanity plate."

"Right. So?"

"And La Cross said it was a Jeep, about ten years old."

"Okay?"

"Ten years ago, the sequence of letters and numbers on California plates that weren't vanity went—number, three letters, then three numbers."

Savannah looked over at Dirk, who was waiting on pins and needles, and rolled her eyes. He mouthed the words "Fluff head." She smacked him on the arm.

"What did we find, Miss Tammy, darlin'?"

"Well, I checked most of the nine hundred ninety-nine combinations of numbers for those last three, missing digits, and I found a black 2001 Jeep that belongs to someone living there on Santa Tesla."

"And it is . . . ?"

"Actually, it's not a person. It's more like an organization. It—"

"Tammy Hart, you are wearin' my nerves to a frazzle! What have you got?"

"The Island Protection League."

"No way! Dr. Glenn's group?"

"The very one."

Savannah turned to Dirk. "And she seemed so nice!"

Dirk shrugged and looked obnoxiously smug. "I told you to take me along when you interviewed her. She never would've pulled the wool over the eyes of a cynical ol' curmudgeon like *me*."

"So, what's the full plate number?" Savannah asked.

As Tammy rattled off the numbers, Savannah wrote them down on a scrap of paper on the nightstand.

"That's wonderful, honey bun," she said. "You did good."

There was a little giggle on the other end, but not the enthusiastic response Savannah expected from her usually overly effervescent assistant.

"How's it going back there?" she asked.

"Okay." Again, the answer was a tad lackluster.

Savannah glanced over at Dirk, who was busy beating and folding his pillow, getting it just right. "Is our little project coming along all right?" she asked.

"Yeah. That's coming along great."

Hmmm. So, if everything's so great, why are you so glum? Savannah thought.

"How's Waycross?" she asked.

There was a long, telling pause. "Okay, I guess. Haven't seen much of him because he's been busy, you know, with that. When he is around, he's . . . well . . ." Another silence. "He's okay, I guess."

Savannah's heart sank, in spite of the intriguing information she'd just been given about the case. "Okay, darlin'," she said. "Excellent work there. I'll call you again tomorrow after I've reinterviewed Dr. Glenn."

"Nighty-night."

"Sweet dreams."

Savannah hung up the phone and switched off the light. Moonlight shone through the mullioned window, casting prison bar shadows across the bed. Every few seconds, the beam from the lighthouse made its round, bathing the room in a momentary silver glow.

"That's some pretty exciting news, huh?" Dirk said. "Finally we've got a halfway decent lead."

"Yeah. I guess."

He turned onto his side to face her. "What's up with you? Usually, you'd be dancing a jig around the room."

"I'm worried about Tammy and Waycross."

"You sound like Granny. Don't worry. They're old enough to behave themselves. And if they don't, they'll be careful."

"That's not what I mean. Quite the opposite, in fact."

"But they were getting along good. Great, in fact. What's wrong with that?"

"Waycross is backing off."

"You're kidding! Tammy's a doll, and hotter than a pistol. She's obviously crazy about him."

Savannah felt a tightening in her throat. Her eyes stung with unshed tears that seemed to well up from out of nowhere.

Not exactly nowhere, she reminded herself. Her tears and her brother's sprang from the same source.

"He doesn't feel worthy of her," Savannah said, her voice catching on the lump in her throat.

"Why the hell not? He's a great guy."

"A great guy from a family tree with some really rotten branches on it," she said.

"Oh."

Savannah could hear the hurt in his voice—a lot of it—echoing in that one word. She had made her statement without thinking. In light of Dirk's recent revelations about his own family, she should have known better. This had to be a painful topic for him, too.

"I'm sorry to hear that," he said finally.

"Of course, something like that shouldn't matter at all," she offered, thinking how lame it sounded.

"But it does."

"Does it?"

"Absolutely."

In the darkness, she could hear him swallow . . . hard.

"It can keep a guy from going after a special gal for a long time. Years even."

Savannah thought of all the years of friendship between Dirk and herself. Years when they were dear friends, but they could have been lovers.

She rolled onto her side, facing him, and gently touched his cheek. "What a shame," she said.

He kissed her, softly and sweetly. "Ain't it though?"

Chapter 21

Savannah and Dirk had been unable to find Dr. Glenn at the office where Savannah had interviewed her before, but a volunteer, who was manning the desk, suggested they look at a nearby lake.

"Once a week, Dr. Glenn goes out there and picks up litter," the woman had told them. "She may be our director, but she isn't afraid to get her hands dirty when she has to."

"I wonder just how dirty she gets her hands," Savannah mused as she drove the Jaguar into a valley between two of the island's largest mountains.

Hills that looked like they had been covered with tawny-beige suede rose on either side of them, dotted with dark green sage bushes here and there. Yellow daisies and bright orange California poppies bloomed in profusion. Alongside the road, a creek burbled over its stony bed, reaching ever inland, flowing to the center of the island. Along its banks grew the occasional grove of ancient, gnarled oaks.

"A little mud on your hands is one thing," Dirk said

as he enjoyed the view from the passenger seat. "Now, if we're talking blood, that's another story."

"I have to tell you, this one surprises me." Savannah shook her head. "You wait till you meet her. Dr. Glenn comes across as a quality person—intelligent, devoted to the well-being of this island. I just can't imagine her hanging out the window of a Jeep, shooting at a police chief."

Dirk sniffed. "Yeah, well, considering who the police chief is, I can imagine myself taking a shot at her. La Cross doesn't exactly bring out the best in people. She's a real battle-axe."

"That's a highly sexist remark."

"Why? What's wrong with it? She is."

"If she were a man, you wouldn't say that. You'd say he had a strong personality."

"Naw. That's not true. I'd hate La Cross no matter what gender she was."

"How much of that is because she insulted your jacket?"

He glanced down and ran his hand lovingly over the old, cracking leather. "The woman's obviously got no taste. In men or in jackets."

"That's true . . . about the 'men' part."

He shot her a look.

"You know what I mean," she added quickly. "Northrop's obviously a jackass."

Up ahead, they could see the creek widening and spilling into a small lake, surrounded by reeds, massive rocks, and a few trees.

"Hey, look at that." Dirk pointed to a rusty black Jeep parked at the end of the road, near the water's edge. "And check out the plate number."

"That's the one," Savannah said, still not quite believing it.

Certainly, over the years, she had been fooled by suspects. Many times, in fact. But this one shocked her all the way to her core. She would have bet any amount of money that Dr. June Glenn was exactly what she had appeared—a woman dedicating her life to worthy causes.

The idea that Dr. Glenn was involved in anything so sordid and violent as these attacks was unthinkable. But there was the evidence, parked right in front of her.

She parked the Jaguar beside the Jeep and turned off the engine. Glancing around, she didn't see Glenn or anyone else, for that matter.

Except for a few seagulls circling overhead, a half-dozen snowy egrets roosting in trees, and a pair of ducks paddling around in the water, the lake was remarkably, deliciously peaceful.

"Well, let's get out and find her," he said. "She can't be far away."

Once they were out of the car, it didn't take them long to spot the doctor. She was standing in the shallows at the water's edge. She had on a pair of rubber boots, which reached up to her knees, and she was bending over, pulling something from among the reeds.

"Is that her?" Dirk asked.

Savannah nodded. "She looks a little different in dungarees, but yes."

She headed in Glenn's direction, with Dirk following close behind.

"Dr. Glenn!" Savannah called.

When the woman turned, Savannah motioned to her. "It's me, Savannah Reid. Can we talk again?"

June Glenn nodded and began to wade through the reeds toward them and the bank. She was holding several soda cans and a plastic grocery bag in her hands.

Savannah was amused and a little surprised to see that she was wearing a bright red sweatshirt with an enormous Mickey Mouse face on the front. The word "Disneyland" was emblazoned over his head.

Dr. Glenn seemed to notice her staring at the shirt, because she chuckled as she stepped up onto the bank and said, "I can't help myself. I'm a big fan. Worked there as a kid and never got over it."

"Hey, don't apologize," Savannah replied. "My granny's in her eighties and still madly in love with Sir Mickey. She'll never get over it either. I'm sure she'd work there now, if they'd hire her."

Glenn walked over to a bag, which was stashed on the bank, and dropped the garbage into it. "Those darned kids," she said. "Teenagers mostly. They come up here to drink, smoke pot, and do God only knows what else. Then they leave their litter behind. We had to rescue a heron last week that was tangled up in some of their trash."

She walked up to them and took off her rubber gloves. "I'm June Glenn," she said, offering Dirk her hand.

"This is my husband, Detective Sergeant Dirk Coulter," Savannah said. "He's investigating that case with me, the one we spoke about the other day."

Savannah watched Dirk as he shook the doctor's hand. His quick eyes swept over her, evaluating her with the same scrutiny he would any street person or recently released ex-con.

Dirk was no great respecter of titles, wealth, degree, or position. All that interested him was whether or not a person was capable of committing the crime he was investigating on that given day.

"Nice to meet cha, Doc," he said in an unconvincing tone.

"Please, just call me June," she said. She turned back

to Savannah. "Obviously, you went to a lot of trouble to track me down today. May I ask why?"

"Something's come up in the course of this investigation, and I need to talk to you."

"Certainly. About what?"

"Your vehicle."

"My Mercedes? Why? What about it?"

"No, not your personal car. That Jeep parked over there. Do you drive it often?"

"Once in a while. When I come to places like this, where I wouldn't drive, well . . ."

"Your fancy car," Dirk supplied.

"Yes."

"Were you driving it this past Sunday morning?" he asked.

"No, but it's funny you should ask."

"Why is that?" Savannah wanted to know.

The doctor reached down and picked up her bag of trash and started to walk toward the Jeep.

"Here, let me get that for you," Dirk said, taking the bag from her hand.

They followed her as she continued toward the old vehicle.

"Because," she said, "even though everyone in the league drives it from time to time, no one in our group used it that morning. Yet, strangely enough, it was missing."

"Missing?" Savannah didn't know whether to be relieved or discouraged. Maybe a bit of both. Relieved that, if she was telling the truth, this could clear Dr. Glenn of suspicion. Discouraged that they would be sitting back on square one, with no suspect.

"Yes. It's usually parked overnight behind our office, where you visited me before," Dr. Glenn said. "But when one of our volunteers went to get it Sunday morning to take a drive on the beach, it was gone. Weirdly enough, the next night, it was back again, sitting in its usual spot."

"Who has keys to it?" Dirk asked.

"Keys? We usually leave the key above the driver's sun visor and the door unlocked." When he looked surprised, she added, "This is Santa Tesla Island, Sergeant Coulter. Thankfully, we live a bit differently here than you do on the mainland."

"Obviously."

"Even stranger still," Dr. Glenn continued, "that wasn't the only time it happened. It was taken a couple of weeks ago. The same way. Also for an overnighter."

"Do you remember the exact date that occurred?" Savannah asked.

"No. I'm sorry. I can't. We just figured one of our volunteers took it without permission and was afraid to own up to it later. But then when it happened again, we were a bit more curious."

"If you were all that curious," Dirk said, "did you consider reporting it to the police? That's what most people do the first time their cars go missing, let alone if it happens twice."

A solemn, unpleasant look crossed Dr. Glenn's pretty face. Her eyes didn't meet theirs when she said, "No. I didn't consider calling the so-called authorities. I'm not a fan of the current police department. We haven't found them to be fair in their dealings with the league, so we have as little to do with them as possible."

They approached the Jeep, and Dr. Glenn started to reach for the handle to open the back door. Savannah put out her hand and stopped her.

"I'm sorry, Dr. Glenn, but I'm going to ask you not to touch this vehicle again until after it's been processed."

" 'Processed'?"

"Yes, for fingerprints."

The doctor looked shocked, even horrified. "Are you telling me that our Jeep is somehow connected to a crime?"

"That's right," Savannah told her. "A rather nasty crime, at that."

"Attempted murder," Dirk added. "Doesn't get much worse than that. . . . Unless, of course, you actually kill somebody."

Two hours later, Savannah and Dirk stood beside the Jaguar and watched as Chief La Cross directed a young woman who was swirling fingerprint dust around the driver's door handle of the Jeep.

Many, many times they had watched professionals perform this task. It was painfully obvious that this technician was an amateur at best.

"Doesn't exactly inspire confidence, does it?" Dirk said as the chief grabbed the brush out of her hand, pushed her aside, and took over the job herself.

"Nope. It doesn't. In fact, it sends hot and cold chills running through my bloodstream. This might be our only shot, and they're blowing it."

"Did you call Ryan and John yet?"

"I certainly did. They said if we get anything, send it right over."

"Good. With their old FBI connections, they'll find out if there's a match anywhere in the system. Heck, they're even faster than Fluff . . . er . . . I mean, Tammy."

Savannah smiled up at him. Maybe there was hope for him, after all.

They continued to watch for as long as they could stand it. Finally, when they saw La Cross apply tape for the fourth time, lift another print, and affix it to a fourth evidence card, Savannah couldn't take it any longer.

"That's it," she said. "She's either gonna give those to me or she isn't. I'm gonna find out which."

She stomped over to the Jeep and Dirk watched as she had a few words with La Cross.

The police chief shook her head and held the cards behind her back, like a kid refusing to share their favorite toys.

Savannah said something else and La Cross wavered, started to surrender the prizes, then snatched them back, then . . . finally . . . gave them up. Savannah took a camera from her pocket, laid the cards on the Jeep's front fender, and, one by one, took several close-up shots of each one.

Then she handed the cards back to La Cross and returned to Dirk, with a big smile on her face.

"Got 'em!" she said.

"So I see."

"Let's get going. I can send these to Ryan on the way."

As they climbed into the Jag, she was already texting like crazy. "Okay," she said as he started the car's engine. "He's got them! Now it's just a matter of waiting."

When they pulled away from the scene, leaving a more-disgruntled-than-usual police chief in their wake, Dirk asked, "What did you say to her to get her to hand 'em over?"

"Nothing much."

"I know better than that."

"I just mentioned that if she didn't share them with me, a certain Los Angeles station was going to hear all

about her affair with Northrop in time for it to be the
lead story on the six o'clock news."

"You're a wicked, ruthless woman."

"Don't you ever forget it."

Savannah figured she did a few things well. She was a
better-than-average private detective, an excellent cook,
and a decent housekeeper. She was a superb cat owner,
and to hear Dirk tell it, a great wife—though time
would tell on that one.

But Savannah was pretty honest when it came to self-
evaluations. She knew that the one thing she did worse
than anything else was wait.

When she had something important or something
difficult, or both, to do, she wanted to get it over and
done with as soon as possible. And cooling her heels
waiting for something to happen that was out of her
control, something that prevented her from getting on
with her dreaded task—it was a pure vexation to her
soul.

However, Savannah had learned that one way to
soothe her spirit and clear her mind was to enjoy a bit
of nature while she waited. Even if it was five minutes in
her rose garden, two minutes looking up at the clouds
in the sky, one minute of stepping outside and feeling
the cool ocean wind on her face—it was often enough
to put her right with the world again.

Or at least lessen her cantankerous mood.

So she decided that while she waited for Ryan and
John to get back to her about the fingerprints, she
would leave Dirk in the lightkeeper's cottage, where he
could take a peaceful nap. That way, he wouldn't have

to watch her pace the floor or listen to her mumble curses under her breath.

Having covered him with the quilt and kissed him on the forehead like he was a kindergartner settling down for an afternoon "time-out," she stuck her cell phone in her pocket and headed for the lighthouse.

After climbing the 137 steps to the top, she had expended a great deal of her nervous energy. And when she stepped out onto the gallery and felt the sea wind swirl through her hair, she was happy she had decided to wait this way.

As she stood at the railing and looked down on the harbor, filled with fishing boats, yachts, ferries, and sailboats and motorboats, she thought about what a crazy honeymoon this had been.

Who else began their married life together chasing a killer?

Who else considered it marital bliss to track down leads, interview suspects, and butt heads with local authorities? No one else that she could think of.

Maybe everyone else she knew led boring lives compared to hers and Dirk's. But as she leaned against the rail, her body tired and aching from all it had been through in previous days, she thought that perhaps "boring" would be a nice change of pace.

But then, she reminded herself, if she'd liked "boring," she probably should have chosen another occupation. Something other than law enforcement and private detecting. Some field where you weren't expected to shoot at anyone, and had every reason to expect that no one would shoot at you.

Maybe in her next lifetime, she'd become a mortician. That would probably be peaceful enough. At least your clients wouldn't talk back to you. Or maybe a first-grade schoolteacher. Then, if you got into a scuffle on the job, you'd probably win the fight.

"Who are you kidding, Savannah?" she heard a voice deep inside ask. *"A pack of wild hyenas couldn't drag you away from this job. It's in your blood. And there's no place in this world you'd rather be than right in the middle of all this mess. Even if it is your honeymoon."*

She shook her head, trying to get rid of those thoughts. But, of course, they were right. The "voice" was always right.

A trio of brown pelicans flew by, nearly at her eye level. It was the closest she had ever been to these strange, exotic-looking creatures, which, in flight, had the appearance of a flock of pterodactyls. As she watched, they swooped down to the sea in unison, fishing its bounty.

Savannah walked slowly around to the other side of the light—because she knew she had to. Although she didn't want to relive it, she had to.

She had to see the place, the stretch of beach, where she had first witnessed Amelia Northrop running for her life.

And there it was, glistening golden in the sunlight . . . as natural and lovely as any bit of sand in the world, the foaming waves rolling onto it and settling in.

Quite a few times before, Savannah had felt a shock at the irony of having a beautiful place become the scene of a terrible crime.

She had walked through fantasy forests where someone had been murdered. She had roamed fragrant, sun-warmed orange groves where rapes had occurred. She had sat on the shores of lakes where brutal acts had led to the loss of life and wondered how such things could happen among such peace and loveliness.

It was as though something sacred had been defiled.

This stretch of beach beneath her was no different. No one should have died there.

Amelia's world may have become complicated and sad in her final days, but she shouldn't have lost her life at another's hands. And Savannah was damned determined to find out who had done it and see him or her brought to justice. She wasn't going to leave this island until it was settled.

"Help me," she whispered . . . to the blood-soaked sand below her, the sun above, the wind caressing her face, and to the Maker of brown pelicans and nature. "Lead me to them. Show me the truth."

As though in answer to her impromptu and informal prayer, the phone in her pocket began to chime. It was Ryan.

"Hi," she said breathlessly.

"Hi. We got it."

Ryan's smooth, sexy voice sounded excited. Her heart rate soared.

"Who is it?"

"There were several, as you could expect. One from Dr. Glenn, another from a gal named Sadie, who does a lot of volunteer wildlife rehabilitation with Glenn. But the one you want belongs to a guy named Harry Jacobsen."

"Who's that?"

"A guy who was busted in 2006 for possession of illegal explosive devices."

"Okay." Her mind raced, trying desperately to fit this new piece into the puzzle.

"You've interviewed him already," Ryan was saying.

"No . . . I don't think so. I—"

"He doesn't go by 'Harry Jacobsen' anymore. Now he's 'Hank Jordan.' "

Savannah grabbed the railing as the adrenaline rush hit her knees and nearly made them buckle beneath her. She closed her eyes and whispered, "Thank you" to the sand, the sky, the wind, and the Maker of pelicans and nature.

"You're welcome," came the sweet reply over the phone. "All you had to do was ask."

When Savannah rushed into the house to tell Dirk the news, she could hear him talking upstairs. Curious, she went up to see who was there.

As she reached the top of the stairs, she heard him say, "I know. I used to feel the same way. I mean, look who I'm married to. I don't have to tell you how fantastic she is."

Savannah paused on the top step. She didn't want to eavesdrop on his conversation, but she couldn't resist hearing just a bit more before either announcing herself or going back downstairs.

"Well, you know what they say," he continued, "she married beneath her. All women do."

Savannah grinned. He had told her that on their wedding day, on the ferry to the island. He'd also told her she was the best person he'd ever met in his life and he was darned lucky to have her.

You could forgive a guy for a lot of chili belches and for leaving the toilet seat up when he said stuff like that.

As a woman—especially as a young woman—Savannah knew you always had to judge a man's motives when he was sweet-talking you face-to-face. You had to ask yourself what he was up to, what he was hoping to get for all that honey he was smearing on so thick. But when a guy said sweet things about you to other people behind your back, you could be pretty darned sure he meant it.

"But you can't worry about stuff like that, dude," Dirk was saying. "If you think she'd be willing to take you, go for it. It's up to her if she's gettin' a deal or not."

A long, silent pause caused Savannah to realize that he was on the telephone.

"Sorry, but you gotta be a little selfish here. What makes you so sure she'd find somebody better than you down the road? She hasn't yet. She might do worse. Hell, she's done way worse than you already."

Ah, Mr. Smoothie all the way, Savannah thought with a sweet ache in her heart as she realized he was giving her kid brother advice about women.

It was all she could do not to run into the bedroom and lay a big smooch on him.

"Listen, I have it from your big sister that Tammy's very interested. So what if your dad couldn't keep his damned zipper closed . . . so what if your old lady's the town drunk . . . that's got nothing to do with you. You're a good kid. So's Tammy. You two deserve to be happy. Go for it!"

In the silence that followed, Savannah's conscience got the better of her and she continued on up the stairs, walking heavy so as to be heard.

She entered the bedroom and saw Dirk sitting on the bed, the phone to his ear. He was wearing his shirt, boxers, and black socks.

Ordinarily, that wasn't a look that set her heart to pit-ter-pattering. But after what she'd just heard, she could have thrown him back onto the bed and ravished him— had he not been talking to her little brother.

He looked up, gave her a wink, and said, "Your big sis just walked in the room. I can ask her the mystery question now, if you want." A pause. "Okay, hold on."

Dirk held the phone away and said, "Your brother wants me to tell you that they didn't have the color you wanted. So, do you want blue or beige?"

Savannah thought for a moment. "Blue."

"Blue," he said into the phone. "Is that all? Okay. You think about what I said, all right? Bye."

He hung up the phone and tossed it onto the nightstand. "What's gonna be blue?"

"None of your business."

"You Reids got some sort of secret? Something's going on behind my back?"

"Behind your back, over your head, up our sleeves— you name it." She sat down on the edge of the bed beside him. "From what I heard coming up the stairs, it sounded like you were playing Cupid."

He laughed and held out his arms to her. "I was certainly trying. Wanna roll around in the hay with Cupid, the god of love?"

"More than life itself. But you and I have more important things to do, boy."

"What could possibly be more important than sex on a honeymoon?"

"Hank Jordan's prints were on the Jeep's door."

"Lemme grab my pants!"

Chapter 22

This time, when Savannah and Dirk marched into the Santa Tesla police station, they didn't even bother with the formalities of stopping at the front desk and waiting to be invited in.

As they hurried by Kenny Bates II, he shouted out, "Hey! You hold on a minute! You can't go back there!"

He came out from behind the desk and stood in front of them.

"No. You don't want to do that," Dirk said.

"If it's the chief you want to see, I-I have to call her on the phone f-first," he stammered.

Savannah stepped up to him, nose to nose, and said, "Move, or I swear I'll hurt you."

Something in her eye must have told him that she meant it, because he moved out of her way and returned to his desk.

They could hear him phoning someone, but they were already at the chief's office door, so the alert did little good.

Dirk knocked once; then, without waiting for an invitation, he opened the door.

Chief La Cross was jumping up from her chair as Savannah entered after him. "Stop right there! How dare you barge into my office like that!" She reached for the phone on her desk and punched a number. "Get in here right now. I have two people who—"

Dirk reached over, took the phone from her, and hung it up. "You don't want to do that," he said. "Believe me."

"Unless," Savannah added, "you want them to walk in here in the middle of you telling us why you lied to us and covered up for Hank Jordan. Maybe they want to hear why their chief would give an ex-con a fake alibi for a murder."

Two large, young cops barged into the room. Savannah recognized them as the two who had been milling about the beach at the murder scene.

But before they could grab Savannah or Dirk, Chief La Cross said, "Never mind, Franklin. It's okay, Rhodes. I've got it under control. You can leave. Close the door behind you."

As soon as the patrolmen were gone and the door shut, Savannah walked over to one of the chairs beside La Cross's desk and sat down. Dirk did the same in the chair on the other side.

"You might as well take off your coat and stay awhile." Savannah tossed her purse onto the desk. "We got plenty to talk about."

"Actually, Chief," Dirk said, "it's you who's gonna be doin' the talkin'. Why did you say Hank Jordan was here at the station all morning on Sunday, when Amelia Northrop was killed, when you—and now we—know he wasn't?"

Savannah looked from Dirk to the chief and was impressed with how convincing his accusation was. Of course, they didn't know any of this for certain. But if you were going to accuse a chief of police of conspiring to murder, you didn't do it timidly.

And Dirk's bluff worked.

La Cross sat down abruptly in her chair and began to shake like a palm tree in a Pacific typhoon. She looked like she was going to burst into tears at any moment.

"Why did you lie for him, Charlotte?" Savannah asked, her voice much gentler than Dirk's.

She often played "good cop" to his "bad."

"Because he asked me to" was the unexpected reply. "And because I was in love with him."

Savannah looked over at Dirk and saw that he was taken aback by this, too. They had both been expecting a denial.

Charlotte and that nasty dimwit, Hank? Really?

The only word that came to Savannah's mind was "yuck."

"Yuck," Dirk said.

There it was. Great minds *did* think alike.

"You were in love with ol' Hank Jordan?" Savannah asked. "Well, I wouldn't have guessed that, but I reckon you must've seen something in him that I didn't."

Chief La Cross looked at her, stunned. Then she turned to Dirk. "What are you talking about? Hank Jordan? I wasn't in love with that slimeball. I was talking about William."

Savannah's brain pulled the emergency brake, skidded to a stop, and did a U-turn. "What? You just said . . . Oh . . . it was *William* who asked you to cover for Hank? To give him an alibi?"

La Cross nodded as tears started to roll down her cheeks.

"How did he talk you into doing something as stupid as that?" Dirk asked with his usual tact.

"He said Hank was innocent, that he had nothing to

do with Amelia's death. William said Hank was with him that morning, and they were doing something that had to do with the casino."

"Like what?" Savannah asked.

"He said he couldn't tell me, that it was confidential and it might put me in a compromising situation if I knew. But he assured me it was all legal and honest."

"And you believed him?"

La Cross began to cry in earnest. It was a sad, ugly sight as she wept bitterly. Harsh, wracking sobs shook her entire body. "Yes, I believed him about a lot of things," she said, choking on her own tears. "I was crazy about him. He told me he felt the same way about me."

Savannah reached into her purse and pulled out a handful of tissues. She handed them to Charlotte, who blew her nose violently into them, then handed them back to Savannah.

She stared at the wad of sodden tissues in her palm for a moment; then she spotted a trash can nearby and quickly deposited them there.

So much for showing compassion to a fellow human being, she thought.

"He was just using me to get his damned casino. He needed some obstacles removed, and as police chief, I could do it. But now that the road's clear for him, he's dumping me."

It occurred to Savannah that as Charlotte La Cross sat there at her desk, sobbing her face off over a guy, Santa Tesla's chief of police looked a bit like a distraught teenager who had just lost her first love.

The thought also crossed Savannah's mind that William Northrop might have, indeed, been the first serious love affair Charlotte had ever experienced. Dirk had suggested that she wasn't an attractive woman by any measure, but, more important, she had a cold, standoffish personality that probably didn't attract a lot of people—friends or lovers.

"Let me get this straight," Dirk said. "Northrop told you that he and Hank knew each other. And that they were together doing some sort of casino stuff on Sunday morning when Amelia was killed?"

"Yes, that's right. But now you're telling me that he wasn't? That he was doing something else?" Charlotte wiped her eyes with the backs of her hands. "What did you find out? Well, Ms. Reid? What was he doing?"

Savannah shot a sideways glance at Dirk. He had that frozen-as-an-ice-cream-cone look on his face. A look she'd seen plenty of times before. It meant he had nothing and wasn't going to be any help. She was on her own with this one.

"Um . . . actually . . ." Her own brain went Popsicle on her, too. "Honestly, we don't know for sure what he was doing that morning. But we did uncover a piece of evidence that would probably represent possible cause, so you could bring him in and question him about it."

Chief La Cross stared at Savannah long and hard. Finally she said, "What?"

"Hank Jordan may be the dude who shot at you," Dirk blurted out. "Those prints you lifted off the league's old black Jeep, some of them were his."

The chief looked dumbfounded. "They were?"

"Yes," Savannah told her. "And Dr. Glenn told us the vehicle was stolen for twenty-four hours, then returned."

"The twenty-four-hour period that both you and William were fired on," Dirk added.

"But I don't understand. William was very nearly killed by those shots. Why would he ask me to provide an alibi for someone who tried to murder him?"

"I don't know," Savannah replied, "but I have an idea. Why don't we go pick up Hank Jordan and drag his mangy, sorry butt in here and ask him real nice. . . ."

"If that doesn't work," Dirk added, "I'll ask him."

Savannah chuckled and said to La Cross, "And he's not so nice."

La Cross shot Dirk a long, scathing look. "Believe me," she said, "I never thought he was."

As they gathered their things and prepared to leave La Cross's office, both Savannah and Dirk reached down and subconsciously checked the weapons in their shoulder holsters beneath their jackets.

"You two won't be needing those," La Cross said as she pulled her own from a drawer and began to strap it on.

"I beg your pardon," Savannah said. "This man should be considered armed and dangerous. We won't be going after him without our weapons."

"You won't be going at all." La Cross's dark eyes went totally black. "This guy shot at me. He's mine."

"Hey! You wouldn't even know about him if it wasn't for us," Dirk snapped back. "We're coming along."

The chief stepped out into the hallway, stopped, and turned back to them. Her chin was elevated several notches, and her hands were on her hips. "You are welcome to wait here at the station house," she said. "Either in the coffee room or a jail cell. Your pick."

Savannah realized they had met their match. Chief La Cross wasn't going to budge on this one. And Savannah realized that if someone had put a bullet in one of her front yard's trees, while aiming at her head, she'd feel the same way.

"Is the coffee any good?" she asked.

"No. But feel free to make a fresh pot."

With that, La Cross spun on her heel, executing a

precision about-face that would have made a U.S. Marine jealous, and marched away.

"Battle-axe," Dirk muttered under his breath.

Savannah nodded. "Yeah. But you have to kinda like her . . . a little bit."

"No, I don't."

Chapter 23

Savannah and Dirk disposed of a pot-and-a-half of coffee and six donuts between them as they waited for Chief La Cross and her team to return with the prisoner.

Waiting . . . without any nature to soothe the anxiety. It was almost more than Savannah could bear.

As her pulse raced, her blood pressure soared, and her anxiety level broke record highs, it never occurred to her to attribute her physical woes to caffeine or sugar intake. No, of course not. It was all La Cross's fault.

"We could have nabbed him, stuck him in a sweatbox, and squeezed a confession outta him four times by now," she said as she paced back and forth in front of Dirk, who was sitting in one of the coffee room's stylish and comfortable plastic lawn chairs.

"Yes, we coulda," he agreed. But not with anywhere near the amount of frustration and angst she was experiencing.

Years ago, she had noticed that in the face of small, daily irritations, Dirk came unhinged. If the woman ahead of him in line at the grocery store had too many

coupons, his life simply wasn't worth living. He would
threaten to do great bodily harm to anyone who cut
him off in traffic, went twenty miles per hour in a forty
zone, or gave him a cheeseburger instead of a ham-
burger.

But when it mattered—really mattered—he was the
quiet in the storm. The guy who couldn't wait three seconds for an Internet page to load on a computer was a
great guy to have around when waiting for biopsy results or a life-and-death verdict to be handed down.

"It'll be okay," he said, now as always. "Don't fret. It'll
all work out."

" 'Fret'? 'Fret'? Is that what you call this? I 'fret' when
a jug of milk in the icebox goes bad. I'm worried sick
here. What if we did all this for nothing, and they let
him slip through their fingers?"

"They'll get him, Van. Sit down and have another
donut."

"You saw how they've handled everything else about
this case," Savannah exploded, letting out all the rage
and frustration that had been building over the past
few days. "They were tripping all over each other there
at the beach. For all of her throwing her weight around,
the chief didn't come up with a single lead on her own.
I swear that's why she was following us. It wasn't to see if
we'd committed any crimes. It was to see if we came up
with anything, because she doesn't know how to conduct a case on her own. They're a bunch of bumbling
idiots around here. This department is a joke. And La
Cross is—"

"Not laughing."

Savannah spun around and saw Chief La Cross filling
the doorway of the break room, directly behind her.
The look on her face told Savannah that she had heard
every word. At least . . . all the worst ones.

"We bumbling fools just brought in the prisoner," La Cross continued dryly. "If you two would like to watch the interrogation, follow me."

Savannah gulped. "Yeah, uh . . . thank you."

"You're welcome."

As Chief La Cross turned and strode down the hallway, Dirk and Savannah fell into step behind her. Dirk nudged Savannah and whispered, "See? What'd I tell you? Things just couldn't be better."

As they watched the game of cat and mouse being played between Hank Jordan and Chief La Cross—with the chief playing the role of mouse—Dirk's initial optimism was fading, and Savannah's worst fears were being confirmed.

Things were going badly. Very badly, indeed.

Jordan hadn't demanded a public defender yet. But that was about the only thing that had gone right so far.

He and La Cross sat across from each other, eyeball to eyeball—so to speak—at a small table in the interview room, which Savannah suspected at times might double as a closet.

She and Dirk sat behind La Cross in one corner, watching. Savannah was mentally imagining the blood as it figuratively rolled from their badly bitten tongues, down their chins, and dripped onto their shirtfronts.

This was agony to watch. And it seriously made Savannah wonder how Charlotte La Cross had ever attained her office.

"Are you really going to stick to that stupid story," La Cross was asking him, "about how you just put your hands on that Jeep when you were walking down the sidewalk that day?"

Hank Jordan was leaning back on the rear two legs of

his chair. His hands were behind his head, where he was toying with his greasy gray ponytail.

"Yep," he said. "I was walking down the sidewalk there in front of Coconut Jane's Tavern and that old Jeep was parked there. The window was down and I saw one of those big nets, the kind you use to catch animals or butterflies or whatever. I was just wondering what it was. So I leaned in and looked. That must be how my prints got on the door."

Savannah groaned internally. La Cross had tipped her hand far too soon by telling him about the prints and then compounding her error by letting him know where they had been lifted.

But the worst mistake she was making was . . . telling her suspect the truth. Every single word the chief had uttered since they'd entered the room was the gospel truth. And both Savannah and Dirk knew you never got anywhere in an interrogation by sticking to the actual facts of the case.

Long ago, Savannah had learned that if there wasn't at least a whiff of pants burning in an interrogation room, you probably weren't making a lot of progress as an interrogator.

She pulled out her phone discreetly and texted Tammy: **La Cross personal cell #?**

She put the phone on vibrate and waited. Less than two minutes later, Tammy texted back the number. Savannah grinned. The kid was fantastic. Savannah sent her a virtual "hug" and composed another message— this time to Chief La Cross.

Step out for a few. Give Dirk a chance.

She heard the chief's phone chime and saw her glance down at it.

Don't blow it. Don't turn around, Savannah thought. *Surely, you have at least one sneaky bone in your body. Use it now.*

Chief La Cross sat still for several moments, thinking, saying nothing.

Just when Savannah thought it was a lost cause, La Cross stood, stretched, and turned to Dirk. "I'm going to go get myself a water. I'll be back in a minute. Can you keep an eye on this one for me?"

Dirk grinned. "Oh, yeah. *No* problem. I'd be glad to keep both eyes on him."

The instant La Cross went out the door and closed it behind her, Dirk was on his feet. He walked over to the chair where she had been sitting, turned it around, and straddled the back.

"Now this is more like it," he said to Hank, who didn't seem to approve of this change in circumstances. "You've heard of the good cop/bad cop routine, Hank, my man? Well, the chief there—she was the good cop. Catch my drift?"

Hank stopped fooling around with his ponytail and squirmed in his seat. He reached for the pack of cigarettes in his shirt pocket; then he seemed to think better of it and started drumming his fingers on his thighs instead.

"Yeah, so what?" he said, trying to sound tough.

Savannah thought he would have sounded a lot badder if his voice hadn't been quavering.

"You go beatin' around the bush with me, the way you were with her the past forty-five minutes, and I'll show you 'what,' " Dirk told him.

"You gonna . . . like . . . hurt me or somethin'?" Hank tried to smirk, but his upper lip quivered and the effect was sadly compromised.

"Well, let's see now," Dirk said, leaning over the table toward him. "I work out at the gym three hours a day."

Lie number one, Savannah thought.

"And I run four miles every evening."

Whopper lie number two.

"And I box at a club in South Central LA every weekend."

Wow! Monster lie number three! Savannah was impressed. Ol' Dirk was on a roll.

"And you," Dirk continued, "wipe off sinks and toilets with a dirty rag, and in your spare time, you throw bedspreads on the ground. So, who do you reckon would come out on top if we decided to tussle in here?"

Hank reached for the cigarette pack again. This time, he pulled it half out of his pocket; then he shoved it back in with a highly agitated look on his face.

Savannah had to admire his fortitude. If ever there was a time to break your New Year's resolution to quit smoking, this would be it. Most smokers in an interrogation hot seat would have had smoke rolling out of practically every orifice of their body by now.

"I told that chief gal how my prints got on that Jeep, and that's all I've got to say to you, too."

"Yeah, but we both know that's a crock, so let's get real. We're burnin' daylight here, and we've gotta get past the 'I didn't do it' BS and on to the 'why I did it' part."

Behind her crossed leg, Savannah had been composing another text. She pushed the button to "send."

Dirk's phone jingled. He pulled it out of his pocket and looked at it. "Oh," he said. "I think this is what we've been waiting for."

Hank looked worried as Dirk opened the text and read it aloud: " 'Suspect Jordan's DNA recovered from

steering wheel and inside driver handle of Jeep—
Moonlight Magnolia Laboratories, McGill, Georgia.' "

Dirk smiled at Hank. " 'Suspect Jordan.' Now, buddy,
we both know that's you. And DNA. You can't get any
better than that."

"When I was . . . um . . . leaning in the window looking, I mighta touched the steering wheel and that handle."

Dirk slammed his fist down on the table, and Hank
jumped like he'd been shot with Granny's Taser prongs
in his backside.

"Don't you even start with that, boy!" Dirk shouted at
him. "You killed that pretty young TV reporter and
you're going away for first-degree murder. You better
start telling me why, or you're looking at the death
penalty here."

Lie number four, Savannah thought. No special circumstances had been proven yet.

However, the lie seemed to work even better on
Hank than on most folks. Savannah wondered if, perhaps, he had a needle phobia. His face turned a distinct
shade of white as he grabbed for the cigarettes in his
pocket, started to tear into the pack, then caught himself and quickly shoved them back into his pocket.

But not quickly enough.

Savannah had caught a glimpse of something odd. It
was a ring of clear adhesive tape around the top—the
kind she used to wrap birthday and Christmas presents.

What smoker tapes his cigarette pack closed? she wondered. And what smoker could resist taking a good,
long drag, when being threatened with capital punishment?

Slowly she rose and walked over to the table.

"Excuse me, gentlemen," she said, standing close to

Hank. "But I was just wondering, Mr. Jordan, would you mind? I really need a smoke. Can you spare one?"

For a second, Dirk looked at her like she had lost her mind. Then she saw him glance away and quickly don his poker face. Of course, he didn't know what she was up to, but he knew enough to go with the flow.

"I . . . um . . . I"—Hank looked like a rat caught in a trap—"I . . . I'm trying to quit," he offered lamely, his hand resting protectively over the pack in his pocket.

"And I think that's plumb admirable. I do," she crooned. "But I'm dyin' here, so if you don't mind. Just one."

Suddenly Dirk was as interested in the mysterious pack as she was. He reached over, brushed Hank's hand away, and tapped it with his fingertip.

"You don't wanna give the lady a cigarette, huh, Hank, my man?" he said. "That's downright ungentlemanly of you."

At that moment, La Cross opened the door and walked back into the room.

Dirk said to her, "Did you search this fella good before you brought him in?"

La Cross's feathers ruffled. "Of course we did. We'd never bring a prisoner in without making sure they're weapon-free."

"How about contraband-free?" Savannah asked.

"What are you talking about?" La Cross responded.

"He's got something there in his cigarette pack that he's guarding like I'd guard a box of Godiva truffles," Savannah told her. "I think you'd best be finding out what it is."

"You can't search my . . . You can't search nothin' of mine without no search warrant!" Hank said, clamping both hands over his shirt pocket with all the drama of a bad Shakespearean actor who'd just been run through with a fake sword onstage.

"Of course I can," La Cross told him as she walked over, placed her hands on his shoulders, and squeezed—hard.

"*Ow!* That hurts."

"So put that cigarette pack on the table and it'll stop hurting," she told him.

Reluctantly, with a hangdog look on his face, he did as he was told.

Savannah snatched up the pack. A second later, she had it unwrapped.

The thing was stuffed with wads of toilet paper, instead of the drugs she'd expected. Some pot maybe? A few bindles of meth perhaps?

She pulled out one bit of tissue after the other and tossed them onto the table. Dirk and La Cross watched her, confusion mixed with expectation on their faces. Hank looked like he wanted to fall through a crack in the floor and never crawl out again.

Finally, Savannah got to the bottom of the pack; all that remained was a small ball of tissue.

When she took it out, she could feel something hard and round wrapped inside.

"Well, now," she said. "What have we here?"

Even before she got it completely unwrapped, she knew what it was by the feel and the shape of it.

It was a magnificent engagement ring. The center stone alone was at least two carats of glistening princess-cut diamond.

"Just lookie here! As pretty a little bauble as I've ever laid eyes on," Savannah said, holding it up to the light and turning it this way and that, watching it sparkle.

She stuck it under Hank's nose. "It appears our

friend Hank was getting ready to pop the question to some lucky lady."

When he didn't reply, she added, "Oh, wait a minute. If Hank here was to work five years, he couldn't pay this thing off. In fact, if he were to sell that motel he works in, he couldn't afford something like this."

"Which means," Dirk said, taking the ring from her hand, "that he probably came by this in an unscrupulous manner. Whatcha wanna bet?"

Savannah was already texting Tammy. She had a hunch, and she needed proof. Something told her the sunshine girl could get it for her pretty quickly.

"It's fake," Hank said. "I won it at the ringtoss on the pier."

"I don't think so," La Cross said, looking it over. "This is a platinum setting and a quality diamond. You stole this."

"I didn't steal nothin', and you can't prove it!"

"Then why were you carrying it next to your heart there in a cigarette pack?" Savannah asked.

"I bought it!"

"A minute ago, you won it," Dirk said. "Make up your mind."

"Just take us to your jeweler," La Cross told him. "You know, the one you shop at on Rodeo Drive. If he vouches for you, no problem."

Hank propped his elbows on the table and buried his face in his hands. "I didn't steal it! Really, I'm telling you the truth. I swear to God!"

"Then how did you get it?" Dirk demanded. "And it better be good."

Hank reached up and pulled long and hard on his ponytail in a nervous gesture, which made Savannah wince. It had to hurt. Finally he said, "Somebody gave it to me, okay?"

"Who?" Dirk asked. "You don't look to me like a guy who'd be gettin' diamonds from women. Or men either."

Savannah's phone vibrated in her hand. Trembling with anticipation, she read the message from Tammy and opened the two pictures that she had sent, as requested.

It was all she could do not to cheer, cry, and laugh out loud, all at the same time.

"Oh, Hank, Hank," she said, showing him the first picture, "look at that. Your ass is grass, and the power mowers are a-circlin'!"

Chapter 24

"What is it?" Dirk asked, leaning over and peering at the small picture on Savannah's phone.

Chief La Cross did the same and looked as puzzled as he did.

But Hank Jordan didn't look confused. He knew exactly what he was seeing there in that tiny image.

Judging from the pallor of his skin, Savannah wondered which he would do first, throw up or faint.

Savannah turned to Dirk. "That first picture is of Amelia Northrop. It's her publicity head shot. And you can see that ring there on her hand."

Dirk held the cell phone practically against his nose and squinted. "Okay, if you say so."

"Okay. For you old folks without your glasses, here's the zoom shot."

She showed them the close-up of Amelia's hand. There was no mistaking the distinctive design of the ring. It was a match.

Savannah pulled the chair she had been sitting in close to Hank and sat down beside him. Summoning as much fake concern and sincerity as she could muster, she said to him, "I believe you, Hank, when you say you didn't steal that ring. I believe Amelia gave it to you."

"Well, I don't!" La Cross interjected. "He took it off her finger just before he shot her there on the beach."

Savannah gazed into Hank's eyes, trying to convey understanding. "I don't believe that, Chief. It'd be one cold-blooded bastard who'd rip a ring off a lady's finger right before he killed her. Now just look at this man. He's not like that."

"That's right!" Hank was so happy to have found an ally. "I wouldn't do something like that. I'm telling you—she gave it to me."

"How did you meet Mrs. Northrop?" Savannah asked as casually as she could, considering that she would have much preferred to just reach out and squeeze his weasely neck until something cracked.

"She came by the motel one day. Said she'd done some research about the people on the island and I interested her."

"I'll bet you did. What happened then?"

"We got to be sorta like friends, and she gave me that ring."

In her best "Big Sister Mode," Savannah reached out and adjusted Hank's collar. "Now, Hank, we know she gave it to you for a reason. Like maybe a payment for something?"

He suddenly looked wary. "Um, no. Nothing like that."

"Oh, I think it was. In fact, I think Amelia had found out that her husband was being unfaithful to her, so she did some research on people living on the island and came across you."

Hank just looked from one of them to the other and

kept playing with his ponytail, so Savannah pressed on. "After doing a criminal background check on you, she probably thought you'd be her best bet."

"For what?"

"To kill her husband and his lover. That's why you wounded Northrop and tried to kill Chief La Cross here. If you'd been a better shot, they'd both be dead, huh?"

When he didn't reply, Dirk chimed in with his own questions. "What happened, Hankie boy? Did Ms. Northrop get mad at you for blowing it and threaten you somehow? Is that why you chased her on that beach and killed her in cold blood?"

"No! That's not it at all!"

"Then you'd better fill us in right now on all the gory details," Savannah told him, "or you're about to go down as one of the ugliest, meanest killers in history. People all over the country are gonna cheer when you get the needle. You killing a pretty young gal like that for no reason, and all."

"It wasn't for no reason! I mean, it wasn't just me! I'm not going to jail all by myself when—"

"When what, Hank?"

"When killing her wasn't even my idea!"

The moment he said the words, Savannah could tell he wanted to take them back. But it was too late.

Her face was only a few inches from his. Her eyes were filling his vision when she said, "Murder for hire is one of those 'special circumstances,' Hank. Punishable by death. You could get the needle for this if you don't give Chief La Cross what she needs here."

A flicker of hope registered on his face. "You mean, if I tell her who hired me, I won't get the needle?"

La Cross started to speak; Dirk reached over, put his hand on her arm, and squeezed.

"You'll not only have to tell her who it was, but you'll have to help us prove it."

"Like set him up? Wear a wire? Get him to confess?"

"Exactly."

"And then I won't get the death penalty?"

"If you aid law enforcement in apprehending all guilty parties in this crime, Mr. Jordan, I'm certain your cooperation will serve to prove your great remorse. I can assure you that your actions will weigh heavily in the scales of justice, on the day you're sentenced."

"What?"

She lost her patience. "Who the hell was it? Northrop?"

"Yeah."

"Why?"

"Because he found out she'd hired me to shoot him and the chief here, and that she'd given me her wedding ring to do it. That really pissed him off."

"Go figure," Dirk mumbled.

"He figured out it was me from some paper she'd left there at the house with my name on it. So the day he got out of the hospital, he called me and offered me a hundred grand to do it."

Jordan shrugged. "I've been broke my whole life. You couldn't expect me to turn down a deal like that!"

"Of course not," Savannah replied evenly. "How did you get her to go to the beach with you that morning?"

"I was waiting for her outside her house, by her car. I told her we had to talk, that I wanted some more money until I could fence the ring. I got her to take a ride with me."

"Once you got down to the beach, what happened?"

"I told her what her husband had done, how he'd offered to pay me to kill her. I told her if she wanted to up his ante, I'd consider it."

Savannah felt her blood temperature plummet. This guy was sitting there, discussing his heinous crime as though describing a fishing trip with his best buddy.

"But she didn't even want to talk about it. She sorta freaked out and jumped outta my car and ran down toward the water. I guess I don't have to tell you two the rest, 'cause you were there."

"You saw us?" Savannah asked.

"Sure. I thought about taking you guys out, too, but I figured it'd be easier just to get away from there. I figured she'd croak before she told you anything. She didn't look like she was gonna make it."

By then, Savannah's blood felt like it had reached subzero. She knew she had to get out of that room before she tied into him and tried her best to kill him with her bare hands. Deep in the most primal part of her being—a part she couldn't deny, but didn't want to have to see with such stark clarity—she wanted to see him dead. As dead as that young woman on the beach.

She also had to leave because if she didn't, she was going to tell him that she had just lied to him. Whether he cooperated and helped them nail Northrop or not, he would probably still be facing the death penalty. She wanted to tell him because she wanted to see the look on his face when he realized he'd just been had.

But she didn't. She didn't attack him, and she didn't mock him. Her determination to control that primal part of herself was the only difference between her and the guy in the chair.

And she *would* be different from him. She *would*.

"He's all yours, Chief," she said.

Then she turned and ran out the door, in desperate need of sunlight and fresh air.

*   *   *

"This is going way better than before," Granny said as she sat in the big, comfortable passenger seat of Ryan and John's surveillance van and watched the action through the windshield.

Behind her, manning two different recording devices, were Savannah and Dirk. Chief La Cross was watching through a small side window with a pair of binoculars.

Directly ahead was William Northrop's big glass house. Hank Jordan was walking up to the front door.

On the lawn a couple of gardeners were raking the flower beds. They looked a heck of a lot like Ryan and John.

Two utility workers examining a nearby telephone pole bore a striking resemblance to the patrolmen Franklin and Rhodes.

"That's true, Gran. It wouldn't take much to improve on our last surveillance job," Savannah replied.

"I thought we weren't going to talk about that." Dirk was still decidedly grumpy about the topic.

"Would this have anything to do with the bruises on your faces?" La Cross asked.

Savannah sniffed. "It was a contributing factor."

La Cross lowered her binoculars and gave them a teasing look. "Good. I thought maybe you'd had a newly-weds' quarrel."

"Hey, don't even talk like that!" Dirk snapped. "Real men don't hit women. Real men hit men who hit women."

"Sometimes real women do, too," Granny added with a snicker.

"Amen," Savannah replied.

"You know, I like you two better than I did at first," the chief said.

"That, too, was an easy improvement. No place to go but up," said Savannah.

La Cross waved an arm, indicating all of Ryan and John's expensive equipment. "This is a nice setup your friends have here. Wish I had something like this." She sighed. "Hell, I'd be happy just to have that gadget that triggered the gate to open."

"Shhh," Dirk said. "I'm getting something here."

He pressed a button on the recorder. A blue graph danced on a computer monitor in front of him as Hank Jordan's voice came in loud and clear.

"Hey, I gotta see you," Hank said. "Right now. We got a problem."

"You can't come here to my home, you idiot!" was the equally clear response from William Northrop. "How did you get through the gate?"

"It was open."

"Well, get the hell out of here now before somebody sees you!"

"No, seriously, we've gotta talk!" Hank insisted. "This guy I know at the motel, he figured out what I did for you, and now he wants in on it, too."

There was a long pause; then Northrop said, "Get in here."

Hank disappeared into the house and the big door closed with a finality that would have bothered Savannah if it had been anyone other than a heartless murderer inside. She figured she should conjure up some concern for Hank Jordan's well-being, but she couldn't.

If a battle ensued, she wasn't sure which party, if anyone, she would be rooting for.

"You told somebody about it?" Northrop was asking Hank. "You had to go and shoot your mouth off to some other moron?"

"Hey, watch who you're calling names here. I didn't tell anybody. He got into my stuff, and he saw the backpack full of money you gave me. Now he's saying if I don't give him half, he's going to the cops."

"So give him half."

"I don't wanna give him half! That ain't enough for doing a murder. Especially of a woman. It wasn't easy killing a woman as good-lookin' as your old lady."

Everyone in the van held their collective breaths for the next response.

Come on, Savannah thought. *Come on, Billy boy. Don't stop now! Dig that grave of yours a full eight feet deep.*

"Listen to me, you stupid ass," Northrop said. "You've gotten all the money out of me that you're ever going to get. Don't forget, if my wife's murder comes back on me, you'll go down for it, too."

"But I—"

"You nothing. You deal with this idiot friend of yours any way you have to, but don't you ever come back to me again. If you do, I swear, I won't even bother to hire somebody to kill you. I'll do it myself! You hear me?"

"Oh, darlin', we hear you," Savannah said, bouncing up and down on her seat. "We *all* hear you! And I can't wait till the jury hears you, too!"

"That's enough. Let's go get him," Chief La Cross said as she opened the van door and jumped out. Dirk hopped out with her.

"You go ahead, Chief," Savannah said. "You've got enough good backup there without me."

La Cross didn't have to be told twice. In a heartbeat, she was running toward the house. Dirk, Ryan, John, and Patrolmen Franklin and Rhodes swept en masse up the sidewalk to the front door with her.

"That's not like you, sweet pea," Granny said, "holding back when it's time to grab the bad guy."

Savannah smiled, watching La Cross charge through

the front door, gun drawn, followed by the rest of her team.

"The chief there's the one who got her heart broken," she said. "He bedded her and betrayed her, and that kills an important part of a woman's soul. She needs this a lot more than I do."

"I love you, Savannah girl."

"I love you, too, Gran. You're the best!"

It didn't take long for Savannah to locate Dr. June Glenn. The entire island was abuzz about the fund-raising gala she had organized, and the festivities had just begun on the oceanfront in the harbor.

Known for its casual lifestyle, Santa Tesla Island wasn't accustomed to having ladies in evening gowns and men in tuxedos stroll her pier. But tonight, the island's elite were doing just that as they sipped champagne, chatted, nibbled hors d'oeuvres, and enjoyed one sultry jazz number after another, performed by a twelve-piece orchestra.

Savannah felt woefully underdressed in her linen slacks and simple button-down shirt. But then, she wasn't here to raise funds, nibble, or sip. She had good news to deliver . . . and a new husband waiting for her back at the lighthouse keeper's cottage.

It was a simple task, locating Dr. June Glenn. As Savannah had expected, the doctor was at the center of one of the largest conversation circles. Wearing a floor-length red gown that draped her slender form, her hair in an elegant updo, she was easily one of the loveliest women present. Interestingly, much of her beauty had to do with her grace and her passion as she presented her point of view to those standing around her.

Something told Savannah she wasn't lecturing them on the weather or sharing the latest fashion tips. Whatever the topic was, Savannah knew it was something important, and she was reluctant to interrupt the business at hand.

But the moment Dr. Glenn spotted her, standing patiently on the sidelines, the doctor left her companions and hurried over to greet her.

"Good evening, Savannah," she said, extending her hand. "I'm so glad you could join us."

"Oh, I'm not joining," Savannah told her. "I just stopped by to give you an update."

Glenn looked concerned. "Not more bad news, I hope."

"No. Very good news. I'm happy to tell you that a suspect has been arrested for killing Amelia Northrop."

"That's wonderful! Who is it?"

"Hank Jordan. It appears your instincts were right about him."

Dr. Glenn's excitement turned to sadness. She shook her head. "People only hurt our cause when they use violent means like that."

"He didn't do it out of concern for the environment. It was murder for hire."

The doctor's eyes widened. "Really? Who paid him?" She thought for a moment. "Was it William Northrop?"

"Yes. He's in custody, too."

"Good."

Savannah smiled. "I guess that solves your problem, too, huh? Now you don't have to worry about his big casino complex destroying your beautiful beaches."

Dr. Glenn turned and looked up at the sweeping hills, which were turning purple in the glow of the setting sun. The lights of the island's homes and businesses were coming on as Santa Tesla's golden daylight charm faded into sparkling nighttime splendor.

"No," she said. "It doesn't solve my problem. I still

have a community in desperate need. That's what all this is about tonight." She waved an arm, indicating the gala. "We have to find a way to bring tourists and businesses to the island. It doesn't need to be a casino. It could be a family-oriented complex, one that doesn't negatively impact the environment." She sighed. "We'll think of something."

Savannah's eyes were warm as she said, "I'm absolutely sure you will. This island is lucky to have you, Dr. Glenn. Both the animals and the people."

"Thank you," she replied, offering her hand in farewell. "This island was very fortunate that you and your husband chose to honeymoon here when you did. Please come see us again, under more pleasant circumstances."

Savannah looked around, taking in the glimmering hills, the pier, the beach, and the harbor. "Don't worry. We will."

Chapter 25

When Savannah and Dirk strolled up the sidewalk toward her door, she looked up and saw the moonlight streaming through the bougainvillea arching across her porch. She breathed a sigh of relief.

It was so good to be home.

Once the case had been closed, the remaining days on the island were a pure delight. Ryan and John had even convinced Betty Sue to allow them a couple more nights at the lightkeeper's cottage.

But, sooner or later, all good things come to an end. Savannah was more than happy to be returning to her house, her kitties, and her mundane, routine life.

"Vacations and honeymoons and trips are all nice, but I think the best part is coming home," she said.

"I think the best part for me is coming to your house and thinking of it as my house now," Dirk told her, slipping his arm around her shoulders and pulling her close against his side. "I keep feeling like I'm just dropping you off and heading back to my trailer."

"Nope, I reckon if you want, we could have a sleepover. I'll blow up the air mattress, and you can sleep on the living-room floor."

"Wow! What an offer!"

She unlocked the front door and prepared herself for what she knew was coming.

She knew.

Dirk didn't.

As they walked into the dark foyer, they heard a slight rustling near the staircase.

"Hey, the kitties are still up," Dirk said.

But no sooner had he spoken than the lights came on and Tammy and Waycross jumped out from under the stairwell, shouting, "Surprise! Surprise!"

Savannah wasn't sure how Dirk was going to take this. He wasn't so big on surprises—let alone surprise homecomings when they were both exhausted.

But when Tammy had suggested it on the phone that afternoon, she had sounded so excited, Savannah hadn't had the heart to deny her.

After all, she and Waycross had worked so hard.

"Gee," Dirk said with obviously feigned enthusiasm, "what's all this?"

"Just us welcoming you two home," Tammy said. "Especially you, Dirko."

He looked very confused and moderately pleased. "Why me? I don't get it."

"You will," Waycross told him. "Savannah's got something to show you."

Dirk turned to her. Now he was totally confused. "You do?"

She grinned and nodded. "I do. Well, actually, the three of us do. Come upstairs."

He allowed her to lead him up the steps as Tammy and Waycross tagged along behind.

"Where are Granny and Marietta?" he asked as they headed down her hallway.

"Marietta went home today," Waycross told him.

"And Granny's at my house in my guest room," Tammy said. "Probably sound asleep by now."

Savannah stopped outside the door of her second bedroom. "Waycross, I think you are the one most responsible for this, so why don't you fill him in."

His big freckled face shining with happiness, Waycross reached for the doorknob. "Well," he began, "my big sister here knew that it was gonna be hard for you— a real man's man that you are—to live here in a woman's house. Her being kinda a girlie-girl decorator, and all that. So she told me how she wanted this done, and I did my best. Me and Tammy, who was like my assistant."

Waycross reached over, put his arm around Tammy's shoulders, and pulled her next to him. "Now the three of us would like to present you with"—he threw the door open with a flourish—"your *man* cave!"

Savannah was as surprised as Dirk when she looked inside and saw that her feminine, ruffles-satin-and-lace guest room had disappeared. In its place was an almost exact replica of Dirk's trailer's living room.

There was the bus seat sofa—though Savannah was thankful to see that Waycross hadn't transported the rusted TV trays, which served as end tables. On new shelves, which lined one wall, were Dirk's Harley mementos. All two hundred–plus of them, including Harley mugs and shot glasses, figurines, ashtrays, bobble dolls, and Christmas ornaments.

On the opposite wall hung his framed Harley tee-shirts, collector plates, and old tin signs.

The third wall also had shelves, and they were lined

with Dirk's VHS tapes—an entire library of *Bonanza* episodes, as well as Sean Connery and Clint Eastwood movies.

Instead of the walls being a rosy pink, they were now pale blue. The lacy curtains had been replaced with simple white shades. And on the floor lay a blue rug with the Los Angeles Dodgers logo in the center.

"*Holy cow!*" Dirk said as he stepped into pure Coulter paradise. "How did you . . . ? When did you . . . ?" He turned to Waycross and Tammy. "You guys did this for *me*? Really?"

"Savannah paid for it," Waycross said. "She told us what to do."

"But they painted the room and moved everything over here," Savannah added.

"And Waycross built all those shelves," Tammy said. "He's really good with power tools! You should see him! He's amazing!"

Tammy gazed up at him with so much adoration that Savannah felt like bursting into tears. Especially when she saw Waycross look down at Tammy with the same affection in his eyes.

Apparently, Dirk's little telephone pep talk had done some good, after all.

"I don't know what to say," Dirk told them, suddenly plagued by some fuzz or something in his eyes. "Nobody's ever done anything like this for me before. I mean, it's just . . . geez, guys . . . it's too much!"

Waycross reached over and wrapped his other arm around Dirk's shoulders and gave him a hearty, sideways hug. "Well, heck, man. You're my brother now."

Suddenly, without any warning, it was a group hug— just one great big knot of sniffling, laughing happiness.

Savannah half-expected Dirk to try to wriggle out of

it. Group hugs weren't really his favorite things. Especially a Reid family hug.

Everyone knew people had been seriously injured during those.

However, he submitted with more grace than she had ever thought him capable of.

"This is cool," he said with typical Dirk articulation. "So cool. It's like I really do have a family now."

Tammy was the first to pull out of the bunch. She reached over and took his hand. "That's true. Since we're feeling all this family love stuff, I have something to give you, too. It's a belated wedding gift, but we have to go downstairs to get it."

Dirk looked around at his new room. "I hate to leave my man cave, but okay. Let's go."

They tromped back down the stairs.

Once in the living room, Tammy led them over to her computer. She sat down in the desk chair and pulled up another chair next to her.

"Have a seat," she told Dirk. "There's something I want to show you."

Savannah stood with Waycross behind them. She was rabidly curious what this present might be. Tammy hadn't mentioned any additional surprises to her. But then, the sunshine girl was always coming up with unique gifts for the ones she loved.

Savannah was so grateful to be counted among that number.

Tammy turned in her chair to face Dirk. To Savannah's shock, she took both of his hands in hers and looked into his eyes. "I want to thank you, Dirk," she began, "for what you said to Waycross. The things you shared with him the other day—it's made a big difference in our relationship."

She beamed over her shoulder at Waycross for a moment. His face flushed almost as red as his hair.

Tammy turned back to Dirk, who was nearly as flustered as Waycross. He mumbled, "You're welcome."

Then she continued. "I hope that you don't mind, but he shared a little of what you told him about you being adopted."

Oh, wow, Savannah thought. There must have been a lot more to that conversation than she had heard.

"He also told me what that awful man who adopted you said about your mother."

Dirk didn't reply. He just nodded and looked down.

Tammy squeezed his hands. "I couldn't bear to think of you living your whole life and not knowing, so . . . I hope you'll forgive me if this is something you wouldn't have wanted me to do, but . . ."

She reached over and flipped on the computer. ". . . but I did some research about your mother. If you don't want to know, I won't tell you, because—"

Dirk sat bolt upright in his chair. "Yes!" he said. "Yes! I want to know. Whatever you found! Everything!"

Tammy did some typing and a Web site came up. "First of all, your mother wasn't a . . . well . . . what that guy said. She was a really sweet girl named Dora. She was just sixteen when she got pregnant by her high-school boyfriend. She was being raised by her elderly aunt and uncle, and they insisted she give her baby— you—up for adoption."

"Are you sure? How do you know all that?" Dirk asked.

"I kinda hacked into some files I wasn't supposed to. Once I had her name, I found some blogs where she'd posted messages. Dirk, she's been searching for you for years."

"Really? She has?" This time, Dirk didn't pretend it

was fuzz in his eyes. Tears spilled down his cheeks, and he didn't bother to wipe them away.

Savannah stepped up behind him, put her hands on his shoulders, and kissed the top of his head.

"Yes, she has," Tammy said. "So has your father."

"My *father*?"

"Yes, her high-school boyfriend. As soon as they graduated, they ran off together and got married. They live in Seattle and have three other grown kids. Two sons and a daughter," Tammy told him.

"Oh, honey," Savannah said, starting to cry herself. "That means you have brothers and a sister of your own!"

"They're quality people, Dirk. They really are," Tammy told him. "And they want you. They've *always* wanted you. Would you like to see their pictures?"

He couldn't even speak. He just gave a quick nod.

With a few more clicks, Tammy had filled the screen with photos of his family: a father, who looked remarkably like him, a pretty lady, with kind eyes, and three siblings—all with a striking family resemblance to him and to each other.

"Your parents just recently retired," Tammy said. "Your mom was a registered nurse for twenty-five years. And you're not going to believe what your dad did."

A few more clicks and the picture on the screen was of a young man, who could have been Dirk, in a policeman's uniform.

It was too much. Dirk was simply overwhelmed.

He turned in his chair toward Savannah and buried his face in her chest. She held him tightly as he wept against her.

"It's all right, darlin'," she said, stroking his hair. "This is such good news. Everything's gonna be all right."

Finally he regained some of his composure and

turned back to Tammy. "Have you . . . have you contacted them yet?"

"No, of course not. It had to be your decision. But I have everything here for you, if you choose to—their addresses, phone numbers, e-mail addresses. I printed out the blogs where your mother posted messages looking for information about you. You can read them first, if you want to."

Dirk leaned over, grabbed Tammy, and gave her a big hug and a kiss on the cheek. "Honey, you don't know what this means to me. You'll never know. But thank you. Thank you so much!"

Tammy smiled at him sweetly. "You're welcome. I tease you a lot, but you know I love you."

"Yeah. I'm kinda fond of you, too."

He ruffled her hair and stood, though he seemed to have wobbly knees. "Gee whiz," he said. "I go from being a grumpy old bachelor, living in a house trailer with nobody, to having a wife, two cats, a man cave, and *two* families. What am I gonna do with all of ya?"

Savannah wrapped her arms around his neck and kissed away the tears from his cheeks. "That's easy, babycakes. You're gonna love us, and fight with us, and tolerate us, and annoy us, and occasionally enjoy us. You know . . . the way other families do."

He smiled, and it was one of the few times Savannah had ever seen Dirk truly, deeply happy.

"It sounds good to me," he said, holding her so close it took her breath away. "In fact, baby, it sounds *very, very* good to me."

Plus-sized P.I. Savannah Reid gets a taste of the high life when she attends a Hollywood premiere on the arm of husband Dirk Coulter. Savannah may be a newlywed, but even she gets weak in the knees when she meets celebrity athlete-turned-movie-star Jason Tyrone. So imagine how she feels when the star's rock-hard body is found rock-hard dead . . .

Some guys have everything. With his stunning looks and dazzling charm, former heavyweight champ Jason Tyrone is America's favorite new action hero. Make that *was*. Once so spectacular in action, the blockbuster idol was found dead in his hotel room after his latest premiere. Despite his chiseled physique, Jason is never getting up again.

Though the autopsy reveals Jason may have gotten his killer body through doping, no one wants to believe the beloved athlete is a fraud, least of all Savannah. Soon she's deeply immersed in the dark world of body enhancing drugs, and wondering if the world-class gym where Jason worked out is really just a front for a lucrative drug ring. Was Jason's death the price he paid for threatening to expose other celebrities caught in the clutch of keeping a flawless image? Or was everyone's obsession with image, Savannah is determined to get to the truth. And for the voluptuous investigator, this time it's personal. . . .

Please turn the page for an exciting sneak peek of the newest Savannah Reid mystery

KILLER PHYSIQUE

coming next month wherever print and ebooks are sold!

Chapter 1

Standing at her bathroom sink, staring at the disgruntled, newly-married woman in the mirror, Savannah Reid rehearsed the speech she intended to give the jury at her murder trial. It would be during the sentencing phase, no doubt, because she fully intended to plead "Guilty."

She was certain that if there was even one semi-persnickety female on the jury, she'd escape the needle.

"You have to understand, ladies and gentlemen, that I spent three and a half long weeks redecorating that bathroom – all in anticipation of his parents' visit. I'm pretty sure I messed up my back permanently by hanging those fancy ceiling tiles . . . the ones that used to be white, but are now all globbed up with dribs and drabs of blue shaving foam. How in heaven's name does a grown man get shaving foam on the ceiling?"

She glanced around at the carnage of her freshly-renovated bathroom and added in her thick, Georgia drawl, "I reckon the same way he got it all over the sink, the faucet handle, the light switch, and the mirror. My dear jury members, you haven't lived 'til you've tried to scrub that stuff off a mirror. It's blue cement. You can take a razor blade and fingernail polish remover to it, and it won't budge."

A brisk knock on the door interrupted her plea for mercy.

"You in there?" inquired a deep, annoyed, male voice.

"Yeah," she barked back.

"You comin' out soon? Or am I gonna have to go downstairs again to do my business?"

She jerked the door open and stood, nose-to-nose, with her beloved new husband – give or take a few inches. "Boy, you and your thimble-sized bladder are ir-ritatin' the daylights outta me."

He shrugged and grinned down at her with a sexy smirk that would have set her bloomers atwitter, were it not for the devastation behind her.

"Hey," he said, "when the dragon needs drainin', what's a guy to do?"

He waited, giving her plenty of time to chuckle, or at least grin. But all he got was an icy blue stare. It was the glacial glare that had made former cop, now private de-tective, Savannah Reid, infamous among suspected mur-derers, robbers, embezzlers, and jaywalkers. Evildoers of all shapes and sizes, including husbands who left the toilet seat up and burped loudly in fancy restaurants, had been on the receiving end of those cobalt lasers.

Rolling his eyes, Dirk moaned and said, "Oh, man. I'm always in trouble. What did I do *this* time?"

Stepping to one side, so that he would have a clear, unobstructed view of the crime scene, she waved an arm to indicate the extent of the damages. "That," she said. "That's what you did. Again."

He gave the room a cursory glance and frowned, ob-viously confused. "What? What's the matter? Did I fold the towel in half instead of perfect thirds? Did I leave the cap off the toothpaste? Am I gonna get shot at sunrise or hanged from the neck until dead?"

She decided not to tell him that she had, indeed, been fantasizing about an execution only moments before. Her own. Society's recompense for premeditated, first degree homicide.

As she watched his eyes dart around the room, registering absolutely nothing amiss, by his own lax nonstandards, her ire rose. "Does this room look neat and tidy to you?" she asked.

"I've seen worse," he replied.

"Yes, I'm sure you have. But not in *my* house. Look at those toothpaste spit specks all over the mirror."

"Hey, happens when I floss. You don't want a husband with lousy dental hygiene, do you?"

"And why did you leave your deodorant, shave cream can, and jock itch powder there on the sink again? I asked you to put them back in the medicine cabinet when you're done with them."

He looked genuinely perplexed. "But why should I go to all that work when tomorrow I'm just gonna have to drag 'em out so's I can use 'em again?"

"Al-l-l that work? Dra-a-ag 'em out? You act like I'm asking you to pick a bale o' cotton in the hot, Georgia sun."

He gave her a sappy, condescending smile that was, no doubt, intended to smooth her ruffled feathers, but in fact, accomplished exactly the opposite. "If I put those three tiny little things away," he said, "will that make my beautiful, new bride happy?"

"I reckon," she grumbled. "And maybe you could wipe off the mirror once in a month of Sundays, since it's you who gunks it all up four times a day."

Sighing deeply, he trudged past her into the room, picked up his offending toiletries and with great cere-

mony, placed them in the medicine chest. He fussed
with the containers for what seemed like forever to Savannah, making quite a show of spacing them perfectly,
evenly, among their neighbors, turning the labels
straight outward, then re-adjusting ad nauseum.

With that delicate mission accomplished, he strode
to the toilet, unrolled a giant handful of tissue, and returned to the sink. Still grinning like a goat munching
sand burrs, he flipped on the sink faucet and wetted the
paper.

As Savannah's blood pressure soared, he calmly, casually, smeared the sodden wad all over the mirror, leaving bits of soggy mess behind. Unfortunately, the blue
blobs of shaving cream remained undisturbed.

Standing behind him, her face turning redder by the
moment, Savannah looked around the room for potential murder weapons and wondered if it were possible to
inflict a fatal wound with a Lady Gillette aloe-moisturiz-
ing bikini line shaver.

"There," he exclaimed, proudly displaying his handi-
work. "Happy now?"

"Plum ecstatic," she muttered.

"Good. And now that I'm in here, I'm gonna choke
the chicken. So, unless you've got some picky-ass directions about how I oughta do that, too, you might wanna
skedaddle."

With her chin a few notches higher than usual, a
grim look on her face, Savannah marched stiffly to the
door. She paused there for a moment as a hundred or
so of Granny Reid's admonitions about "living in har-
mony with the man the good God gave ya" and "over-
lookin' the better part of a husband's transgressions
bein' the path to domestic tranquility" danced through
her head.

She could take the high road and just walk out without saying another word. That would be noble, virtu-
ous.

Blessed are the peacemakers, and all that good stuff.

Dirk was, after all, a decent man. He loved her. He'd
put his crap away with a smile – okay, a smirk – on his
face and kinda, sorta cleaned up when she'd asked him
to. What more could a woman ask, really?

Yes, she would put away her anger and choose the
path of peace.

Virtue, after all, had its own reward . . . mostly in the
form of self-righteous gloating.

Then she heard a sound behind her that made every
muscle in her body kink into a knot. A merry little tin-
kling sound.

Not the sound of liquid hitting water. Oh, no. It was
the unmistakable merry little melody of pee hitting tile.

She whirled on him with a vengeance. "Dammit all,
Dirk! At the shooting range, you score 49 out of 50
shots from 25 yards—standing, kneeling *and* prone!
But you can't hit a dadgum toilet that's two feet away?"

He stood – chicken partially choked, dragon half
drained – a look of shock and confusion on his face.
"What?"

"If I were to paint a bull's-eye on the bottom of the
bowl, do you reckon it'd improve that piss-poor aim of
yours?"

He thought about it. Long and hard. Then, having
given it all due consideration, he solemnly nodded,
smiled and said, "It could. Yes, I think it might at that.
Good idea, babe. You get on that right away."

"You . . . ! You . . . ! I oughta . . . ! A-a-u-u-gh!"

She stomped out of the room and slammed the door
behind her, rocking the house to its foundation.

As she strode down the hallway, she could hear her groom laughing his butt off on the other side of the bathroom door.

Yeah, well, at least somebody's enjoying all this wedded bliss, she thought.

"Laugh it up, Fuzzball," she muttered as she went into the bedroom to get dressed for their big night out. "I'll getcha back. One way or the other."

Granny Reid had told her many times, "Don't let the sun set on your wrath, Savannah girl. No matter how bad the squabblin's been that day, come nighttime you always make it right 'tween you and your man before you lay your head on your pillow to sleep."

Savannah had no problem with that sage advice. It would be at least seven hours or more before they retired for the evening. Surely, she could arrange some soul-gratifying form of revenge before then.

Nope, she had no intention of going to bed angry. Come nighttime, she intended to be giggling on that pillow and rubbing her hands with glee.